'Til
Death

Books by Carol J. Perry

Witch City Mysteries

Caught Dead Handed

Tails, You Lose

Look Both Ways

Murder Go Round

Grave Errors

It Takes a Coven

Bells, Spells and Murders

Final Exam

Late Checkout

Murder, Take Two

See Something

'Til Death

Haunted Haven Mysteries

Be My Ghost

'Til Death

CAROL J. PERRY

Kensington Publishing Corp.
www.kensingtonbooks.com

KENSINGTON BOOKS are published by

Kensington Publishing Corp.
119 West 40th Street
New York, NY 10018

All Kensington titles, imprints, and distributed lines are available at special quantity discounts for bulk purchases for sales promotion, premiums, fund-raising, educational, or institutional use.

Special book excerpts or customized printings can also be created to fit specific needs. For details, write or phone the office of the Kensington Sales Manager: Attn.: Sales Department. Kensington Publishing Corp., 119 West 40th Street, New York, NY 10018. Phone: 1-800-221-2647.

The K and Teapot logo is a trademark of Kensington Publishing Corp.

First Printing: May 2022
ISBN: 978-1-4967-3143-2

ISBN: 978-1-4967-3144-9 (ebook)

10 9 8 7 6 5 4 3 2 1

Printed in the United States of America

For Dan, my husband and best friend.

CHAPTER 1

Scott Palmer tapped urgently on the glass partition that separates my office from the WICH-TV newsroom, while in front of my desk the Fabulous Fabio attempted unsuccessfully to coax a reluctant pigeon back into a frayed top hat, and on the phone my Aunt Ibby tried once again to explain to me why she thought a prospective tenant for her soon-to-open Airbnb might be a wanted criminal.

Not all of my days as program director at the Salem, Massachusetts local television station WICH-TV began with such confusion, but recently quite a few of them had. I'm Lee Barrett, née Maralee Kowalski, thirty-five, red-haired, Salem born, orphaned early, married once, and widowed young. At that moment, I lived with my aunt, Isobel Russell and O'Ryan, our gentleman cat, in the old family home on Winter Street.

That was soon to change. I was happily engaged to be married to my longtime policeman beau, detective sergeant Pete Mondello, and in the midst of making plans for our June wedding. The ceremony would be held at Salem's Old Town Hall. It's a beautiful Federal-style building built in 1836 in the historic heart of downtown Salem. Our reception would be a short distance away in Colonial Hall at Rockafellas in the Daniel Low building. This cornerstone of Salem history was once the largest jewelry store in America. I'd be wearing my mother's altered and updated gorgeous 1980s Priscilla of Boston champagne satin gown and it, as well as my maid of honor and bridesmaids' dresses, were ready for final fittings. I'd asked my best friend, River North, the station's late-show movie host, to be my maid of honor and bridesmaids would be WICH-TV pals, receptionist Rhonda and weather girl Wanda, Pete's sister Marie, and former student Shannon Berman. I'd been Shannon's maid of honor at her marriage to Salem artist Dakota Berman. We'd picked a Sunday for the wedding when the programming is mostly off-site, so none of us at the station had to work, and Shannon was a brand-new stay-at-home mom. Rupert Pennington, director of Salem's newest school, the Tabitha Trumbull Academy of the Arts (known around Salem as "the Tabby") where I'd once taught a course in television production, had agreed to officiate at our ceremony. Mr. Pennington was also a close friend—and occasional date—of Aunt Ibby's.

I'd moved downstairs to my childhood bedroom while my cute apartment on the third floor of the Winter Street house was in process of being converted to a bed-and-breakfast while Pete and I searched for a home of our own.

Scott's glass-tapping was more annoying than the piti-ful pigeon-cooing, so I swung my swivel chair around and faced him through thick glass. *What do you want?* I mouthed.

Call me, he mouthed back, forming the thumb and two-finger approximation of a phone receiver. I nodded and pointed to the phone at my ear, where my anxious aunt was still speaking. *Later*, I signaled, spinning the chair back toward the struggling magician.

"I can tell that you're busy, Maralee," my aunt said. "We'll talk about it when you get home."

"Okay. Love you," I told her, and turned my attention to Fabio. Although his skill as a magician is questionable, his talent as a creator of extraordinary culinary confec-tions—especially wedding cakes—was unparalleled in Salem. I'd seen and tasted examples of his work and had long ago decided that if and when Pete and I married, we'd surely have a Fabulous Fabio cake for our recep-tion.

A beaming Fabio, having successfully coaxed the bird back into the hat, sat in the chair opposite me. "See that?" he said. "The kids are going to love it." The "kids" he re-ferred to were the live audience of "little buckaroos" who appeared daily on WICH-TV's most popular children's morning show—*Ranger Rob's Rodeo*.

Fabio's cakes were, not unexpectedly, much in de-mand. There was a waiting list. We were on it—but Fabio had made it clear that a single guest spot with Ranger Rob would *guarantee* my perfect cake on the date we'd chosen. With fingers mentally crossed, and high hopes that Fabio would give the little buckaroos one of his bet-ter performances, I signed the contract his agent had drawn up, and he signed the order for the quadruple-layer, buttercream frosted, vanilla cake with astonishingly realistic sprays of fondant roses and daisies and pansies and ribbons and butterflies—topped with a custom-designed bride and groom and a yellow striped cat that looked just like our O'Ryan.

I wished Fabio and his cooing companion a good day, punched Scott's number into my phone, and watched through the glass as he answered. "What's up over there?" I asked.

Before I was promoted to the station's program director I was a field reporter. That's the job Scott has now. I have to admit that sometimes I still miss the edge-of-your-chair, race-out-the-door-at-a-moment's-notice, day or night excitement of my field reporter days. But the orderly routine and normal working hours of program director, along with the challenge of pleasing the varied tastes of the WICH-TV viewing audience, had been a welcome change for me. It's also a perfect work schedule for married me!

"Got a question for you," Scott said. "Are you still in touch with the boss man over at the Tabby?"

"Mr. Pennington? Sure. He's going to perform our wedding ceremony. I see him fairly often. Why? What's up?"

"There's a little buzz going on—unverified, naturally—that one of the new instructors over there has quite a prison record."

"Oh?"

"Heard anything about it?"

"No," I said, "but if the person has served his time, what's the problem?"

"Okay, Miss Goody-Goody. What if he—or she—was a mass murderer or a serial rapist?"

"He or she probably wouldn't be out of prison," I reasoned. "Anyway, isn't it a matter of public record? Why are you asking me?"

"My contact—a student at the Tabby—says that this new hire of Pennington's who calls himself Fenton Bishop looks just like a photo of Michael Martell he saw in one of those true-crime magazines, only older. Ring any bells?"

"Nope. The name Michael Martell isn't familiar at all and the only Fenton Bishop I've heard of is the mystery writer."

"Yeah. That must be him. He's teaching writing anyway. But Martell was convicted twenty years ago of killing his wife."

"He's been released?"

"Right."

"And you think he's in Salem using this other name?"

"Right."

"So what?" I asked, wondering what all this had to do with me, especially since I already had a lot on my plate. "If this person has paid his so-called debt to society, why shouldn't he work at any job he's qualified for?"

"Will you just ask Pennington if it's true?" he pleaded.

"Call him and ask for yourself. Here. I'll give you his number."

He held up one hand. "Already tried that. All I get is the old 'no comment.'"

"Listen, Scott. I have a lot to do. I'll ask Mr. Pennington next time I see him," I promised. "He'll probably give me the 'no comment' answer too. Bye."

I ended the call before he could object. My immediate project was figuring out when we could schedule a magic-themed show for *Ranger Rob's Rodeo* and then how to wangle an invitation for Wanda the weather girl to appear on a new national reality show called *Hometown Cooks*. The show features a competition between local cooking show hosts like our Wanda, whose *Cooking with Wanda the Weather Girl* is a regional favorite. She's even authored a cookbook of her own. Besides all that, I needed to do some serious house-hunting with Pete.

We had an after-work appointment to look at a house on Winter Street, just a short walk from Aunt Ibby's. It's a two-bedroom condo, built back in the 1800s. It shares a common central wall with another almost identical house next door—sort of like those row houses in Baltimore, except that this is the only one built that way in the neighborhood. Pete was a little nervous about the 1830s date on the place, but as I reminded him, Aunt Ibby's house was built in the same time period and it has all the modern amenities, as well as the old Salem charm. I hoped the condo would be similar, partly because I love the neighborhood and mostly because it would be an easy commute for O'Ryan. He wouldn't even have to cross any streets to visit us, and my aunt and I definitely planned on shared custody of our remarkable cat.

It was nearly five o'clock when I locked in a date for a magic-themed show for *Ranger Rob's Rodeo*. I'd signed up two sponsors to do special presentations for the show. Christopher Rich, the owner of Christopher's Castle, one of Salem's largest witch shops featuring all things magical, was delighted to be included. Captain Billy Barker owns the Toy Trawler toy store and is a regular sponsor of the show. He happily agreed to provide Magic 8 Balls for all the little buckaroos in that day's audience, plus advertising some of the many boxed magic games and instruction books in his inventory. Katie the Clown, Ranger

Rob's regular sidekick, would work with Paco the Wonder Dog on some amazing new dog tricks. Our boss at WICH-TV, station manager Bruce Doan, was on board with the idea. So far, so good. Since I no longer had a kitchen of my own, I'd agreed to meet Pete for an early dinner at the Village Green before our appointment at the condo, so my pursuit of Wanda's *Hometown Cooks* debut would have to wait a little longer.

I locked my office, said good night to WICH-TV's office receptionist Rhonda, and stepped into the elevator—known more or less affectionately as "Old Clunky"—and rode down to the first-floor lobby. I'd parked my rental car—a red 2021 Chevrolet Blazer SUV—in my assigned space in the station's harbor-front parking lot. I still hadn't decided on a replacement for my recently totaled Corvette Stingray. Pete insisted that I needed something a lot safer and surely more practical than my gorgeous Laguna-blue convertible dream car. I knew he was right, but making the choice was more difficult than I'd imagined it might be.

The Village Green restaurant is in the Hawthorne Hotel, just across the Salem Common from Winter Street. Pete's unmarked Ford Police Interceptor Utility was already parked in the Hawthorne's lot. I pulled the red Chevy in beside it and hurried inside. Pete stood and waved from across the room, then gave me a quick hug when I reached the table.

"Am I late?" I asked. "Crazy busy day."

"Nope. Just got here myself. They've got the seafood chowder tonight."

"My favorite," I said.

"I know."

"I love it that you know me so well," I told him.

"I'm getting there," he said, "but you're still full of surprises."

"I guess I like that too," I admitted, not exactly sure what kind of surprises he meant. One fairly recent surprise that both of us are still struggling to accept, is the fact that I am what's known in paranormal circles as a *scryer*. My best friend River North calls me a "gazer." River happens to be a witch, so she knows about such things. Anyway, I'd learned that I have the strange ability to see things in shiny objects—things that have happened, or are happening, or could happen in the future. River calls it a gift. I don't think of it that way. I admit, it's come in handy a few times, but most everything it's ever shown me has been about death and dying.

Pete smiled and took my hand so I knew he meant the happy kind of surprises, like my learning how to cook his mom's recipe for lasagna, or my teaching his two nephews how to play cribbage. "You're pretty excited about the Winter Street condo, aren't you?" he said.

"Oh, I am. Did you get a chance to look at the Zillow photos I forwarded to you?"

"The wide floorboards look great," he said, "and the kitchen seems to have everything we want. I like the fireplaces too—if they work."

We ordered our dinners: a bowl of that famous seafood chowder and a house salad for each of us. I told him about my meeting with Fabio, and my hopes that his magic tricks would appeal to Ranger Rob's young audience.

"He'll be fine," Pete said. "Even when he messes up, he's funny. And the important thing is we get the cake. Right?"

"Absolutely," I agreed. "It's guaranteed. Contracts signed. Magic show approved by Doan. And wouldn't you know, just at the same time I was negotiating buttercream frosting and a disappearing pigeon, Aunt Ibby called, all upset about a prospective tenant for the B and B."

He frowned. "What was her problem?"

"She just has a funny feeling about him," I told him. "Then Scott Palmer called, wanting me to check with Mr. Pennington over at the Tabby about somebody they've hired over there that Scott thinks might be a murderer or something." Our orders arrived and I dipped into the chowder, spooning up a lovely pink shrimp. "Say, do you know anything about some creepy new guy in town?"

I didn't actually expect an answer. Pete very rarely discusses police business with me, especially since I work for a TV station. But now that I'm not a reporter anymore and hardly ever in front of the cameras, he's been a little bit less guarded about it. He broke some crackers into his chowder and looked at me thoughtfully.

"A disappearing pigeon?" he asked.

CHAPTER 2

I clearly wasn't going to get any information from Pete about either the Tabby's new hire or Aunt Ibby's prospective tenant. Were they both talking about the same creepy guy or was there more than one new suspicious character lurking around in Salem?

I dutifully explained the failed pigeon-in-the-hat trick as best I could, and returned the conversation to the condo. "It's listed as two bedrooms, two-and-a-half baths," I said, "but there's another room that could easily be an office, and there's a nice closed-in sunporch in the back. There's room in the yard for two cars."

"Sounds good." He looked at his watch. "Want to have coffee and dessert now or shall we come back later to talk it over after we check the place out?"

"We may want to leave a deposit tonight if we both love it," I reminded him. "We don't have a lot of time before the wedding." I wasn't kidding. "Unless we want to come home from our honeymoon in Maine and move into my old bedroom, we don't have a lot of choice. The lease on your apartment will be up, and mine might already be rented to some wanted fugitive or other by then." I tapped my handbag. "I brought my checkbook, just in case."

"Good thinking," he said. "Then we can start combining your furniture and mine and figure out what new stuff we might want to buy."

"I know. I'm excited about having our own place, yours and mine."

"Me too," he said, reaching for the check. "Let's go buy a condo."

"If we both love it," I said.

"If we both love it," he agreed.

We left my car in front of Aunt Ibby's house and continued down the street in Pete's Ford. We'd barely parked when our real estate agent, Joanne, stepped out of the house and greeted us from the granite front step. "Welcome," she called. "You're right on time. We have about an hour before the next couple arrives." She opened the green-painted door wide and stood back to let us inside.

The front hall revealed a staircase straight ahead as well as an exposed brick wall. The floor, as Pete had mentioned earlier, was of polished wide boards—the kind one only finds in houses of a certain age. On the right, a door led to a living room, which seemed light-filled from tall windows even in that early-evening hour. Here was a white mantel fireplace, recessed into yet another mellow brick wall. A perfect-for-an-office room and a cute powder room were nearby and an arch brought us to the kitchen with its stainless steel appliances, quartz counters, center island, gray-painted cabinets, some with glass doors. I could visualize my 1970s Lucite kitchen set tucked into the neat dining alcove, adjoining a sunroom, where my antique painted carousel horse would feel right at home, surrounded by plants. I was ready to write a deposit check then and there and we hadn't even seen the bedrooms. I sneaked a peek at Pete, trying to determine what he felt.

He wore what I call his "cop face." Unemotional. Unreadable. Did that mean he was unimpressed, or was it meant to hide his excitement at finding this absolutely perfect place for us to begin our life together? Hoping with all my heart that it was the latter, we followed Joanne up a flight of stairs, these of the twisty variety, reminding me of Aunt Ibby's back staircase. A master bedroom with another fireplace, two big closets and its en suite bathroom was beyond gorgeous and a second bedroom had its own bathroom too. "There's some attic space on the top floor—unimproved, slanty ceilings, no heat or air," Joanne said. "You're welcome to use it for storage if you like. It's completely empty."

"Thanks," I said. "I'm sure the two floors you've shown us will be plenty of space for us." Pete smiled and nodded—cop face gone. How could he not be in love with this home?

He was, it turned out, just as crazy about it as I was. It didn't take long for an offer to be made, papers signed, "earnest money" deposited, a few selfies taken in the kitchen and beside the living room fireplace, and hands shaken all around before we hurried back down Winter Street to share the good news with Aunt Ibby.

"Does it already have a cat door or will you have to install one?" was her first question. I had to admit that we hadn't noticed one nor had we asked about putting one in.

"Assuming that our offer is accepted," Pete said, "we'll make sure O'Ryan has access. No doubt about that."

We were in my aunt's cheerful kitchen where O'Ryan had joined us at the round oak table, sitting in one of the captain's chairs. "*Mmrupp*," he said in an agreeable cat tone. So the cat-door question was settled.

I showed Aunt Ibby the pictures of the empty rooms I'd shot with my phone. "Oh look, Maralee!" She pointed to a photo of the sunroom. "Your bentwood bench will look beautiful in this room—and your carousel horse too."

"I know," I said. "Already thought of that. And Pete has furniture in his apartment that will work with a lot of my other pieces."

"My furniture is all cast-offs from my mom's house and Donnie and Marie's place," Pete said. (Yes, Pete's sister and brother-in-law are named Donnie and Marie.)

"Exactly," I agreed. "Along with a few new pieces, we'll have just the look we're both comfortable with."

"I guess so. Ms. Russell—Ibby—you must be figuring out furniture for the new B and B," Pete said. "How's that coming?" It's taken a long time for Pete to use her first name and sometimes he forgets.

"Slowly, but surely," she said. "Pete, about the B and B, I've been meaning to ask if there's some way to have the Salem police check on a prospective tenant. I don't want to rent those rooms to just anybody. After all, I live here too."

"Sure. It can be done. Do you have a name and address for this person?"

"Just the basics," she said. "He's only called once and

I didn't give him much information. I just have a funny feeling about him."

"Is he a teacher?" I asked, remembering Scott's questions about the new Tabby instructor.

"He didn't say. Just that he was relocating to Salem and needed a temporary address until he gets settled in his new job. What do you ask?" She tilted her head to one side, using her wise-old-owl look.

"Probably not important," I said. "Just a coincidence. Scott was asking about a new teacher at the Tabby. Fenton Bishop."

"Fenton Bishop?" My aunt's green eyes widened. "The mystery writer?"

"I don't know anything about it," Pete said. "Anyway, Lee. You don't believe in coincidences."

"Neither do you," I countered. "So will you check on the new man in town? Scott called Mr. Pennington and got a 'no comment.'"

Aunt Ibby sat up straighter. She and Rupert Pennington have been unofficially "keeping company" for years. "If Rupert has hired *the* Fenton Bishop, you'd think he would have told me. He knows how I love mystery books."

"Okay!" Pete held up both hands. "I'll see what information Pennington has and we'll find out if you're both wondering about the same person. It's probably nothing, but if it'll make you feel better I'll see what I can find out. Did you get the guy's name and phone number, Ibby?"

"Of course. He's Dr. Martell. He gave me a cell phone number."

I looked at Pete, who looked at the floor. "And you say he's a doctor?"

"He didn't give me his full name," she said. "He has a

PhD in education so maybe he *is* the same person Scott Palmer asked about. I can give you his phone number. Maybe Dr. Martell *is* Rupert's Fenton Bishop. And maybe he's the same Fenton Bishop who writes mysteries."

"And maybe he's the same Dr. Michael Martell that Scott says killed his own wife twenty years ago," I said.

I heard my aunt gasp.

"To tell you the truth, babe," he said, "I'm sorry I haven't been taking your questions about the new teacher more seriously. The answer is I don't know. A twenty-year-old murder is way before my time in law enforcement. Twenty years ago I was playing peewee hockey and not paying any attention to the news. I'm not familiar with it at all—but I sure will look into it now."

"A murderer?" my aunt murmured. "Fenton Bishop a wife killer?"

"Even if he is the same person, Aunt Ibby," I reasoned, "he's apparently served his time, been paroled, or whatever happened to make him a free man."

"True," she said. "Maybe he didn't actually kill anybody after all." She fixed Pete in her best librarian stare. "But you'll check into it?"

"Sure thing, if it'll put your mind to rest. You know you're not obliged to accept anybody as a tenant. If you don't want this guy to stay here, just say no."

"I want to be fair. And Fenton Bishop writes such wonderful books." Her tone put an end to that portion of the conversation. "Now about your belongings, Maralee. They're perfectly safe where I've had them stored in the attic until you're ready to move them."

I'd wished silently for an alternative storage space. I don't like anything about that attic and I avoid going up those stairs whenever I can. However, this time it made sense. The attic was clean, dry, and orderly—not the dusty hodgepodge of cast-off articles it had been before the fire, which had almost taken Aunt Ibby's and my lives—along with that of our brave cat. Even so, I wasn't crazy about the idea, but I'd pasted on a smile and agreed to it anyway. Pete had already arranged to store his things at his parents' house.

"I have some stickers for you, Lee," she said. "You too, Pete. Kitchen, living room, bedroom and a lot of blank ones for you to fill out—so the movers will know where to put the boxes and furniture on moving day."

I thanked my super-efficient aunt. "What am I going to do without you when I move?" I intended for the question to sound playful, but deep down I meant it.

"Let's all hope that your offer on that house will be accepted," she said. "I'm sure you'll do just fine, but I'll be just a few houses away in case you ever need me." That made me wish doubly hard that the house would be ours.

"I've been thinking about that cat door for O'Ryan," Pete said, stuffing his package of stickers into his pocket. "Is this one of those historical districts where you need permits for things like that? There's one of those 'Built in eighteen-thirtysomething for Captain somebody-or-other' signs on the outside."

"I think it will be all right," Aunt Ibby said. "Your house is of the same period as this one and nobody has questioned our cat doors."

She was already referring to it as "your house." I liked that—and hoped fervently that it was true—cat doors and all.

CHAPTER 3

It took a few days, but our offer was officially accepted. We scheduled a final inspection, contacted a home insurance agent while real estate agent Joanne made arrangements for the transfer of the property deed. We hadn't yet established an official move-in day, but it was definitely time to get started on the furniture-and-packed-box labeling process. Joanne had provided us with careful graph paper–scale drawings of each room, so I knew I'd be able to get a good idea of what would fit where. Now all I had to do was climb those stairs to the attic and get busy with measuring tape and stickers. I was in my childhood bedroom, where O'Ryan snoozed on a window seat. "What do you say, cat? We have a couple of hours before I have to go to work. Want to come upstairs to the attic with me?"

He opened sleepy eyes for a brief second, then squeezed them shut. I took that as a "no, thanks," but per-

sisted. "Come on. We're going to figure out what to take
with us to the new house." Recognizing my insistent
tone, he yawned, stretched, hopped down from the window seat, and followed me out of the bedroom.

We climbed the stairs to the third floor, standing for a
moment outside the once-orange feng shui–inspired door
to my recently vacated apartment. The door, along with
its hinged cat entrance, had been returned to its original
off-white and muffled sounds of renovation activities
came from inside. Aunt Ibby was in the process of adding
a second bathroom and reconfiguring the kitchen, with an
eye toward making the space into two smaller apartments, more suitable for the B and B–type facility she
pictured. I turned, facing the other off-white door in the
hallway—the one leading to the attic. "Okay, O'Ryan.
Here we go." I turned the glass doorknob.

The stairway leading up was fairly new. Nothing
fancy. Plain risers and treads painted gray with railings
on each side. A long string was tied to a railing, and attached to a bare bulb overhead. I pulled the string, dimly
illuminating the long room above. As usual, I imagined I
smelled smoke from that long-ago fire—even though I
knew every bit of charred wood had been removed years
ago.

"Okay, O'Ryan. Let's get this over with," I said, stepping onto the new-looking, dust-free wooden floor—
which, once I got past my imaginary smoke thing, smelled
like the building materials aisle at Home Depot: plywood
and pine boards and fresh sawdust. A stack of brown cardboard boxes on my left were already lettered as to their
content with black marker in Aunt Ibby's precise librarian's script. *Clock and watercolor prints* told me that my
vintage Kit-Cat Klock with its googly eyes and wagging

tail, along with colorful framed prints of fruits and vegetables—more feng shui on the advice of my friend River—were carefully wrapped inside. Other boxes were marked *fiesta ware* and *wineglasses* and *coffee maker*.

"We're already off to a good start," I said, "thanks to my aunt." My package of labels in hand, I moved toward the larger shapes indicating furniture at the attic's deepest recesses. Here I pulled on another string, lighting a bulb in that part of the long room.

I wrote *living room* on a label and stuck it to the front of a zebra-print wing chair. That's O'Ryan's favorite chair and I almost expected him to jump onto the seat and curl up for a nap, but he seemed to know this was business and moved with me to the next piece, a glass-fronted barrister's bookcase that got an *office* sticker. I marked each piece of the headboard, footboard, box spring and mattress that made up my king-sized bed with a *master bedroom* label. My much-loved bentwood bench was destined for the sunporch and so directed. Next came my kitchen pride and joy, a 1970s Lucite table and four matching chairs, followed by assorted side chairs, end tables, coffee table and my gorgeous carousel horse.

"Let's just go with the main pieces for now," I told the cat, "then we'll see what Pete has and what we might want to buy new. Then we can come back here and pick up the miscellaneous stuff. Maybe Aunt Ibby can use some of it in the B and B and whatever is left can go to Goodwill." I turned around in a circle. "Wait a minute. Where's my bureau?"

O'Ryan made a dash for a corner. "*Mmrupp*," he said. I followed and found him sitting atop the bureau I remembered from early childhood. Of course, it wasn't exactly that bureau, but an amazing duplicate we'd been lucky enough to find on WICH-TV's *Shopping Salem* show. The original bureau, with its intricate secret compartments, good-sized drawers, and lift-up mirror had been destroyed in the attic fire, and I certainly wasn't about to leave this one behind. I labeled it *master bedroom* before lifting the lid housing the beveled mirror, making sure it was intact.

Bad idea. The whirling colors and flashing lights that always accompany a vision appeared on the mirror's surface. My first instinct was to slam the lid shut, to make whatever the mirror was about to reveal go away. But I knew that whatever it was would still be there—in that mirror or some other reflective object. I'd get the message, no matter what. River says that the pictures I see in shiny things can show the past, the present, or even the future. With a sigh, I watched the now-familiar light show and waited for the unwanted, but inevitable revelation.

I recognized my kitchen right away—not the one in the new house, but the one currently being renovated. This room was part kitchen, part living area divided by the counter. The space where my kitchen table and chairs had been now displayed a couch and coffee table. There was a new clock where my Kit-Cat had been—a plain, round-faced timepiece—which showed 10:15.

That was it. I stared at the image for a full minute. Nothing moved. Nothing changed. I was aware that O'Ryan, seated on the top shelf of a nearby I-wouldn't-be-caught-dead-with-this-thing-in-my-house three-tiered corner whatnot, was focused on it too.

"*Meh*," he said—which I believe means the same thing in cat language as it does in English: "Meh." The vision was a big nothing.

"I agree," I said and closed the lid. O'Ryan jumped down from his hideous perch and we both headed for the staircase. When we stepped out onto the burgundy-carpeted third-floor landing, I realized that I'd been holding my breath. "Whew," I said. "It's always a relief to get out of there." I looked at my watch. We'd been in the attic for only about half an hour. Wait a minute. The kitchen clock in the vision had shown 10:15. Definitely not the present. Was it showing me the past or the future?

I paused in front of the freshly painted door to my recently vacated apartment. Maybe the unfamiliar kitchen set and round clock *were*, in fact, in there. *Maybe the clock simply hasn't been set properly. I should go inside and check.* O'Ryan beat me to it by scooting through the cat door. I gave a polite tap to alert any workmen who might be in the kitchen, then turned the knob. The room was empty—of workers, furniture, or clock. O'Ryan dashed back into the hall and I closed the door quietly.

Aunt Ibby isn't fond of hearing about the unbidden visions. Pete isn't either. He calls it "seeing things" and I avoid talking to either of them about my strange "gift" unless it's absolutely necessary. River is the only other person in my life who even knows about the things I see—and she *loves* talking about them. This particular picture showed a portion of my aunt's B and B in-progress, though. Maybe she needed to hear about it— however "Meh" it might prove to be.

Okay, I told myself. *No furniture, no clock on the wall, and the appliances are just as they have been ever since she surprised me with the apartment.* So the vision must be a look into the future. "Ten-fifteen," I murmured aloud. O'Ryan looked up at me. "What do you think? AM? Or PM?"

"*Meh*," he said again, then strolled toward the stairs leading down to the second floor. I followed, stopping to drop the remaining labels in my bedroom, then hurried down the wide main staircase leading down to the foyer and the entrance to Aunt Ibby's living room. "Aunt Ibby, it's us," I called, though by that time O'Ryan had already announced our presence by bounding past the dining room and on into the kitchen.

My aunt stood beside a wide counter, wielding a wooden spoon over a large Bennington bowl. She wore a pink bib apron with *I Love Cats* printed on it. "Come in, my dears," she called. "Coffee's on and there are fresh blueberry muffins cooling in the pantry." In addition to her talent as a research librarian and tech whiz, she's also a marvelous cook. O'Ryan headed for his red bowl, where she'd already placed a handful of kitty snacks. I accepted the coffee and muffin invitation and looked over her shoulder, as she stirred enthusiastically whatever was in the bowl.

"What are you making?"

"Just whipping up a little something for this evening. Pistachio nut cake. The Angels are coming over."

"Sounds yummy," I said. The Angels are three Salem women—Aunt Ibby, her high school classmate Betsy Leavitt, and dear friend Louisa Abney-Babcock—who see themselves as amateur sleuths: a sort of senior-citizens cross between *Golden Girls* and *Charlie's Angels*. No kidding—and they take themselves very seriously. They meet every week to watch *Midsomer Murders* and, more often than not, to talk about getting involved in matters that are generally none of their business. I had a good idea that this evening's meeting would involve Fenton Bishop and Dr. Michael Martell.

"You're welcome to join us." She waved the spoon in my direction. "You might enjoy it. Tonight's episode is about a couple who are doing some house hunting. Like you and Pete were."

"Thanks. I think I will—not so much to see the show but to keep an eye on you three," I admitted with a smile. "Glad our house hunting is over though, and I've even started putting stickers on the pile of stuff in the attic."

"Good for you." She poured the silky batter into a tube pan, put it in the oven and started the timer. "There. This'll be ready in fifty minutes. Timing is everything in cake baking."

Time. A clock. Ten-fifteen.

I decided that I might as well tell her about the vision. *Stop. I can't just jump into it. Need to prepare her.* "Aunt Ibby," I began. "Do you . . . have you . . . already bought furniture for the B and B?"

"I have." She sounded pleased with herself, held up one hand and began counting on her fingers. "I found a really nice couch along with a coffee table at the church thrift store. They'll be delivered tomorrow. I stopped by HomeGoods and grabbed a few small appliances. Coffee maker, knife rack, toaster, wall clock; nothing fancy. I'm keeping everything simple—plain-Jane—impersonal, you know. Would you like to see them? They're in a carton in my office. It's just a few basics."

"Sure." I swallowed the last sip of my coffee. "I'd love to take a peek. Guess I'm kind of nosy."

"Not at all. The kitchen's only half the size that yours was, and won't have the character yours had. But then it's just a temporary shelter—not a home. Go along now and look. Come back and tell me what you think."

O'Ryan and I headed for the office, just off the living

room—a big, light space that served as my playroom when I was little. Gone are the Disney characters stenciled onto the walls, the kid-sized table and chairs, the porcelain tea set and the dollhouse. Now my aunt's business domain is a marvel of mellow cherrywood furniture and all manner of high-tech equipment. The large carton stood partly open on a long, polished table, along with a potted Christmas cactus, current issues of *Library Journal*, *Consumers Digest*, and *Cat Fancy*.

Toaster, coffee makers—both drip and Keurig—as well as knives were, as she'd said, simple—but top quality. The clock, the actual object of my interest, was exactly as I'd expected. Its plain, round, white face displayed the correct time, not 10:15. But if it was some kind of foreteller of the future I needed to tell her about it.

"No time like the present," I mumbled to the cat as we walked back to the kitchen.

"*Mmruupp*," he agreed.

So I did. Her response was what I knew it would be: thoughtful and reasonable. "So that's all it showed you? Couch and coffee table and a clock showing 10:15? No activity? No people at all?"

"That's right."

"Thank you for sharing that, dear. We'll—um—watch for anything significant about such a picture. The Angels will be arriving at around seven-thirty. See you then?"

CHAPTER 4

It was a few minutes before 7:30 that evening when O'Ryan and I started down the stairs to the first floor. Some chatter and laughter from Aunt Ibby's apartment announced that the Angels had arrived. The cat scooted on ahead of me, darting into the kitchen.

"There's O'Ryan," I heard my aunt say. "Maralee must be right behind him."

"Hello, Lee!" Betsy met me in the doorway, enveloping me in a Joy-scented hug. Louisa's greeting was less effusive, but just as warm. "So happy you could join us. I've seen the previews of tonight's show. It's about house hunters. I understand you and your fiancé have been doing the same."

"We were," I agreed, "and we've found one we both love—right down the street from this one."

"How exciting," Betsy said. "Although I'm sure your

house won't feature murder, like the one on TV always does."

"I'm sure it won't." I looked at the nearby counter where the pistachio nut cake, generously sprinkled with powdered sugar, was displayed on a footed Fostoria cake plate. "And chances are it won't feature beautiful desserts like this one either."

"You and Pete are always welcome to share desserts with me—but speaking of murders, have you girls heard about the new teacher at the Tabby who they say might have murdered his wife?" My aunt's green eyes sparkled. "I think it's something we might want to look into."

"I was about to mention it myself," Louisa said. "There was some talk about it at the bank this morning. Seems the fellow tried to open an account with some sort of pseudonym."

Louisa sits on the boards of several banks, so she would know about such things.

"Was it Fenton Bishop?" Betsy wanted to know. "I heard that his name is Fenton Bishop."

"It's possible that he might have *two* names," Aunt Ibby offered. "Fenton Bishop and Michael Martell."

"So did one or the other of them murder his wife?" Betsy asked. "This sounds intriguing."

Aunt Ibby picked up the cake. "Shall we go into the living room? It's almost showtime. Maralee, would you get the wineglasses? There's a nice bottle of wine chilling in the refrigerator." She headed for the living room, looking back over her shoulder. "And I have no doubt that the poor woman was murdered."

The Angels have held their meetings for a long enough time that a certain protocol has evolved. Conversation ceases during the program, but is allowed during commercial breaks. That conversation is limited to observations about the program's plot as it plays out on screen. At midpoint in the story I'd figured out that the old rundown house the couple had found was not going to work out well for them. Inspector Barnaby would have to ride to the rescue pretty quickly.

We sipped our wine and snarffed down the wonderful cake and tried to outdo each other on clues we'd spotted. I'd figured out that it had something to do with the piano, but didn't know what. Nobody else did either. Back to the screen.

After the satisfying ending of the show we got down to the discussion of Salem's newest mystery. We'd already determined that Bishop and Martell were one and the same. All of us loved the idea that Fenton Bishop was the pen name of Michael Martell, and that as Bishop, the murderer had written some really good murder mysteries while he was in prison.

"I've put a request for his entire series into the county's library system," my aunt explained, "and as long as we have my laptop handy right now, what do you say we check out the newspaper coverage of Martell's recent discharge from prison."

Without waiting for an answer she opened the laptop and her fingers flew over the keyboard. "Yep. Here it is. '*Wife killer released from prison after serving twenty years.*' It says that before he killed her he had a very successful antiques business."

"That must be where he got the idea for the Antique Alley Mystery series," I offered. "I wonder if his publisher knew he was in prison."

"Looks as though we have more questions than answers," Betsy said.

Louisa agreed. "Did anyone ever come up with an alternate conclusion? Could someone else have killed Mrs. Martell?"

"Not only that," my aunt put in, "How did he pay for such an extensive education? Do prisoners get scholarships? What do you say, Angels? Shall we dig deeper into this and see what we can come up with?"

"I can look into all of the financial aspects of Mr. Martell-Bishop's life," Louisa offered. "Perhaps his book royalties paid for his education."

"Interesting idea," Betsy said. "I'll check out friends who knew him—and his wife—twenty years ago."

"I can access all the public records involving Martell *or* Bishop," my aunt announced. "All the way back to his great-great-grandparents and even further if need be."

I shook my head. "You three are a wonder," I said. "The CIA and the FBI could take lessons."

"True." All three nodded agreement while typing into their respective smartphones.

"Oh look," Betsy said. "I checked the census for around twenty years ago and found their address. Now we'll see who their neighbors were. There's probably still some good gossip to find about such a high-profile case."

"Lee, in your position at the station you must have access to all kinds of media material about the case—from twenty years ago right up to the present," Louisa suggested. "Would you have time to dig into it for us?"

My immediate reaction was something like, "Hey, I'm not an Angel. Count me out," but I didn't say it. Instead I wimped out. "I'll see what I can find," I promised halfheartedly. "I'm not sure how far back the archives go."

"Good enough," my aunt pronounced. "I think we're

off to a good start. If any of you find anything I ought to know about this fellow, please call me right away. After all, I'm thinking of inviting him into my house."

"I wouldn't do it," Betsy declared. "After all, he *did* kill somebody."

"Allegedly killed somebody," my aunt countered. "Pete says he probably plead not guilty at the time."

"Most of them do," Betsy agreed. "I think their lawyers advise them to no matter what. But it seems to me that Lee has quite enough on her plate, what with planning a wedding and finding a home in addition to her responsibilities at the station, without helping us work on our case."

She was right, of course, and I fought back the urge to smile at the casual reference to "our case," as though they were the real Charlie's Angels solving a real mystery. But wimpy me just mumbled something about "doing what I can to help," said good night to all, and left for my room. O'Ryan chose to stay with the three wannabe detectives.

Once upstairs I called Rhonda to check on the fittings for the bridesmaids' dresses. She and Wanda and Shannon would be wearing pale lavender silk in a style as close as we could get in street length to my mom's converted vintage Priscilla of Boston. River's maid-of-honor dress would be nearly identical to the others in a deeper shade of violet. We'd ordered bouquets of blush pink roses with baby's breath. Fittings had gone perfectly, Rhonda reported, and all of the dresses would be available for pickup the following weekend. My gown, freshly cleaned and with the puffy sleeves and five-foot train removed, was already hanging in Aunt Ibby's closet along with the lacy, beaded Juliet cap I'd chosen to wear instead of a veil. We'd carefully saved the sleeves and train, though, in case some future daughter or granddaughter might want to make alterations to suit some future style.

I'd worn a veil when I married Johnny. My dress had been a lovely off-the-rack sample-size Vera Wang from David's Bridal Shop. I'd had one attendant and carried a bouquet of orange blossoms. There hadn't been time for complicated alterations and shipping my mother's dress to Florida—it was race car season and we'd scheduled our day between major NASCAR events. It was a beautiful, perfect wedding. The happiest day of my life. Unfortunately, the dress and veil were lost in that devastating attic fire, while my mother's gown had long been safely stored—along with several now-very-out-of-fashion fur coats and stoles—at a local cold storage facility.

Everything is going according to plan. Cake. Flowers. Dresses. Reception menu at Rockafellas confirmed. Have we forgotten anything?

My phone dinged. Pete. "Hello, my love," he said. "How was movie night with the Angels?"

"Fine," I said. "Creepy story about a charming young couple who buy an old house and the usual murder and mayhem happen."

"Oh-oh. I know a charming young couple who just recently bought an old house," he said.

"I know them too," I said. "*They* will live happily ever after."

"Promise?"

"Absolutely."

"Good. I called Joanne about the cat door. She just called me back. No problem. We just can't mess with the front of the house, but the sunporch was an add-on in the fifties and we can put O'Ryan's door there."

"Perfect," I said. "Everything seems to be going along beautifully. Did you and Donnie and the guys get the tuxedos taken care of?"

"Piece of cake."

"A Fabulous Fabio cake, of course."

"None other. I miss you. Wish I could come over." He sounded sad.

"Me too. But having you stay overnight in my own apartment just isn't the same as inviting you into my childhood bedroom. There are still stuffed animals lined up on the window seat," I told him. "Watching."

"Creepy," he agreed. "Can you get away for lunch tomorrow? I've got a little paperwork to show you about the new schoolteacher. You can decide whether to show it to your aunt or not."

"Anything bad?"

"Not bad. Kind of unusual."

"I should warn you. The Angels are checking up on him too. What do you bet they'll come up with everything you have and even more?"

"I know better than to bet against those three," he admitted. "Pick you up at Ariel's bench at noon?"

"See you there," I said. "Love you."

CHAPTER 5

Ariel's bench is a comfortable, sturdy wooden bench, a pleasant place to sit overlooking one of the prettiest parts of Salem Harbor. It's located at the edge of the WICH-TV parking lot, next to the low granite seawall. It was placed there by a local coven in memory of Ariel Constellation—a witch who once hosted a late-night show called *Nightshades*. O'Ryan (she'd named him Orion) had been Ariel's cat—some say her familiar—and in Salem a witch's familiar is always respected and sometimes feared.

Aunt Ibby and I adopted O'Ryan after Ariel's murdered body was found in the water near where the bench is now. I also inherited her late-night call-in psychic show. The cat turned out to be wonderful. The show not so much, but that's another story.

A few minutes before noon I stepped out of the darkened TV studio onto the sunny parking lot. I paused, waiting for my eyes to adjust to the brightness. Pete had already arrived. His unmarked black Ford was parked nearby and he sat on Ariel's bench, back toward me, his arms outstretched across the top rail, face upturned toward the sun.

I tapped him on the shoulder. "Getting a head start on a tan?"

"Oh, hi, babe." He patted the seat beside him. "Join me. This is nice."

I sat and leaned toward him for a somewhat longer-than-usual in-public kiss, then pointed to a manila folder on his lap. "The new schoolteacher?" I asked.

"Not a lot." He opened the folder. "This is just some pretty basic stuff from back when he was sentenced. Looks like it was an open-and-shut case. He made a plea deal—twenty years for pleading guilty to second-degree murder."

"What happened? How did he kill her? And why?" I asked.

"She was shot. Why? Jealousy, apparently. They hadn't been married very long. High school sweethearts. He suspected that she was having an affair. He spotted her car outside a motel. Went home and started drinking, then went back. He had a gun. Found out what room she was in. Knocked on the door, but she didn't answer." Pete sighed and shook his head. "He fired three shots through the door. Hit her with all three. She died a few hours later in the hospital."

"He served the whole twenty years," I said. "No parole?"

"His choice. He said he was guilty and intended to serve his sentence." Pete shuffled the pages forward to what looked like a diploma. "He didn't waste his time in prison. He got permission to take some online college courses. He earned several degrees—one in English. He even wrote a few books. Mysteries. Murder mysteries. He's definitely qualified to teach creative writing at the Tabby, if that's what your aunt is concerned about."

I didn't speak for a moment, trying to visualize the murder, the guilty man, the hours of study behind bars. *Twenty years is a long time to repent.* "I'm not sure. I know she read his books. Liked them all. But should she rent space in her house to a killer?"

Pete shrugged. "Don't know. He never caused any problems in prison. Seems really sorry for killing the woman."

"Did they ever find out? Was she?"

"Was she what?"

"Having an affair?"

"There was nobody else in the room with her. She checked in alone." He closed the folder. "You can keep this. It's okay if you share it with your aunt and the Angels. It's all a matter of public record anyway. Ready for lunch?" I was, and we headed for Red's on Central Avenue. It's a fifty-year-old restaurant housed in a seventeenth-century house. I had a chicken salad club sandwich and Pete ordered a cheeseburger. "No more talk about murder," I said. "We've got a wedding in a couple of weeks, a new house to furnish, and a honeymoon to plan." I held out my left hand, admiring my beautiful diamond engagement ring. "I'm so lucky. So happy."

He covered my hand with his. "I'm the lucky one."

"Any new ideas about the honeymoon?" I asked. We planned to leave right after the reception. We'd use the Chevy unless I got through car shopping and finally decided on the replacement for my Corvette. It would be a short honeymoon—just ten days. Neither of us could take much more time away from our jobs. We'd decided to head north, up the coast of Massachusetts and New Hampshire to Maine, more or less playing it by ear, stopping when and where we wanted to. Our first stop would be at Loudon, New Hampshire, for the stock car races, then through the White Mountains and up into Maine. Other than the race, we hadn't made any specific plans.

"I was thinking about stopping at Clark's Trading Post. I haven't been there since I was a kid."

"I loved Clark's too," I said. "The trained bears. Great idea. Both of our work lives are so scheduled, won't it be wonderful to go where the road takes us, stop when and where we feel like it?"

"Seize the day," he said.

"Exactly," I agreed. "My idea of the perfect honeymoon. And if everything works out right, we'll come home from our perfect honeymoon and move directly into our perfect house."

"I guess that means there'll be furniture in it."

"I've already put the stickers on mine. All set to go. By the way, your bed or mine?"

He grinned. "Yours, definitely. It's king-sized and mine's only a double. I'll go over to my mom's and do my stickers tonight," he promised. We split the tab and left Red's. When we pulled into the WICH-TV parking lot he made the cross-over-the-heart sign as soon as we'd stopped. "Cross my heart."

"We just need the basics. We can shop for extra stuff later," I said. "We'll be fine. Home sweet home." I opened the car door and stepped out. "Is it okay if I show the report on our killer to Scott?" I held up the folder. "He'll be buggin' me about it."

"Sure. Like I said, it's all public record. It'll save him some time looking it up. No big secrets in there. I'll call you tonight."

The buggin' from Scott began even sooner than I'd expected. The tapping at the glass began as soon as I'd closed my office door behind me. I replied to the tap with an exasperated, mouth-open, arms-outstretched "What!"

He gave the universal forefinger-pinkie-next-to-the-ear *call me* sign. I slapped the folder onto the desk and fished the phone from my purse. "Yes, Scott."

"Did the boyfriend spill anything about Dr. Martell and Mr. Bishop?"

I pointed to the folder. "Some basic information. He said I could share it with you. Give me a minute to make a copy and you can have it." I pulled out the stapled-together sheets, removed the staple, and fed the pages into the copier. I knew Scott was watching through the giant window, his nose pressed against the glass like a kid at a candy store. As the copier whirred out duplicates, I replayed in my mind the words he'd just spoken. They'd been uttered in an unnatural sort of singsong rhythm. "Dr. Martell and Mr. Bishop. Dr. Martell and Mr. Bishop."

I knew right away what was going on in Scott Palmer's devious little mind. He was going to compare my aunt's potential new tenant, the Tabby's new instructor, to Robert Louis Stevenson's *Dr. Jekyll and Mr. Hyde*.

I voiced the thought out loud. "Dr. Jekyll and Mr.

Hyde," I said, wondering if Scott could lip-read through the glass. He could. Big smile and hands raised, he pointed to the EXIT sign in the newsroom, and walked quickly toward it. I re-stapled the original report and slid it into the top drawer of my desk. By the time I'd stapled the duplicate he was at my door.

"Brilliant, isn't it? Dr. Jekyll and Mr. Hyde? He killed the lady when he was Mr. Hyde. What do you think? I'm sure Doan will go for it. I'm surprised that his defense lawyers didn't think of it." He reached for the copy I'd prepared.

I handed it to him. "They probably would have—if he'd had 'Doctor' attached to his name back then. He didn't get the doctorate until later. My aunt is looking at the old newspapers. She probably has all the skinny on the trial by now."

"Call her?"

"Uh-uh. I gave you enough for today. Do your own research. See you later." I laughed and prepared to get back to my own job as program director. Since I was planning to be away from my desk for ten days, I needed to make sure that all of the programs originating from the WICH-TV studio would be set go on the air—on schedule, on time. First on my to-do list was to get an audition tape made for Wanda's bid to star on *Hometown Cooks*. The weather reports were part of the news schedule, so I didn't have to worry about most of those. *Cooking with Wanda the Weather Girl* was scripted and produced by Wanda and videographer Marty McCarthy. River's late-night movie and tarot-card reading show, *Tarot Time with River North*, ran like clockwork on its own. I needed to firm up the guest schedule for *Ranger*

Rob's Rodeo Monday-through-Friday shows for kids, and make sure the *Saturday Morning Business Hour* and *Shopping Salem* had everything they needed.

"I can do this," I whispered to myself, with more confidence than I felt, and got to work.

CHAPTER 6

Amazingly, almost everything on my pre-wedding to-do list was checked off, except for the final arrangements for Wanda's audition tape. We needed to do an actual on-air tape—a real-time weather report for Salem, Massachusetts—done in the newsroom with the maps on the green screen, the radar readings, all the usual bells and whistles. The problem here was the fact that our Wanda bills herself as a "weather girl," and her on-air wardrobe consists largely of short shorts and crop tops. The *weather girl* tag and the brief outfits were both totally politically incorrect, but done with tongue-in-cheek good humor and beloved by WICH-TV viewers. Station manager Bruce Doan had decided that for Wanda to have a chance at a spot on *Hometown Cooks* we needed to somehow identify Wanda as a meteorologist and climatologist—both of which she actually is—and dress her "appropriately."

No doubt regular viewers would be confused. We decided to try it out on the 11:00 news broadcast and rather than leave anything to chance, I'd called Pete to let him know I'd be working late, then I planned to come back to the station to watch in person. (We'd already selected one of her *Cooking with Wanda the Weather Girl* shows where an extra-large apron and chef's hat changed her look sufficiently, and shortened the title to *Cooking with Wanda.*)

Handsome nightly news anchor Buck Covington introduced the weather as usual, but this time he said "Welcome our staff meteorologist Wanda with your up-to-date greater Salem area forecast." Wanda appeared, stunning in a sleekly fitted pinstriped business suit and buttoned-up shirt, long golden hair in a neat chignon. I watched every second of it on the newsroom's big-screen monitor. I needn't have been concerned. Everything went off beautifully. Wanda looked gorgeous and sexy in a very classy way and delivered the weather professionally and accurately without relying on a single provocative pose.

I continued to watch as the *Breaking News* banner flashed across the screen and Buck introduced Scott Palmer. *Good for Scott*, I thought. He'd scored a hard-to get special report spot on the nightly news. I remembered how thrilled I'd been on the several occasions when I'd earned that honor as a field reporter.

Scott had done his homework. The breaking news was a carefully worded story about a twenty-year-old murder and a century-old Gothic novel. He'd used the straightforward police transcriptions about the killing. He described how Michael Martell had been a model prisoner, seemed to sincerely regret his crime, studied for years to obtain several degrees. With what passed for admiration in his voice, he told the audience that—using the pseudonym Fenton Bishop—Martell had written and sold successful murder mystery books. I guessed that he'd been able to talk with Mr. Pennington too, because he mentioned a course in creative writing the ex-convict doctor was qualified to teach in Salem schools.

With his trademark long stare into the camera, Scott launched into a smooth retelling of Robert Louis Stevenson's tale, managing to suggest that it might be possible for this man, with no prior record of violent behavior, who had long ago in a jealous rage killed a woman— might possibly be cursed with an unpredictably dual nature—outwardly good, but sometimes shockingly evil. Then he repeated the words I'd heard earlier. "Dr. Martell and Mr. Bishop. Dr. Martell and Mr. Bishop," then, eyes downcast, dropped his voice dramatically. "A twenty-first- century Dr. Jekyll and Mr. Hyde? It's unlikely that such a thing could really happen. We pray not."

My first thought was for Aunt Ibby, hoping she hadn't been watching. What a terrible thought to put in people's minds. Scott had probably covered his rear with that "unlikely to really happen" tag at the end, but it was a mean thing to do to a person who'd done his time and was ready to return to society. I was sorry I'd shared my info, as basic as it was. I ducked out of the newsroom, meaning to avoid him and hurried down the dark corridor toward the *Tarot Time with River North* set. I knew River would be there, preparing for her midnight-movie show. I'd once hosted my own late show, *Nightshades*, from that same studio space.

If River was surprised to see me, she didn't show it.

Sitting in her trademark wicker fanback chair, makeup perfect, she wore a royal-blue satin sheath dress, a large rhinestone clip in the shape of a spider on one shoulder. Silver moons and stars sparkled in her long black hair.

"Hi, Lee. Good to see you. What's up?"

"Good to see you too. Did you watch the news?"

She shrugged her shoulders, making the spider glitter under the overhead lights. "No. You know I never watch it. Too depressing, even though looking at Buck is always fun." River and Buck Covington were dating. Sometimes the handsome anchor dropped in on River's show to shuffle the tarot deck when it was time for her to do a live reading for a caller.

"I had to supervise a special taping of the weather. I guess you know Wanda's in the running for a national reality show about cooking," I explained. "I hung around for the news. Scott did a piece on Michael Martell."

"We all hope Wanda gets that cooking show gig." She placed a deck of cards on the table in front of her. "Martell killed his wife a long time ago, right? I read something about it in the newspaper. They said he used his time in prison to get an education."

"He did, but Scott's report may have put him in kind of a bad light," I said. "Hope it doesn't hurt him in his new job as a teacher."

Another spider-shimmering shrug. "Well, he *did* kill somebody. Not everybody is going to like or trust him."

She was right, of course. "That's true," I admitted, "and it was an opinion piece, and Scott used a proper disclaimer."

"So. No harm done." She glanced at the studio clock. "We have time for a fast pre-wedding reading. What do you say?" She tapped the tarot deck with a silver-polished forefinger.

"Might be a good idea." I sat in the chair opposite hers. "I was going to tell you about something I saw in a mirror today."

She placed the queen of wands, the card she always uses to represent me, in the center of the table, shuffled the deck, then extended it toward me. "What did you see?"

I cut the deck into three piles as I described the kitchen setting I'd seen, and River began to lay out the cards in a familiar pattern. She bowed her head. "May the power of the stars above and the earth below bless this place and this woman, and me, who are with you." The first card she turned over was the ten of cups. I'd seen it before in other people's readings. It had never come up for me before and I was happy to see it.

"The ten of cups," River began. "There couldn't be a more appropriate card for a bride-to-be." The young couple face toward a rainbow, stretching their arms in gratitude, and little children dance near a small house. "Lasting happiness is ahead for you, my friend." She flipped the next card over. "The two of pentacles," she announced. "The man is juggling two circles, trying to decide which one to accept. This card tells you that you can handle more than one situation at a time." She smiled. "But you know that. You do it all the time in your job." She glanced around and dropped her voice. "And you do it in your private life a lot too. Please be careful."

"Do I detect a little warning?"

"Not a warning, really. It's just that something you need to juggle may be difficult to get started. Sometimes this juggler brings a helpful message, so watch for that." She turned the next card over. "Pentacles again. The page. He's looking at a pentacle that seems to be floating above his hands." She looked up at me. "You mentioned a teacher. The page usually represents somebody who's involved with learning. This would be a kind person. No worries here."

Next came the page of wands. "Here's another message bringer—probably something in the mail for you."

Then came the six of wands, picturing a boy giving a girl a cup full of flowers. "Gifts coming your way," River said. "No kidding. Wedding gifts, most likely. The picture shows children. A childhood acquaintance may show up with a present for you. Or you may get an inheritance. Cool, huh?"

Marty wheeled her big camera onto the set. "Sorry to interrupt, kids, but we need to get this show on the road."

River quickly picked up the cards, replacing them in the deck and shuffling them once again. "Sorry, Lee. We'll finish later. So far, looking good. Happiness, presents, old friends. Looking good all around."

"Hope so," I said. "Any thoughts on my mirror vision?"

"Secondhand couch and a clock?" she asked. "Sorry. I can't read your visions like I read the cards. I have an idea the clock might be the important part, though. Ten-fifteen, you said?"

"Right."

"Watch for those numbers. Might be something other than time."

"I hadn't thought about that. Could be money or an address or practically anything."

"Yep. Watch for it. Gotta go to work now." She faced the camera. "See you later."

Marty waved from under the camera hood. "See ya later, Moon." Marty still calls me "Moon" because back when I played a psychic, I called myself "Crystal Moon" and some of the WICH-TV staff haven't forgotten it. I stepped away from the lights, back into the cool darkness of the long, black-walled studio.

CHAPTER 7

When I was doing the late-movie show at WICH-TV I became accustomed to driving home in the wee hours of morning. It had been a while since I'd done it, and I'd almost forgotten how different midnight Salem looks as compared to noontime Salem. The parking lot was nearly empty. Someone was asleep on Ariel's bench. A few lights twinkled red, white, and green in the harbor—boats moored or moving, buoys marking the channels. A distant air horn sounded, helping to guide mariners on the darkened sea. I tiptoed past the bench, not wanting to wake the sleeper. My regular parking spot at the far end of the lot seemed miles away and my heels made an echoing click-click as I hurried toward it, welcoming the flashing taillight signaling that the Chevy was unlocked, ready to roll and take me home. I eased out of the lot onto Derby Street, turned onto Hawthorne Boulevard past the Salem Common, and made a quick left turn to take me home.

As I pulled the Chevy into our garage, waited for the suspended yellow tennis ball to hit the windshield, I thought for the umpteenth time about getting a new car. Another high-powered, two-seat convertible like my beloved Corvette Stingray was out of the question. Pete wanted me to have something with plenty of safely features. "For our kids," he explained, but I knew it was also because of my very recent experience of being intentionally run off the road by a killer. That episode had cost me my beautiful dream car and I'd been darned lucky that it hadn't cost me my life. It was enough to convince me that a super safe car was probably a pretty good idea.

Maybe I'll even surprise Pete with a new ride for our honeymoon trip. "I'll do something about it today," I told myself. I locked the garage and walked along the solar-lighted path past Aunt Ibby's garden, where shapes of trees and bushes—friendly and familiar in the daytime—loomed like crouching, branch-waving creatures. I was glad to hear the *click* of a cat door. O'Ryan trotted toward me, gave a trilling purr, and fell into step at my side. "Look, O'Ryan," I said, pointing to a lighted second-story window. "Aunt Ibby is still awake. I'll bet she's waiting up for me like she used to do when I was in high school."

We exited the wrought iron gate onto Winter Street, climbed the front steps of the house together and I unlocked the door, resecured the alarm system and, the cat still beside me, started up the wide polished staircase to the second floor. My aunt's door was ajar, leaking a sliver of light onto the maroon carpet in the hallway. I tapped gently and pushed the door open.

"I'm home," I said. "Thanks for waiting up."

"Oh, hello, dear." She held up a paperback book. "Just catching up on my reading. A new Tasha Alexander arrived today. How did your late taping go? I thought Wanda looked especially lovely. That's a whole new look for her, isn't it?"

"Very much so. It'll be interesting to see what the reaction of her regular weather fans will be. I stopped by to spend a few minutes with River."

"Oh? She's showing *Cat People* tonight. O'Ryan and I watched it on YouTube a couple of weeks ago." She gave a dismissive wave. "He didn't care much for it. Did you get a chance to mention your recent vision to her?"

"I did," I said. "She thinks the time may be the important part—only not just as time. It's the numbers ten and fifteen or some combination of them that might be significant. What do you think?"

"I prefer not to think about such things at all." She closed her book and put it on the bedside table. "River is more knowledgeable about things mystical than I. Let's just be on the lookout for those numbers, just in case they're important for some reason." She hadn't mentioned seeing the late news, so it was possible that she'd missed Scott's barely veiled suggestion that her prospective new tenant might be some sort of a weird split-personality case. I wasn't about to bring it up.

"I'm thinking about doing some car shopping tomorrow," I announced. "Something safe, you know? I might surprise Pete with it. We can make our honeymoon road trip the shakedown cruise."

"Excellent idea," she agreed. "Anything particular in mind?"

"Just so it's safe, a nice shade of blue, and has a good sound system," I said. "I'm not hard to please. Nighty-night." I stepped back into the hall. O'Ryan was already curled up at the foot of my aunt's bed, eyes squeezed shut, pretending to be asleep. I passed the small guest room between my aunt's bedroom and mine, opened my door and switched on the overhead light.

The crocheted canopy top, starched white dust ruffle, and puffy pink quilt presented a welcoming bedtime vista. My aunt had even turned down the covers, revealing cool pink sheets. I took a fast shower in my teensy bathroom, tossed my clothes down the laundry chute, pulled on a plaid nightshirt and climbed into bed.

I thought about River's idea that the numbers ten-fifteen could mean just about anything. A date? October fifteenth? A price? Ten dollars and fifteen cents? One thousand and fifteen dollars? An address? Number ten Fifteenth Avenue? Part of a phone number? A password? A license plate? The numbers danced through my head with the general effect of counting a thousand and fifteen sheep. I was sound asleep in minutes.

Alarm clock and cell phone rang at the same time: Six o'clock. I hit the snooze button on one and greeted Pete on the other. "Good morning. I wish you were here."

"I wish I was too. How'd last night go? I meant to watch the weather to see how Wanda cleans up, but I fell asleep."

"Wanda cleans up real nice," I told him. "She looked gorgeous and delivered the weather report complete with isobars and ozone layers. Impressive. I guess you slept through the news too?"

"Yep. Did I miss something?"

"Scott did what almost amounted to a hit piece on Michael Martell. Hinted at a Dr. Jekyll and Mr. Hyde split personality."

"On what grounds?"

"None. He made it clear it was unlikely that it could happen, but he planted the seed anyway."

"Is your aunt upset about it since Martell might be moving into your apartment?"

"She missed it too. I didn't bring it up."

"Probably won't amount to anything anyway," he said. "How's the to-do list coming along?"

"Mine's almost finished," I said. "How's yours?"

"Did stickers. Do you think we'll have room for my big leather recliner?"

I'd seen him happily watching football many times in that worn old chair. "Absolutely," I said. "We'll make room."

"Want to go to breakfast?" he asked. "Maybe we can tie up some loose ends."

"Sure. Want to pick me up or shall we meet at the place?" "The place" is what we call our favorite breakfast restaurant. It's located in one of Salem's side-street neighborhoods in a neat but nondescript two-story house. There's no name on the building, just a vertical red neon OPEN sign in a front window. Patrons usually include night-shift workers on their way home, day-shift workers on their way to work. Nurses, taxi drivers, cops, firefighters, the occasional kids' hockey team with early ice time. Good, homestyle breakfasts and lunches and hardly ever any tourists.

"Meet you there. About seven?"

"Perfect. Love you. Bye."

A lot of my clothes were packed away in boxes and

garment bags in anticipation of moving. The closet in this bedroom contained an assortment of jeans, shoes, boots, handbags, a couple of dresses, some sweaters, jackets, and shirts. My job as program director allowed me to dress casually—different from my always-camera-ready stint as a field reporter. There hadn't been room in the closet for my wedding dress, so for now it hung in Aunt Ibby's roomy walk-in.

By 6:45, bed made, teeth brushed, curly red hair tamed somewhat, dressed in jeans, green silk shirt and tan booties, I was ready to go. I tucked my phone into my favorite hobo bag, checked to be sure my checkbook was there in case I wound up buying a car, and headed out for breakfast with Pete.

Pete was already waiting on the front steps when I got there. We walked inside together. The waitress called us by name, indicated the day's specials on a blackboard, led us to our favorite booth in the back of the room, and poured us each a mug of steaming coffee. We ordered our usual. Veggie omelet for me and ham and eggs for Pete. Home fries for both. We lingered over coffee, making scribbly sketches on paper napkins of furniture placements in our new home.

Pete's phone buzzed. "Sorry, babe," he said. "Gotta take this." He gave a couple of nods, a few cop-voice "yessirs." A long, listening, pause. "Be right there," he said and put the phone back in his pocket. He picked up the check and stood. "That was the chief. I guess he saw the news last night. Take your time and finish your coffee. I'll call you later."

"Is this about Scott's dumb report?"

"Yep. Chief wants to take another look at the Martell murder."

CHAPTER 8

"You're early," Rhonda commented when I checked in at the reception desk. "Getting a head start on that to-do list before the wedding?"

"Breakfast with Pete," I explained. "The to-do list is actually in pretty good shape. Dresses, flowers, cake." I ticked off the items on my fingers. "Guest lineup for Ranger Rob show almost complete, papers for house offer signed, demonstration tapes for Wanda done. Today I'll make sure about the music for the reception and maybe buy a new car."

"We've already had a few calls on Wanda's new look," she said. "What kind of car?"

"What do they say about the new Wanda?" I asked. "Pete thinks I need a safe car."

"Fifty-fifty so far on Wanda," she said. "Too soon to tell which way it'll go. Are you thinking of another convertible?"

"Definitely not a convertible," I promised. "You saw the pictures of what was left of my Corvette. I'm thinking four-wheel drive, automatic emergency brakes, blind-spot warnings, all-terrain tires, roll bar—the works."

"Well, if anyone around here knows cars, you do."

It was true. Being married to a NASCAR driver had made me into a real car buff. Pete calls me a gearhead. I love all kinds of auto races—the speed, the sounds, even the smells of the track. I read *Motor Trend* and *Car and Driver.* I adored my beautiful Corvette Stingray for the big powerful engine (0 to 60 MPH in 3 seconds), the sound of the exhaust, the exotic sports car design—but it admittedly wasn't a practical car for city driving, especially during New England winters. Pete was right about the importance of safety—and my recent accident had made a believer out of me too.

"Business before pleasure," I said. "Program planning first, car shopping as time allows. Is Ranger Rob in yet?"

"He's here, horse and all. Katie the Clown and Paco the wonder dog are here too."

"Good. How about Scott Palmer?" I thought again of what Pete had said about taking another look at the Martell murder. Did Scott have any idea of what his irresponsible comments about an old story may have put into motion?

"Not here yet. He worked overtime last night. He'll be late this morning."

I worked overtime too but I'm here. "I'll be on the Ranger Rob set for a while. After that, I'll be in my office," I said. "If I get everything done, I may sneak out for a while to visit an auto showroom or two."

"Miss Efficiency, that's you."

"Sure." I ducked out the metal door leading down to

the studio and clattered down the metal stairs. I didn't exactly feel like Miss Efficiency, but so far I thought I'd
done pretty well in designating who'd be responsible for
what while I was away. I had a good team to work with
and, after all, it would only be for ten days. It wasn't as if
I was even going to leave New England. I'd be able to be
in touch with the station every day.

Well before I'd reached the soundstage for *Ranger
Rob's Rodeo*, I could hear the excited chatter and laughter
from Rob's little buckaroos. Every weekday morning, a
dozen boys and girls are invited to be part of the show.
They're seated on stage and get to meet and pet Rob's
beautiful palomino Prince Valiant and Paco the Wonder
Dog. I watched as Katie the Clown and Rob skillfully involved the kids in funny skits, which always held an up-
beat message. I stayed for a while, waiting for the new
commercial for Captain Billy's toy trawler to run. Professionally produced, with Captain Billy himself providing
the voice-over, it ran for exactly one minute. Perfect. No
worries about this popular morning show.

Up the metal staircase to the newsroom next, to catch
Wanda's morning weather forecast. No one would ever
guess that Wanda had stayed up late. In her usual weather
girl garb this morning, long blond hair in an over-one-
shoulder braid, she wore hot pink shorts and a barely-
legal matching halter top. It was going to be interesting to
see which Wanda the viewers preferred. Scott wasn't at
his desk yet. A glance at the news monitor told me why.
There he was, facing a couple of young women, apparently doing a field report in front of the Tabitha Trumbull
Academy of the Arts.

I hurried into my own office and turned on my TV. I
didn't want to miss a word of this. The Tabby locale told

me that he wasn't about to let go of his crazy Dr. Jekyll and Mr. Hyde fantasy. He introduced the two, both first-year creative writing students. "How do you feel about having a convicted killer as your instructor, Maryanne?" he asked the first one. "How do you feel that your teacher, who calls himself Fenton Bishop, is really Dr. Michael Martell—confessed murderer?"

"He seems really smart," she replied. "He doesn't talk about his past at all, except about how he wrote his first book while he was in prison."

The second woman spoke up. "I think it's kind of scary, in a way. But I know we're safe in school and any-way, they wouldn't have hired him if there was anything wrong." Her eyes widened. "Would they?"

It was the kind of question Scott relished. He ran with it. "An interesting question, Susan." He used his most se-rious, big-network reporter voice. "Twenty years is a long time. Some folks are wondering if there were any similar killings happening in the area back then—killings still unsolved today."

That sounds a lot like what Chief Whaley is looking into.

Scott pushed his luck with Maryanne. "Does it worry you at all, Maryanne?"

Maryanne didn't back down. "No. I read his mystery novels. They're so good. I'm working on a murder mys-tery myself. He seems like the perfect instructor for me."

"Well, thank you, ladies." Scott looked into the cam-era. "Stay tuned to WICH-TV, folks, for more on this on-going story."

What ongoing story? You're making it all up! I doubted that the rest of the news audience would buy into Scott's fantasy any more than the young Tabby students had. I hoped not. I was sure that by then Aunt Ibby had heard the story—and I also hoped that, like Maryanne and Susan, she'd give Dr. Martell the benefit of the doubt.

By noon, I'd arranged for an hour-long presentation by a well-known UMass business professor as backup in case something went wrong with the scheduled *Saturday Morning Business Hour*, and contacted old friend and publicity hound, Chris Rich, who could always be counted on to promote his shop, Christopher's Castle, at a moment's notice in case one of the *Shopping Salem* guests canceled. There was plenty of the afternoon left for car shopping, and to please Mr. Doan, I'd combine it with a courtesy call on one of our advertisers. Pete had mentioned a Jeep as a safe enough vehicle for "our kids," so I decided to start at the nearby Jeep dealership.

Whatever vehicle I decided on, I planned to simply write a check for it. I'd paid for the Corvette that way too. Between the inheritance from my parents and Johnny's insurance along with expert advice from Aunt Ibby's financial managers, I've become what may be considered a fairly wealthy woman. For a long time I'd been afraid to tell Pete about that—afraid it would scare him away. Once we became engaged, though, I had to tell him, and he's okay with it. He says he's glad he doesn't have to worry about college for our kids.

Two hours later I drove off the lot in my new four-door hydro blue pearl Jeep Wrangler with every safety feature I could think of—from all-terrain tires to automatic emergency brakes to power winch—and a few I'd never heard of. It had been in the center of the showroom floor—the complete deluxe safety package with body-on-frame construction and solid axles. The V-8 engine and eight-speed transmission made me happy and the custom sound system with three-ohms speakers and dual-lever tweeter volume adjustments made me even happier. It even had leather seats. I happily wrote a hefty check for the full amount, cranked up the sound, and drove back to the station with Stevie Nicks playing full blast.

Word spreads quickly in a TV station—after all, news is our business. I'd parked the Jeep in my accustomed space next to the seawall and before I'd reached the studio door, Marty, Rhonda and Chester—the custodian/night watchman/handyman—were already outside. "The manager of the Jeep dealership called Doan about your new ride," Rhonda explained. "He says it's top-of-the-line loaded with everything. Let's have a look."

The four of us paraded back across the lot. I opened everything—doors, hood, glove box, console—and stood back, accepting comments and compliments all around. A few more coworkers arrived, but before too much longer someone commented that we'd better get back to our jobs. So my workplace new car show-and-tell session was over, but I could still hardly wait to surprise Pete and Aunt Ibby.

I called my aunt, just to be sure she'd be there when I got home. "Guess what I did today?" I began.

"You bought a new Jeep," she exclaimed. "When are you coming home? I can hardly wait. Betsy says it's blue. Is that right?"

"Betsy? How did *she* know about it?"

"Hairdresser. Wanda was there getting a new do. She got an email from somebody at the station with a picture of your Jeep and showed it to Betsy. It's hard to keep a secret these days, isn't it?"

"Apparently," I agreed, disappointed that my surprise

was spoiled. "Did Betsy mention what Wanda's new do looks like?"

"Short; quite sophisticated, according to Betts."

"I guess she didn't send a picture?" I was hopeful.

"No picture," she said. "But I'll bet Wanda is embracing her new, smarter, more professional persona. What do you think?"

"You may be right. I just hope Mr. Doan approves of the change." I hesitated, uncomfortable about bringing up Scott's crazy theory about Dr. Martell and Mr. Bishop. "Did you watch Scott's piece about the new teacher at the Tabby?"

"I did. What is that boy thinking? Dr. Jekyll and Mr. Hyde, indeed. Doesn't make the least bit of sense. Those students saw right through it." She made a *tsk-tsk* sound. "I'm sure Rupert won't be swayed by such nonsense. Those girls seemed to like Michael as a teacher."

Michael? My aunt is on a first-name basis already with the prospective tenant? "I agree," I told her. "I'll be on my way home in a few minutes. I'll park in front of the house. I'm not ready to hide my new toy in the garage yet."

"I can hardly wait," she said. "O'Ryan and I will be watching for you from the front hall. Have you told Pete about it yet?"

"I'm hoping to surprise him, but as you said, it's hard to keep a secret these days. Anyway, I'm going to call him and ask him to come over."

"I'll bet he doesn't know about it yet." Soft giggle. "Unless he has the same hairdresser as Wanda and Betsy."

CHAPTER 9

I called Pete and asked him if he could come over to Winter Street for a little while. I pretended I had some questions about the outside of the new house and thought we should do one more fast walk-by. He agreed right away, said he'd be there in about half an hour, and unless he was a better actor than I thought he was, I was pretty sure he had no idea of what I was up to.

My aunt and cat, as promised, waited in the front hall for me to pull up in front of the house, and together they spilled out of the house and down the stairs before I'd even come to a full stop. O'Ryan hung behind, crouching on the bottom step, while Aunt Ibby approached the Jeep, putting a tentative finger on the hood. I stepped out. "What do you think?"

"It looks very big," she said, "and tall, very blue and—well—a bit intimidating."

"But safe?" I asked.

"Oh, absolutely safe." She pointed to the winch on the front of the Jeep, then waved her arm to include the whole front end. "I guess there's a big powerful engine in there."

"There is," I promised. "I think Pete will approve."

I certainly hope so.

I opened the doors, inviting her to come inside, to touch the smooth leather and breathe in the new-car smell. I showed off the space-age look of the instrument panel, opened the glove box and the console, demonstrated the sound system by playing a bit of Pavarotti. My phone buzzed announcing a text from Pete: **On my way.**

"Pete's on his way," I told my aunt. "Let's wait for him on the steps with O'Ryan." So the three of us were lined up in a row when Pete arrived, my aunt and I standing expectantly, O'Ryan still in his cautious crouch. Pete parked behind the Jeep, the broad smile on his face telling me he liked what he saw even before he climbed out of the unmarked black Ford. I ran to meet him. "What do you think? Do you love it?"

He walked around the Jeep. Slowly. By then the smile had been replaced with cop face. "Pop the hood, will you, babe?" I did.

"Start 'er up."

"Okay." I did.

The smile returned. "You got the whole extreme terrain safety package."

"And then some," I agreed. "Pass inspection?"

"It's even better than I expected." He slid into the passenger seat, reaching over to take my hand. "Your safety means more to me than anything else in the world. I worry about you every second that I'm away from you. I love you."

I fought back tears at the sentiment in his words. "I love you too," I said, then sat up straight. "Wait a minute. What do you mean, 'It's even better than you expected.' You *expected* this Jeep? You knew about it?"

His expression was sheepish. "Not exactly. Friend at the rental company mentioned you'd returned the Chevy. I guessed you'd found a replacement for the Corvette. I hope I didn't spoil your surprise?"

"Not at all," I said, meaning it. His loving words had more than made up for the rental company tip-off. By then Aunt Ibby had joined us at curbside, and O'Ryan had ventured onto the sidewalk. "Well, let me lock up this beauty and we'll take that walk by our new home."

"Is there anything wrong down there?" he asked.

"Not at all. I'd like to take a peek at the sunporch and think about the cat door for O'Ryan."

"Come on back and join O'Ryan and me for a little supper," Aunt Ibby offered. "And we have a new batch of RSVP responses from your wedding invitations to go over."

"We'll be right back," I told her. Pete and I walked down Winter Street, turning our heads occasionally, looking back, admiring my gleaming new ride. We reached the one-of-a-kind row house and Pete pulled his phone from a pocket. "Let's take a selfie in front of our half," he said. The two sides are a mirror image of each other. That is, they share a common wall in the center of the building. Our front door is on the far left and the other side has its front door on the far right. We stood close together on the low granite doorstep, smiled into the camera, then ducked into the narrow path beside the house leading to the backyard. "I feel as though we're trespassing," I said.

"I know," he said. "I won't feel as if it's ours until we have keys to all the doors." He jiggled the doorknob to the French door on the sunroom. "This must be where we're allowed to install O'Ryan's entrance."

"Maybe we can just remove one pane on the bottom row and put a cat door there." I scooched down close to the doorjamb and peered through the glass. Boom! Flashing lights and swirling colors. I tried to stand, but a feeling of vertigo kept me focused on the image beginning to take shape. It was a child's shoe, a black patent leather shoe in the style they call "Mary Jane."

I squeezed my eyes shut, reaching up for Pete's hand, grasping it, struggling to my feet. That particular image brings bad memories.

"Are you all right?" Pete put a steadying arm around my waist. "You look kind of wobbly."

"Seeing things in the glass," I admitted. "Made me a little dizzy. I'm okay now."

Pete knows about the visions, but he's always been uncomfortable talking about them. "Want to tell me about it?"

"Just an old shoe," I said. "Darn visions don't make the least bit of sense."

"They do eventually, though, don't they?" he said. "You'll probably figure it out after a while."

"I know." I tried to shake the shoe picture away. "Meanwhile, I think as long as O'Ryan doesn't get fat he'll fit through that space just fine."

"I hope he'll like the new house."

"I'm sure he will. As long as we bring along his favorite zebra-print wing chair and his special red food dish, he'll be fine." I moved toward the path leading back onto Winter Street. "Shall we go take advantage of Aunt Ibby's supper offer?"

"That'd be hard to turn down," he said. We made our way down the street, laughing as we each took more than a few backward glances at our home-to-be. I knew I'd been less than straightforward with that "just an old shoe" remark. Little-girl–sized Mary Janes held a particularly bad memory for me, one I didn't care to discuss with anybody at that moment.

Maybe later, I told myself. Then again, *maybe not.*

O'Ryan peered out at us from the window beside the front door. I used my key to let us in and he made joyous, purring circles around our feet while the good smells from the kitchen welcomed us. "We're home," I called, realizing as I spoke that before long *home* would be another place altogether. I paused as we passed by the Sheraton table in the foyer, where more than a dozen identical small cream-colored envelopes almost filled an antique oval silver tray. Aunt Ibby had been correct about the new batch of responses from our wedding invitations. Ours was to be a small wedding, as Salem weddings go. We planned on about 150 guests. Pete's family is considerably larger than mine—he even still has both sets of grandparents—so I expected that most of the RSVPs would be from his extended family and friends. I have a few relatives from my father's side of the family, none of whom live nearby, and only a couple of distant cousins from my mother's and Aunt Ibby's side. There are high school and college friends of mine who still live in the Salem area, and of course there's my WICH-TV family. I'd been especially pleased when a good many acceptances had already arrived from students from the TV Production 101 classes I'd taught at the Tabby.

Supper that night was one of my favorite soup-and-salad combinations—a thick, rich corn chowder sprinkled with salt pork bits and a bright and beautiful Cobb salad with Aunt Ibby's own homemade poppy seed dressing. Dessert was Pete's favorite—her double-fudge brownies that had won blue ribbons at who-knows-how-many baking contests, along with big scoops of vanilla ice cream and a generous drizzle of hot fudge sauce.

"I noticed a pile of envelopes on the table," I said, savoring the last crumb of my brownie. "Shall we go over them after the dishes and check the yeas and nays off the list?"

"Good idea," she said. "There are a few out-of-state postmarks. I hope some of the cousins are going to join us."

"Hope so," I said. "We usually only get to see each other at Thanksgiving or Christmas. I'll load the dishwasher while you get the checklist. Pete, want to grab those envelopes on the hall table?" We each hurried to our assigned duties, then returned to the table. Aunt Ibby handed Pete a letter opener.

"I recognize the handwriting on this one." Pete held the envelope with thumb and forefinger. "My mom. Wouldn't be surprised if she wrote *It's about time* on it." He slit the envelope. "Yep. My parents. Two for the *yes* column."

"Got it," my aunt said. They established a rhythm. The *swoosh* sound of the opener slicing paper, Pete calling out a name, a "yes" or "no" and the number of guests followed by Aunt Ibby's acknowledgement that she'd posted it. Sometimes there was a snatch of conversation about the respondent. "It'll be good to see them," or "Too bad they can't make it," or occasionally, "Who's that?"

One of the "who's that?" comments came from me.

Pete had mentioned a Maine postmark and the name Doris K. Raymond. "Regrets from Mr. and Mrs. Raymond." He handed the card to my aunt.

"Doris is your father's sister. Your aunt," she said, studying the note. "They sent you a gift card from Macy's for a hundred dollars."

"That's nice. Did I ever meet her? Or Mr. Raymond?"

"I doubt that you'd remember them. Doris and Bill Raymond. They came to your parents' memorial service. Since then we've exchanged Christmas cards. That's about it. I sent them items about you from time to time— like your high school graduation. They sent a check and I made sure you wrote a proper thank you note. Remember?"

"Vaguely. You've had me write quite a few of those notes over the years to long-lost second cousins I'd never met. I wish now I'd paid more attention. They live in Maine?" I asked.

"Yes. As a matter of fact, your folks had been visiting Doris and Bill on their island before their tragic accident." She looked down and made a check mark on her sheet.

"Wow. They have their own island?" Pete asked.

"They sure do." She nodded. "There's even an old lighthouse on it. Quite an historical site, as I recall."

"No kidding. Maybe we should drop in on them while we're in Maine," Pete said.

I laughed. "Hard to drop in on an island when you're on a road trip," I reminded him. "But we could call them, maybe invite them to join us for dinner when we're in the neighborhood."

"Good idea," Pete said. "Do you have their number, Ibby?"

"I'm sure I do."

"Good." Pete held up three envelopes. "Look at this. Three Mondellos in a row. Bet they're all acceptances."

"I had a phone acceptance from my cousin Rita," Aunt Ibby countered. "She and her husband and all three of their kids will be there."

"Some of the WICH-TV people did phone acceptances too," I said. "Good thing the Sunday schedule is mostly canned infomercials, church services, and network programs. The place runs on a skeleton staff, so I'm pretty sure most of my friends from work will be there."

We finished our RSVP count and showed Aunt Ibby our latest selfie. "That's a handsome front door," she said. "But did you figure out where O'Ryan's door will be?"

"There's a French door on the sunroom," Pete told her. "We figure we'll just take out a pane of glass at the bottom and put it there."

"A French door is so nice," my aunt said. "Those clear panes let in such lovely light."

Sometimes they let in things you don't want to see.

CHAPTER 10

When the call from Joanne came I was in Rhonda's office checking my schedule on her whiteboard. "Can you and Pete get away at around noon to meet me at the title company?"

"It's final? The house is ours?"

"Sure thing. There are a few papers to be signed and notarized and the title and keys to your new kingdom are yours." I heard the smile in her voice. "Will you call Pete?"

"I will. Right now."

"Your house?" Rhonda was all smiles too. I punched in Pete's number, nodded *yes* rapidly and waited for him to pick up.

"Pete? Joanne called." I knew my voice was shaking. "She wants to meet us at the title company at noon. Okay?"

He said the same thing I'd said. "It's final?"

"Yep. We just need to sign some papers and they give us the keys. To our 'new kingdom,' Joanne says."

"Want me to pick you up or meet you there?" Pete asked.

"Let's go together. Pick me up at quarter to twelve?"

"Ariel's bench. Quarter to twelve. Listen, I have something to show you."

That made me curious. "A surprise? Or are you going to tell me what it is now?"

He laughed. "I'll tell you now. I know you'll pry it out of me anyway. I looked up your Aunt Doris's island. It's enormous. Over two hundred acres. They call it Pirate's Island."

"So my aunt and uncle actually *own* a whole island?"

"Nothing unusual about that. There are more than four thousand islands off the coast of Maine. A bunch of them are privately owned."

"Wow," I said. "I'm impressed. I didn't know I had such interesting relatives."

"Everybody has interesting relatives," he insisted. "Didn't I ever tell you about my great uncle Vinnie? He was almost killed in the great molasses flood of 1919 when he was five years old."

"I don't believe you ever mentioned him." I waited for the story.

"Vinnie and his three sisters went to a bakery in the North End—Boston, you know, to get some cannoli for their mother and *whoosh!* They heard an explosion and this huge tidal wave of molasses came from a giant vat and swallowed little Vinnie. Some people actually drowned in molasses that day, but Vinnie's sisters pulled him out and saved his life. He said he had a cough for about a year afterwards—and he always swore that on hot summer days you could still smell the molasses in the North End. True story."

"I believe it," I said. "Some hot day this summer let's go there and get cannoli and see if we can smell molasses."

"You're on. So, does an uncle who survived an historic event beat an aunt who owns an island?"

"Maybe. Yeah, it probably does. I'll ask Aunt Ibby to see if she can dig up something juicier than mere island ownership," I promised. "I'll see you out by the bench in a few and we'll go get our house keys."

I shared the bench with a man wearing neatly pressed gray slacks and white open-at-the-throat shirt. Business casual, I thought, but a well-thumbed copy of *Destination Salem* on his lap and expensive-looking camera focused on the harbor view before us shouted *tourist*. "Excuse me, miss." He lowered the camera. "Could I ask you a favor?"

"What can I do for you?" I asked.

"Would you take my picture with this great view behind me? I have plenty of pictures of scenery but few with me in them. Someday I might want to prove I was here." I recognized him as soon as he smiled.

"You're Dr. Martell," I blurted as I reached for the camera. "I mean, sure. Of course I will." The smile faded as he stood, handed me the camera, and walked to the seawall. He turned, facing me. "Try to get that beautiful sailboat in the frame, would you?"

I nodded, took a couple of shots and silently handed the camera back to him. *Should I apologize for blabbing his name out like that?* I froze, embarrassed.

The gentle smile was back. "It's okay," he said. "I'm

getting used to it. The publicity. Actually, I was sitting here trying to work up the courage to go inside." He jerked a thumb toward the building behind us. "I've agreed to an interview with a reporter. Scott Palmer. Know him?"

"Yes. Yes, I do." I was relieved to see Pete's car pulling onto the lot, glad I wouldn't have to elaborate. "Well, here comes my ride. Nice to meet you. Good luck with your interview."

"Thank you, Miss . . . ?"

"Oh." I extended my hand. "Lee Barrett."

He shook my hand, gave a tiny bow, turned and headed for the front door just as the black Ford Utility came to a stop. Pete rolled down the passenger window. "Wasn't that . . . ?"

"Sure was." I slid into the seat. "Dr. Martell has an interview booked with Scott."

Pete grimaced. "That's not a good thing, is it?"

"I don't know," I admitted. "It depends on how they each handle it. Dr. Martell is obviously very smart—brilliant, maybe—and Scott knows how to conduct a straightforward, careful, honest interview. On the other hand, Dr. Martell has been away from the real world for a long time—and Scott can be really aggressive with his questions if he wants to."

"Do you suppose they're doing it live? For the noon news?"

I looked at my watch. Ten minutes to twelve. "I hope not, but I'll bet they are. For Martell's sake, I hope Scott's not going to press that Jekyll and Hyde nonsense. I mean, how do you flat-out just ask someone if they killed some other people before the murder they were arrested for?"

"Would Dr. Martell know about everything he did

when he was Fenton Bishop?" Pete asked as we parked in front of the title company's Federal Street office.

"Fenton Bishop was just a pseudonym he used for writing mystery stories," I said, "not a real person."

"Maybe," Pete said. "Let's go in and get our keys."

It didn't take long. Some more name signing and initialing of papers and copies of papers, some congratulations and thank-yous all around and the half-a-house on Winter Street was ours. We decided to drive over there right away to try out our new keys.

Pete held the front door key in ready position, then paused. "Is this the part where I carry you over the threshold? Or is that after the wedding?"

I didn't hesitate. "Now is good."

"Feels right to me too. They say carrying the bride over the threshold protects her from evil spirits." He turned the key, pushed the door open with his foot, and lifted me into his arms. A passing car tooted the horn. We both laughed and I waved over Pete's shoulder. He stepped into the hall, lowered me carefully until my feet touched the polished wide floorboards. Long, happy kiss—then we ran from room to room like excited kids.

"We can start moving furniture in right away," he said. "I'll borrow Donnie's truck and get mine started this weekend."

"Aunt Ibby has already hired a mover to take care of the major stuff of mine," I said. "Everything has to be moved down three flights of stairs—too tricky for amateurs. The new Jeep is big enough to handle smaller things, though—pictures and lamps and plants. I can hardly wait to get started."

"We're going to get a lot of use out of that Jeep," he said. "I'm glad you bought it."

"Me too," I said, with a moment's silent sadness at the loss of my gorgeous Corvette. "It's surely useful, and sturdy and safe."

"All that," he said. "Want to stop and tell your aunt we're officially neighbors now?"

"Let's," I said.

Pete made a U-turn onto Oliver Street and pulled into the gravel parking area beside the garage in Aunt Ibby's yard. We walked together past the fenced garden toward the back door, where O'Ryan waited to greet us. "How does he always know which door we're going to use?" Pete wondered as we approached the house.

I shrugged. "I don't understand how he knows a lot of things." It was true. From the moment I first saw the big yellow cat—when I tripped over him in the WICH-TV parking lot just after I'd discovered Ariel's body floating in the harbor—I'd been aware that he was no ordinary house cat. I pulled keys from my purse as O'Ryan treated me to a series of affectionate figure eights around my ankles. "I have my key," I said, turning it in the lock as O'Ryan darted through his cat door.

"I still have mine too," Pete said. "I guess I'll have to give it back now that your apartment is going to be an Airbnb." The twisty staircase to my third-floor apartment was just inside the short hall. The entrance to Aunt Ibby's kitchen was a few feet away. Pete and I had used this entrance much more often than we'd used the more formal foyer on the Winter Street side of the house.

The sound of the Mamas and the Papas' "Monday, Monday" issued from the kitchen, along with the aroma of something delicious baking. I knocked, but by then O'Ryan had already scampered through that cat door, announcing our presence. "It's Pete and me, Aunt Ibby," I called. "Got a minute?"

"For you? Always," she said, pulling the door open, then wiping her hands on a red-and-white–checked apron with *Crazy Cat Lady* embroidered in black.

"We are officially homeowners!" I threw my arms around her. "We can move in right away."

"I'm so happy for you both," she said. "There's going to be a lot of moving activity around here. My first third-floor tenant will be arriving as soon as the new kitchen appliances are hooked up."

"Good for you," Pete said. "The front apartment or the rear one?"

"I suggested the rear one," she said, "since he has a car and the easiest parking is in the backyard. But I told him he could have his pick," she said. "Since he was first to apply it seems only fair."

"He," I repeated. "So you're renting the first one to a man?"

"Dr. Martell," she said. "Rupert recommends him very highly."

CHAPTER 11

"Coincidentally," I said, "I met him this morning. Just before noon."

"You met Dr. Martell? Where?"

"At the station," I said. "He was there for an interview with Scott Palmer."

"You know, since you aren't doing your field reporting anymore, Maralee, I don't watch TV in the daytime much anymore." She glanced up at the clock. "It's not twelve thirty yet. Do you think I've missed it?"

I sure hope so. "Probably," I said.

She reached for the remote and the small wall-hung TV over a shelf full of cookbooks glowed to life. A serious-looking Scott Palmer faced Michael Martell. My aunt frowned. "I certainly hope he's not going to mention that ridiculous Jekyll and Hyde idea."

"So, Dr. Martell," Scott intoned. "I understand that you'll be teaching creative writing at the Tabby."

"Yes, indeed." Martell smiled into the camera. "Classes have already begun. My students seem very receptive. Teaching has long been a dream of mine."

"While you were incarcerated, you mean."

Oh-oh. Scott's going to be snarky.

"Of course, but even before that." Dr. Martell's tone was even. Polite. "I studied journalism at university many years ago."

"Before your marriage, you mean?" Scott leaned forward, scowling slightly.

"Yes. Before that."

"Before your wife's death."

"Of course."

Scott leaned back in his chair. Long pause.

Too long. Bruce Doan hates dead air.

He continued questioning. "You wrote a mystery book. Several murder mystery books."

Martell smiled again. "Indeed I did."

"You wrote them while you were in prison? Under an assumed name—the same name you're using as an instructor here at the Tabby."

"Yes. Fenton Bishop. I've written some more scholarly tomes under my real name."

Scott looked surprised. "I didn't know that."

Martell shrugged. "They were in some fairly obscure publications about antiques. I'm an authorized antiques appraiser." He looked into the camera again. "I'm still writing mysteries under Fenton's name."

Scott's expression brightened. "You say you wrote those

mysteries 'under Fenton's name.' Do you think, perhaps, of Fenton as a person other than yourself?"

Martell smiled, chuckled softly. "What a strange idea—but perhaps I do. Maybe I wear my antiques-expert writer hat when I'm working on nonfiction analytical topics, and my Fenton Bishop hat for more lighthearted work."

"You consider murder lighthearted?" Scott's tone was smug. "Really?"

Still smiling, Martell answered. "It's fiction, Mr. Palmer. Not meant to be taken seriously. It's make-believe. Just like the works of Stephen King or Agatha Christie . . . or Robert Louis Stevenson."

The music signaling a commercial break swelled. Noon news anchor Phil Archer thanked Scott and Dr. Martell for "an interesting interview" and invited viewers to stay tuned for traffic and weather.

Aunt Ibby turned off the TV with an authoritative *click*. "I think I'm going to like my new tenant. He put Scott in his place about the Stevenson book, all right, and did it like a perfect gentleman. What did you think, Pete?"

Pete used his cop voice. "The man has served time for what he did. He's earned his teaching degrees. He's free to earn a living."

"I think it's interesting that he's written on other topics," I said.

"I do too." Aunt Ibby wore her wise-old-owl look. "I mean to encourage him to keep doing both types of writing—that is, if he's interested in my opinion at all."

Pete spoke again, this time with cop face *and* cop voice. "Ms. Russell—I mean Ibby—it may not be wise to interact with these short-term, Airbnb people, other than as the landlady. Remember, this is simply temporary housing for these folks. They're not here to make friends."

He's warning her. My phone vibrated. "Oh-oh. Text from Rhonda. Doan's on a tear about Wanda's new look. I'd better get back to the station. Pete?"

"We'd better not keep him waiting, then." He smiled. Real smile, cop face gone. "Let's go." He pulled the back door open, holding it for me. "Keep this door locked, Ibby."

"You tell me that all the time," she said, returning his smile. "I will."

We hurried past the garden and climbed into Pete's car. "I hope he takes the rear apartment," I said.

"You do? Why?"

"He'll enter and leave using the back door, the back stairs. He won't have any access to the rest of the house."

"It's a B and B," Pete pointed out. "A bed-and-breakfast. I assume she'll be serving breakfast in her kitchen for both apartments."

"Oh boy. You're right. What do you think—about Dr. Martell living there? Have you learned anything about him that I should be worried about?"

"It sounds as if you already are worried." He reached across the console, patted my knee, and eased out of the driveway onto Oliver Street. "And no. I haven't found anything that we didn't already know. As I said before, he's served his time, he's earned a teaching degree and he's free to earn a living."

"You sounded worried too."

"I worry about her in general. She and those girl-friends of hers are—well, nosy. They'll be digging into this poor guy's life the minute he gets there. Probably even before he arrives. He may not appreciate it."

My first instinct was to jump to the Angels' defense, but I stopped to think about what Pete had said. *He may not appreciate it.* What if Scott was right? What if there was even the tiniest germ of truth to the Jekyll-Hyde idea? If there was, I certainly wouldn't want my aunt and the girlfriends to say or do anything to upset the new tenant.

"Mr. Pennington says the man is perfectly okay," I mumbled.

"Pennington is probably absolutely right," Pete said, "and I already told you I haven't turned up anything in Martell's record that says otherwise. I'll get in touch with his parole officer, just to be sure."

"So we can stop worrying about it." I was hopeful.

"You'll worry about Aunt Ibby for as long as she lives," he said. "You love her. She's an important part of your life. She worries about you too. So do I. You're both intelligent, grown-up women. She'll be fine. You will too."

"You're right," I said. *I hope you're right*, I thought.

Ariel's bench was unoccupied when we reached the station. Pete and I exchanged a quick kiss across the console. "See you tonight?" I asked.

"Sure. We'll do something. Love you," and he was gone.

CHAPTER 12

"**D**oan's looking for you," Rhonda warned as soon as I arrived in her office.

"About Wanda's makeover?" I asked.

"If that's what you call it. I think she looks great. Better than ever. Doan's worried about the fan base." She made a face. "Worried about the ratings. The sponsors. They all loved her the way she was."

I wasn't too concerned about it. She'd only had a haircut and tried on a new suit, for heaven's sake. "She'll be fine. If the fans want the old Wanda back, there are wigs, hair extensions," I said. "Will you buzz Mr. Doan and tell him I'm here?" Rhonda tapped the console, said a few words, then waved me toward the manager's office.

"Go right in. He's expecting you."

"I'm sure he is." I tapped on the door and pushed it open.

"Ms. Barrett—what the hell have you done to my weather girl? You've got her all done up like one of those FOX-TV anchorettes."

"I haven't done anything to her, sir." I spoke calmly. Softly. "You asked me to tone her down a bit for an audition tape for the network show. The haircut was her own idea."

"Yeah, well, I talked to her. She thinks she's a meteorologist now. She wants to wear that schoolteacher getup for the six o'clock news tonight."

"She *is* a meteorologist," I said. "She has a master's degree in meteorology from Penn State, and one in climate science from BU. She even interned for a semester in Texas as a storm chaser. Why not let her try it for tonight? If the audience doesn't like it you'll hear about it soon enough."

"I guess you're right. It won't do any harm to let her try it."

"Of course it won't—and Mr. Doan, Wanda in form-fitting pinstripes doesn't look like any schoolteacher you or I ever had."

That brought a grin. I left his office on that positive note and headed downstairs to my own little glass fish-bowl beside the newsroom. I phoned Wanda and left a message that she was free to revisit the new Wanda for the evening news—and to use the company credit card for another outfit if she liked—and I was sure she'd like.

I looked through the glass wall to the newsroom. Scott hadn't yet returned from his noon shoot. I thought back to my own days as a field reporter. It was quite likely that he'd be on his way to another assignment by now—and yet another one after that. The immediacy of actually being there as news unfolded in real time is a thrill I'll never forget.

I shook away the moment of reflection, spun my chair around, faced my desk, and concentrated on my current job. There are plenty of advantages to being program director. For starters, it pays better and the hours are regular. Working a normal nine-to-five schedule was certainly going to be more convenient for married me than the be-available-24-7 life of the field reporter had ever been.

Still, nagging thoughts about Scott's current fixation with the twenty-year-old murder of Michael Martell's wife, and the fact that my beloved aunt was about to invite the man who'd committed that crime into her home, wouldn't go away. I opened the top desk drawer, pulled out the report Pete had given me, smoothed out the pages, and began to read.

It was, as Pete had indicated, a cut-and-dried account of the event itself. Basically, it said that someone at the motel had reported gunshots. When police arrived the shooter, who identified himself as Michael Martell, was sitting outside the door, the gun still in his hand. The motel manager unlocked the door and police found a woman on the floor bleeding profusely from three bullet wounds. She was transported by ambulance to a hospital, where she was later pronounced dead. Martell admitted the shooting and was arrested without incident. He was detained at Essex County prison, awaiting trial. His court appointed lawyer entered a not guilty plea for him. That, minus a lot of whereases and heretofores, was about it. According to what Pete had told me earlier, about Martell refusing parole and wanting to serve all of his time, the man had been a model prisoner.

It looked to me as if he was entitled to his freedom—to his writing career—to live wherever he liked. I put the pages back into the folder, made a hanging file marked *Martell* and put it under M in the file cabinet and told myself to forget about it.

Of course, myself didn't listen. I'd been a reporter for too long. I did, however, put thoughts about Martell/Bishop on the figurative back burner while I turned my attention to the things I was being paid to do.

The *Shopping Salem* host had left a message requesting a thirty-second promo. During June she'd be featuring various types of home furnishings from A to Z—"accent tables to zebra rugs" she claimed—and where to find them in Salem. Looked like a made-for-me assignment. Between us, Pete and I had the basic pieces for our new house, but we were going to need some things to tie the whole look together. I returned the call and made an appointment for camerawoman Marty and I to visit a few furniture venues—both new and vintage ones.

Katie the Clown from *Ranger Rob's Rodeo* morning show asked about doing a segment on rescue pets and the *Saturday Morning Business Hour* host had submitted a requisition slip for a paper shredder. I called Animal Aid and arranged for us to film their cutest residents available for adoption, fighting the growing urge to adopt a puppy myself and okayed the business guy's request. So far, so good for the morning's work.

My self-congratulatory moment was interrupted by a call from Aunt Ibby. "Michael has decided on the back apartment," she said. "When you come home this evening, would you drop off your keys to the back door and the back apartment so I don't have to bother to change the locks?"

"Uh, sure," I agreed. *So they're definitely on a first-name basis.* "Will he be moving in soon?"

"The appliances will be all hooked up by the middle of the week. It's just a narrow little galley kitchen, you know. Convenient for a single man, I should think."

"Just right for a short-term residence," I said. "How long does he plan to be there?"

"That's kind of open-ended. He's in a hotel now, so he's anxious to move in."

"You say Mr. Pennington vouches for him, right?"

"Absolutely. The Angels do too, and you know how good they are at vetting somebody," she said with a little giggle. "Betsy went all the way back to his high school yearbook and Louisa says his credit rating is sterling. See you this evening. Don't forget the keys." She was gone, and the Martell/Bishop matter zoomed off of the back burner—even one on a narrow little galley-style stove—and right back into my worry zone.

I checked out with Rhonda at exactly five o'clock, tiptoed past Doan's office, and rode Old Clunky down to the street level. From the sidewalk my new Jeep looked a lot different than the Corvette had, over in the corner of the parking lot, silhouetted against the blue of the harbor. I jumped, startled, when I heard Scott Palmer's voice from behind me.

"I like the new wheels," he said. "That's one badass-looking Jeep. Got everything but a gun rack in the back window. You expecting trouble?"

"Trouble? Not me," I assured him. "You saw what was left of my last car. Safety first, this time. It's cool though, huh?"

He fell into step beside me. "Very cool, for sure. I hear our local jailbird celebrity is moving into your old homestead. That right?"

I stopped walking and faced him. "*Jailbird celebrity* is pretty cold, don't you think?"

He gave me that familiar long, silent stare. "Well," he finally said, "he did spend the past twenty years in jail."

"Twenty years is what the state required. He did it. Debt paid."

"You're not worried at all about him living in your aunt's house?"

"Not one bit," I fibbed. "And you have no good reason to spread your nutty idea about a split-personality killer. There's no evidence at all to point to such a thing."

"Ratings." He gave an offhand shoulder-shrug. "The audience likes that kind of stuff. It's an investigative piece. I never actually *said* that he was guilty of any other crimes besides wife-killing. It's an interesting possibility, though."

"It's mean," I told him and quick-walked to my new and very cool Jeep.

CHAPTER 13

Pete and I had agreed to do something after work and the something we decided on was moving some of our small items into our house, and placing them in the rooms where we thought they belonged. We agreed to meet at seven, giving me time to return the keys to Aunt Ibby, get myself invited to her place for dinner, and to watch the six o'clock evening news where the new Wanda would be on display.

First of all, I handed over my key to the back door and the back apartment—saving Aunt Ibby the time and expense of new locks, but causing me a moment's discomfort. *What if someday I really need to get in there because of an emergency?* I couldn't think of what emergency it might be, and anyway I still had a key to the front door, so put the thought aside. I'd already prepared a small cache of items and cartons that would fit easily into the

Jeep and stashed them on the second-floor landing. I'd parked on the Winter Street side of the house and carried them, one or two at a time, down to the foyer. O'Ryan trotted along beside me on each trip—whether he thought he was being helpful or just because of catlike curiosity about what was going on, I don't know. Before long I'd packed a couple of lamps—both table and floor types, two occasional tables, about fifty potted plants, three cartons of books, and an assortment of vases, figurines, and other decorative tchotchkes into the Jeep. I tossed in a few throw pillows to keep things from shifting, locked the car, and headed back to Aunt Ibby's kitchen with the cat in the lead.

Pete had arrived at the new house ahead of me. His brother-in-law Donnie's pickup truck was parked at the curb, tailgate down. The front door of the house stood open. I could hear voices coming from inside. I stepped into the hallway.

"Pete? You in here?"

"I'm in the den," came the reply.

I couldn't remember which room we'd designated as the den, so I followed the sounds of conversation to one of the rooms I'd thought of as perfect for an office. I passed a stack of cardboard boxes, a goosenecked desk lamp, and a pair of tall kitchen stools in the living room. "Hi, babe. Look." Pete stood on a wooden chair straightening a wall-hung TV—the source of the voices I was hearing. I recognized it as the set from his apartment. "She just fits and the cable connection was already set up." He stepped down from the chair. "As long as I had the truck I thought I might as well move the TV and my recliner along with some of the other stuff."

Sure enough, the recliner was there, angled toward the TV and looking comfortably at home. "You're right," I said. "It makes a perfect den. Since you have the truck, want to go back to my place and pick up my old glass-front barrister's bookcase? It will just fit there under the window, and we might as well get the carousel horse too. We can put it in the sunroom and arrange my plants around it. And maybe my bentwood bench too, okay?"

It was well past nightfall and we'd already made several trips up and down Winter Street. By the time we emptied Donnie's truck of its last load, two rooms in our new house were already beginning to look like home—the sunroom and the newly christened den.

We made the final return trip to Aunt Ibby's, truck empty, Pete and I dusty and a little bit sweaty, but satisfied with a job well done. A vintage Lincoln was parked just behind my Jeep.

"Whose car is that?" Pete asked. "I know it doesn't belong to one of the Angels."

"I don't know. Aunt Ibby didn't say anything about expecting company."

"I hope it's not somebody looking to rent a room." He frowned. "She should make it clear that the place is shown by appointment only."

"She has. The rooms aren't even ready to be shown yet," I said. "Want to come in with me? To be sure everything is okay?"

"Yes, I do." Cop voice. He parked the truck close to the Lincoln. Close enough so that the old car wouldn't be able to move unless the Jeep or the truck moved first. "Got a key?"

"Right here," I said, the key already in my hand.

O'Ryan's fuzzy yellow head was pressed against the glass in the window beside the door. I climbed the steps, Pete close behind me as I pushed the door open.

"Holy smoke! What's all this?" Pete waved his arm at the stack of boxes that all appeared to be smiling at us.

"Wedding gifts," I explained. "It looks like this almost every day lately. We're keeping the Amazon truck busy. As we unwrap them, Aunt Ibby logs them in so we can send prompt thank-you notes. They're all on display in the dining room. Come take a look."

"After we check on your aunt," he said, "and whoever that Lincoln belongs to."

"You're right," I agreed. "Aunt Ibby, it's me." I stepped into the living room, expecting the usual answering call from the direction of the kitchen.

"Yes, dear. We'll be right down." My head snapped around. The voice came from above. Pete looked upward too. *We'll be right down? Who is* we? My aunt leaned over the third-floor railing, still-red hair bright in the light from the overhead chandelier, a tall, smiling man at her side.

Michael Martell.

Within a minute my aunt and her escort had joined us in the foyer. "I believe you and Michael have met, Maralee," she said. "Michael, please meet Pete Mondello, my niece's fiancé." Maralee, Pete, this is Dr. Michael Martell."

Our "how-do-you-dos" echoed one another and we shook hands all around. "My aunt tells me you're looking at the B and B space, Dr. Martell," I said.

"I am," he said, the smile still in place. "It seems to suit my need for temporary housing perfectly." He looked down at my aunt. "A mutual friend tells me that Ibby's breakfasts alone are worth the price of the rent."

They're not just on a first-name basis. This is nickname familiarity. I was vaguely uncomfortable about it. I sneaked a glance at Pete. He wore his cop face with a tight-lipped smile. I almost expected him to demand ID from the man. "You plan to be in Salem for only a short time then, sir?"

"No, indeed," Dr. Martell responded with a chuckle. "I expect to be in this fair city for at least two years. That's the extent of my contract with the Tabitha Trumbull Academy of the Arts. I'm in the market for something more permanent. Perhaps a condo—maybe a town house." He cast a fond look in Aunt Ibby's direction. "Meanwhile, I look forward to a quiet, simple abode in this fine old home—along with some home-cooked breakfasts."

"We just bought a home," I told him. "We'll be glad to recommend our agent. I'm sure she can find something you'll like." *So you'll want to move out of here ASAP.*

"Thank you, Ms. Barrett. I'd appreciate that." He moved toward the door. "Good night, Ibby, Mr. Mondello."

"I'll walk out with you, Dr. Martell," Pete said. "I'm afraid my truck may have blocked your vehicle."

Dr. Martell gave a silent, but polite nod. Pete opened the door. "Good night, Michael," my aunt said. "I'll call you tomorrow just as soon as the appliances are hooked up."

I joined O'Ryan at the tall window beside the door and watched the two men descend the stairs. At the bottom, Pete opened his wallet, holding it open for Martell to see. I knew he was displaying his badge, and wished I could hear the conversation. I decided it couldn't have been anything very serious, since both of them smiled, shook hands again and Pete climbed into the truck and backed it up. Martell waved as he drove away.

"What was all that about?" I could hardly wait to question Pete when he came back inside. "Why'd you show him your badge?"

"Friendly gesture," he said. "Gave him my card too. Any friend of your aunt is a friend of mine." He winked. "Besides, I wanted him to know Ibby has a friend on the force who keeps a close eye on her at all times."

"Thank you, Pete," my aunt said. "Now would you like to open a few gifts? They're starting to pile up."

"Good idea." He picked up four of the boxes, two under each arm, and I did the same. My aunt carried the remaining one package and single file, we marched into the dining room. The long mahogany table with its white linen tablecloth already held an assortment of gifts worthy of a department store display window. Small appliances and utensils shared space with sparkling crystal glassware and china. We'd shared our wish list with several stores and clearly our friends and relatives had paid attention. "Our house is going to be well accessorized," I said. "Look. That's the air fryer I wanted."

"There are quite a few gift cards too," my aunt said. "I have everything cataloged so you know who gave you what. The monogramed thank-you cards have arrived too. This wedding is going to be perfect."

I slipped my hand into Pete's. "Let's open some more boxes."

CHAPTER 14

We opened the nine boxes and a few envelopes, dutifully exclaiming over each one, while Aunt Ibby carefully filled out names and addresses and gift descriptions in her distinctive librarian's bold backhand in a white moire covered notebook. "I'll arrange all these lovely things on the table later. You two run along. You've had a busy day."

"I'm just going to put the Jeep in the garage and go upstairs to bed," I said, "and I'm sure Donnie wants his truck back." I looked at Pete.

"Right," he said. "I'll see you tomorrow, Lee. And Ibby, keep your doors locked."

My aunt smiled at the familiar admonition and promised, as she always does, that she'd double-check all the doors before she went to bed. I didn't say so, but I always checked them too, just in case. Pete and I shared a fairly decorous front-door kiss and said good night.

On the way back from the garage I hurried past the garden and the neat row of tall hedges leading to the wrought iron gate opening onto Winter Street. O'Ryan waited for me on the front steps. I unlocked the door, followed the cat into the foyer, relocked it, and made sure the household alarm system was activated. The first-floor lights were all out so I assumed that my aunt had already gone to her bedroom. O'Ryan started up the staircase and I followed.

I was surprised to see that the door to our second-floor, book-lined study was open, spilling light into the hall. O'Ryan dashed into the room and I followed. "Aunt Ibby?" I called. "May I come in?"

"Of course, dear child." She sat behind the big mahogany desk that had once belonged to great-grandfather Forbes. "I hope you won't think I'm being terribly nosy, but I'm just doing a little research on the kind of degrees one can get while in prison."

"Checking on Dr. Martell's credentials?" I asked.

"Well, in a manner of speaking, yes."

"And?"

"His degrees are from fully accredited college programs, and he worked very hard to earn them," she said. "It seems that if a person is in prison and cannot have access to a computer, he has to find a school that will allow snail-mail classes."

"Time consuming," I said. "I don't suppose there are many."

"He found a reputable Midwest university that still offers them. All of his degrees in English are from there. Of course, Michael already had his bachelor's degree before he was imprisoned."

"What about his other degrees? The ones he needs for his antiques articles?"

"No degrees at all. Completely self-taught from library books. Those articles apparently stand on their own merit."

"Impressive," I said. "The more we learn about him, the better he looks."

"I agree." She returned the book she'd been reading to its shelf. It was a section I was familiar with. Criminology. I'd spent the past few years taking online classes in the subject. Most home libraries aren't set up with the Dewey decimal system, but ours is. I even recognized the book she'd selected: Number 364-1523. *True Crime.*

"Impressive," I said again. "Well, I'm off to bed. See you in the morning."

I tried hard not to make anything of my aunt's evening selection of reading material. She is, after all, a research librarian.

"Come on, O'Ryan," I said to the cat. "Time for bed." He followed me down the hall to my bedroom, hopped up onto the window seat and peered out into the night. I changed into pajamas, set my alarm, climbed into bed and turned on the TV. Wanda had reverted to her weather girl wardrobe—black short-shorts and yellow-and-black–striped crop top with bumblebee deely bobbers calling attention to her new short hairdo. Much different from her six o'clock meteorologist persona.

"Almost time for River's show, O'Ryan," I called to the still window-seated cat. He loves River. Almost reluctantly, and with a couple of backward glances toward the window, he joined me on the bed. River's scary movie for the night was *The Spiral Staircase*, one of my all-time favorite serial killer horror movies. "Come snuggle up next to me, O'Ryan," I said. "This isn't one I like to watch alone." Obediently, he curled up on the pillow beside me. We watched the first commercial, waited for River to introduce the film and to give the phone number for viewers to call for on-the-air tarot readings.

The black-and-white movie is accompanied by a particularly creepy musical score. I was tempted to hide under the covers as the eyes of an unknown person watched a mute Dorothy McGuire from the shadows as she pauses in front of a mirror. The commercial break was welcome and I was happy to see River, stunning tonight in a slim gold satin sheath. Buck Covington had joined her on the set and shuffled the tarot deck with the skill and flair of a Las Vegas dealer. He'd clearly been practicing, since his appearances with River had become audience favorites and boosted her ratings—pleasing Mr. Doan greatly.

"I consecrate this deck to bring light wherever there is darkness," River said, as the overhead camera focused on the beautiful cards and she began to tell her caller what they revealed. She advised the caller that sheer will and determination don't always make things happen. She advised that love and consideration would help life run more smoothly. "Such good advice," I told the cat. "For everyone."

O'Ryan favored me with a quick lick on the end of my nose, left the pillow and returned to the window seat. "What is so interesting out there, nosy cat?" I asked and nosy me followed him across the room, kneeling on the cushion beside him, shielding my eyes from the room light behind me, and trying to figure out what he was looking at. It didn't take long. The Lincoln was back, parked in front of the house as it had been earlier. By now it was after midnight. Too late to call Pete?

Never.

It took a couple of rings before he answered. "Did I wake you?" I asked.

"Yep. What's going on? Are you okay?"

I told him what I saw from the window. "I think he's been there quite a while," I said. "What should I do?"

"Turn off your bedroom light for one thing," he said. "I'll be right over. Are all the doors locked? Is your aunt okay?"

"She was reading in the study earlier. I'll go and see if she's still there." I'd already turned out the light, slipped my feet into slippers and opened my door. I tiptoed into the hall. I saw that the study door was closed and so was my aunt's. "Looks like she's gone to bed," I reported.

"Go back to the window and see if he's still there." I crossed the room, pausing to mute the TV where Dorothy McGuire has found a corpse in the basement. O'Ryan hadn't moved. I joined him. The Lincoln was still there. I told Pete.

"I'm on my way."

"You're not going to use your siren, are you?" I asked.

"No siren. Just a friendly wellness check."

It seemed like a long time before I saw the Ford round the corner of Winter Street, but a check of my clock told me it had only been ten minutes. There'd been no activity from the Lincoln. A glance at the silent TV showed Buck Covington cutting the deck as River prepared for another reading.

O'Ryan and I, like a couple of voyeurs, were glued to the window. I wished the Lincoln had been parked closer to the streetlamp so that we'd have a clearer view of whatever was about to happen.

CHAPTER 15

As Pete had promised, there were no sirens, but with red, white, and blue lights flashing, the cruiser pulled up behind the old car. Pete approached the driver's-side window and in a moment, the interior light of the Lincoln gave the cat and me a better view as Michael Martell climbed out of his vehicle. There was no TV-like scene of a pat down or hands on the roof of the car or anything like that. The two men appeared to hold a brief conversation. Then surprisingly to me, they shook hands. Each returned to his own vehicle. Pete drove away. Martell remained where he was.

I reached for my phone. It rang before I could punch in Pete's number.

"What the heck was all that about?" I demanded. "Why is he still out there?"

"An abundance of caution, I guess," Pete said. "According to Martell, he went back to his motel and got to thinking about the apartment being available as soon as the appliances were hooked up in the morning. Ibby hadn't asked for a deposit and he wanted to be sure he'd be first in line. So he got up and drove straight back there. He says he left a message for his parole officer about where he was going and why."

"But Aunt Ibby had told him he could have the apartment he wanted."

I could almost see Pete's familiar shoulder-shrug. "I guess twenty years behind bars changes a man. Makes him less trustful. He wants to be sure nobody else comes along and offers her more money for the place."

"That's sad," I said. "Aunt Ibby's the one taking a risk. He's the ex-convict. She'd be hurt if she knew he didn't trust *her* word."

"Let's not tell her."

Hesitantly, I agreed. "Okay. Thanks for checking on him. I was worried."

"You were right to call me. Anyway, this underscores the fact that I was serious when I said we keep an eye on Ibby at all times."

"That's true. Good night again. I love you."

"I'll call you later. Love you."

I climbed back into bed, but O'Ryan maintained his vigil at the window. The silent TV screen showed Ethel Barrymore armed with a gun. Yawning, ready for sleep, I turned off the set. I'd seen the old film enough times to have memorized the ending. "Good night, O'Ryan," I said. "Wake me up if anything interesting happens out there."

The alarm clock clanged at seven. The cat was sound asleep at the foot of the bed, indicating that nothing inter-

esting had happened. I opened the door to the hall so that
O'Ryan could go downstairs and out the cat door to do
his morning business in the garden while I showered and
dressed for the day. A quick look out the window told me
that Martell's car was gone. Good news. By the time I got
downstairs, O'Ryan was already in Aunt Ibby's kitchen,
hunched over his red bowl, enjoying his breakfast. Aunt
Ibby was, as is usual at this time of day, busy working the
Boston Globe crossword—in ink.

"There's a nice spinach quiche in the warming oven,"
she said. "Help yourself. You'll notice there are a couple
of pieces missing." Shy smile. "Darndest thing. Michael
phoned me at six-thirty asking if he could drop off his deposit check. He wanted to be sure the apartment would be
his. Imagine that? I'd promised him it would. Anyway, I
jumped into my clothes, put on the coffee and grabbed
the quiche out of the freezer. He joined me for breakfast,
then went along to his new job at the Tabby." She sighed.
"I wish he'd just believed me when I told him the place
was his in the first place."

I took a bite of quiche and repeated what Pete had said.
"I guess twenty years behind bars changes a man. Trust
issues, I suppose."

"Makes sense." She pointed toward me with her pen.
"You should know this one. What's an eight-letter word
ending in *d* for something that controls fluid flow into a
transmission?"

"Solenoid?" I offered.

"That works. Thanks," she said. "Let's take a look at
the weather and see which Wanda we've got today." She
reached for the remote. "I like the new look. What do you
think?"

"I don't know," I admitted. "She's gorgeous either

way, but I think *she* likes the new Wanda. She was back to the cute bumblebee outfit last night though."

Phil Archer gave the traffic report and introduced the Geico insurance commercial. After the little lizard delivered his speech, a hybrid Wanda appeared on the screen. The sleek new haircut was unencumbered by bee antennae. Four-inch platform heels complemented long, slim black pants. An unbuttoned black suit jacket revealed no shirt, but a matching vest which, in turn, revealed some magnificent cleavage. Straight-faced, Phil introduced her as WICH-TV's "crack meteorologist."

"Something for everyone," my aunt commented.

"I wonder what surprises she has in store for us on the cooking show," I said. "I'd better get going." I gulped the last of my coffee and left via the back door, remembering to lock it behind me.

"You're early again," Rhonda said when I arrived at the station. "Doan isn't even here yet."

"Wanda's taping a cooking show this morning," I said. "A romantic breakfast for two. I need to check on her choice of costume, and to approve the new title graphics. Besides, maybe I'll surprise Pete on our honeymoon with a romantic breakfast."

"Just order room service," she advised. "Have you firmed up the honeymoon destination plans?"

"Not exactly. We've tentatively added an island visit though."

"An island? Like Bermuda?"

I laughed. "Nothing so glamorous. It's one of those big islands off the Maine coast. Turns out my dad's sister and her husband own one of them. Pirate's Island. Ever hear of it?"

"Nope. Let's take a look." She tapped on the keyboard

in front of her and the big monitor screen over her desk came to life. She's supposed to have it tuned to WICH-TV all the time, but whenever Mr. Doan is out of the office, the screen remains dark. "Google Earth probably has an aerial shot of it. Have you looked?"

"I meant to. Just haven't had time. Whoops. Is that it?" I gazed at the screen. "It looks huge."

"It is. That looks like an airstrip right down the middle." She enlarged the picture. "Sure. That's what it is. And there's a lighthouse. That looks like a boat dock too. You say your aunt owns it?"

"So I've heard. It makes sense there'd be an airstrip. My parents were visiting there by plane just before they—um—they died."

She zoomed again and the roof of a house appeared. "Big house," she said. "It's right on the edge of a cliff."

"Nice," I said. "Thanks, Rhonda." I glanced up at the gold sunburst clock on the wall. "I'd better get down to the kitchen set and make sure Wanda's chosen outfit is more homemaker than home-wrecker if she's going to qualify for *Hometown Cooks*."

I needn't have worried about it. Wanda was attractive and professional in slim black pants and immaculate white chef's coat. Her hair was partly covered with a traditional white hat, just puffy enough to signify her chef status, and jaunty enough to be cute. She'd nailed it. I didn't need to hang around for the taping. I climbed the metal stairs back to the reception area, intending to pick up a requisition slip for the new paper shredder, feeling confident about Wanda's shot at national TV.

I was surprised to see that Rhonda's monitor still displayed Pirate's Island. Now the scene had been expanded to show the coastline of the state. Rhonda had spun her chair around and her attention was focused on the screen. I was surprised. "Something special about Aunt Doris's island?" I asked.

"Interesting, not special." She pointed to the upper half of the monitor, where the Maine coastline began. "Look at it. Reminds me of a poem I had to learn in first grade. '*The breaking waves dashed high on a stern and rockbound coast. And the woods against a stormy sky their giant branches tossed.*' It must look just like it did back in the Pilgrim days. All rocks and trees."

I wasn't surprised that Rhonda remembered a poem from first grade. She's one of the smartest people I know and sometimes I suspect that she has total recall— remembers *everything* she's seen or read. I turned away from the screen. Suddenly light-headed, I closed my eyes. "I don't want to look at it." I felt behind me for one of the purple-upholstered chrome chairs. My stomach ached. The bridge of my nose stung as I fought back tears.

Rhonda turned her chair so that she faced me and at the same time turned the monitor off. "Lee! What's wrong. Are you all right?"

"Yes. No. I don't know. Looking at that coastline made me sad. Made me almost seasick." I put my head down in my lap. "What's wrong with me?"

Rhonda was at my side in an instant, kneeling, her arms around my shoulders. "Was that where . . . you said your parents died in a plane crash after they left the island . . . was that the place?" She was right. It was exactly the place and I remembered exactly how and why I recognized it.

It was only a few years ago that I learned that I was a scryer. Apparently, I've been blessed—or cursed—with that dubious gift since childhood, but I'd successfully somehow blocked it for most of my life. The visions had begun to reappear when, along with O'Ryan our wonderful cat, I'd inherited Ariel Constellation's obsidian ball. That black surface held disturbing pictures within its depths that nobody but me could see.

I'd told Aunt Ibby what was going on when the visions began. She took charge, bringing me upstairs to the fourth-floor attic, pulling open a bureau drawer. "I hope I'm doing the right thing, Maralee," she'd said and handed me a small shoebox. "I think you need to remember some things if you're ever going to make sense of what's happening to you now."

I removed the lid and pushed aside blue tissue paper. The tiny black patent leather shoes were still shiny.

CHAPTER 16

Little Maralee Kowalski loved Sundays. She and Daddy and Mommy and Aunt Ibby would get all dressed up and go to church. Sometimes it was Daddy's church, with the pretty colored windows and the man who said funny sounding words. Sometimes it was Aunt Ibby's church, with the plain windows and the man in a black suit. It didn't matter to Maralee. She liked both churches. The music was nice and, anyway, if she didn't want to listen to the man talk, she could watch the pictures in the toes of her Sunday shoes.

Then one day Mommy and Daddy went on vacation. Maralee stayed at Aunt Ibby's house. On Sunday morning Aunt Ibby helped her get dressed in her prettiest dress. Maralee wore ankle socks with lace on them and her shiny patent leather shoes.

"You may sit on the front steps, Maralee," said Aunt

Ibby, "while I bring the car around. Don't get dirty, will you?"

The little girl sat quietly and, to pass the time, looked to see what pictures might be in her shoes. First, she saw the little cloud. That always came first. Then the swirling colors and the twinkling lights. Then the pictures. The child clapped her hands together in delight when she saw the image of a yellow airplane.

"Daddy! Mommy!" she whispered happily.

She saw the cliff. "Watch out, Daddy!" she cried.

She saw the flames.

CHAPTER 17

Rhonda handed me a glass of cold water.
"Thanks," I said. "I'm okay now."

"Is that what it was?" she asked again. "The place where your parents died? I didn't know. I mean, I never would have brought that picture up. I'm so sorry."

It was my turn to comfort her. "Not your fault at all. There's no way you could have known." I'd never told Rhonda about the visions. No one except Aunt Ibby, Pete, and River knew about the damned things. "I'd just never thought about it being a particular place. It's about time I faced it. Pete and I will be in Maine next week. We should go there. Put flowers or a wreath or something next to the cliff. I should go every year. Memorial Day, maybe. Heck, Pete and I go out to Misery Island once a summer to put purple pansies on a little dog's grave. I should do at least that much to honor my parents." I knew

I was babbling, but the rush of memory had been over-whelming. I was glad no one else had been around be-sides Rhonda. I sipped the water.

"That's a good idea." She spoke softly. "Going to the place where they died might give you some kind of clo-sure."

"I believe it would. Going to the island where they spent their last days is a good idea too. Meeting my Aunt Doris might be important. She can tell me what kind of kid my dad was."

"Do you have any memories at all of them?"

"Oh, sure. I was almost five when they died. Daddy had a yellow Corvette. I remember riding in it. I remem-ber pony rides too, and a birthday party, and going to kindergarten. My mom and dad took me to church some-times." I strained to remember. "And we had a pretty house in North Salem. It's gone. There's a dollar store there now. I don't recall anything about the funeral, al-though Aunt Ibby says I was there. She says after that I never spoke a word for about six months."

"Wow. That must have been a big shock to a little kid. Sounds like you had some kind of PTSD."

I nodded. "Wouldn't be a bit surprised if I did."

Rhonda looked toward the glass door. "I hear Old Clunky starting up. That would be Doan. You sure you're okay?"

"I'm sure," I said, "but I think I'll duck out of here and head back to my office." I darted for the green door, clos-ing it behind me just as Old Clunky stopped on the sec-ond floor. I'd completely forgotten my requisition slip, but I wasn't about to go back for it. I clattered down the metal stairs, emerging next to the newsroom just in time to literally bump into Scott.

"Whoa, Moon. Where are you off to in such a hurry?"

"Heading for my office," I said. "Busy day."

"Yep. Me too," he said. "Francine's got the mobile unit warming up. We're going over to Essex Street. They finished the restoration of the big clock in front of the old Almy's department store and today's the rededication."

"Nice story. You through with the Jekyll and Hyde thing?"

"Yep. Couldn't find a damn thing to keep it going. Nothing there. According to his parole officer the guy's practically a saint." He started for the studio outside door. "Anyway, Doan told me to knock it off."

"Good," I said. "Tell Francine I said hi." I watched his retreating back and thought about that big old clock— wondering idly if the hands would be positioned at 10:15. Wondering too why just as Scott was through asking questions about Michael Martell, I was busy thinking some up.

With my wedding day just short of a week away, I wasn't lying when I'd told Scott I had a busy day ahead of me. As program director I had a lot of responsibility for filling much of the airtime within the ten days I'd be gone. There were still a few guests to line up for the shows that required guests. I needed to assign food-shopping duty to someone who'd keep Wanda's studio kitchen properly stocked with necessary items for her live cooking show. I called Howard Templeton, Mrs. Doan's nephew, who'd dis-placed me as field reporter, to see if he'd be needing guests, props, or anything else during the time I'd be gone, and Chris Rich could always be counted on to fill in on short notice for just about any Salem topic for any given show. He'd mostly be faking it, but he did it in such an entertaining way, nobody minded.

Young Howie said not to worry, that he had everything on his end handled and Chris, as expected, would be delighted to appear on any show, any time. Aunt Ibby called and asked that I stop on my way home at Shaw's Market and pick up a few things. She read off a list of items and I dutifully wrote them all down. There were more than a few. "Use the front door, dear. I've already given Michael the key to the back."

"Appliances all hooked up?" I asked.

"Yes. Everything's shipshape. You'll hardly recognize the place. Michael will be moving in tomorrow. I'll give you a peek at it later tonight."

Rhonda managed to keep me occupied all the way up to twenty minutes past five o'clock, even though I'd hoped to leave early. I was just a tiny bit annoyed because it seemed to me that some of the assigned duties that had found their way onto Rhonda's whiteboard under my name could easily have been taken care of by someone else on the staff—for instance, *inventory paper cups and plates in the break room* and *get comparative bids on classified ads in all Essex County newspapers.*

Complimenting myself on being a good team player, I completed my tasks, stuffed Aunt Ibby's shopping list into my purse and left. I couldn't help noticing that most of the nine-to-five employees' vehicles—including Rhonda's—had already left the parking lot. I may have been pouting a bit and harboring a poor-me attitude as I drove onto Derby Street and headed for Shaw's.

My mood did not improve. Had my aunt selected one item from each and every aisle in the place? It certainly seemed so. Cheese from the deli. Apples from produce. Cupcakes from bakery and so it went all the way to vitamins from the opposite end of the store. Took me twenty minutes before I got to the checkout line, which was naturally jammed with people who, like me, have to shop after work.

With two tightly packed reusable bags stashed in the back, I aimed the Jeep toward home, remembering my aunt's instructions to turn onto Winter Street—instead of Oliver Street, which would have been much more convenient. "Heck," I grumbled to myself, "if I still had my back door keys I could park behind the house and pop the groceries into Aunt Ibby's kitchen in a minute instead of doing it the hard way."

I carried the two bags up the front stairs, putting them down on the top step while I fumbled in my purse for the keys. O'Ryan watched serenely from the side window, at the same time grooming his whiskers with one paw. I stuck my tongue out at him, pushed the door open, brought the bags inside, and closed the door behind me. "Must be nice to be you," I told him, and started through the darkened living room toward the kitchen, a bag under each arm, with the cat leading the way.

Odd, I thought. *There's no light on in the kitchen. No sounds either.*

I stopped walking, just listening. O'Ryan stopped too. "Aunt Ibby?" I called softly. No reply. I tried again. Louder, this time. "Aunt Ibby? You here?"

I heard a crash, a whispered curse. O'Ryan, startled, darted across my feet toward the dining room. I dropped both bags and ran toward the sound.

CHAPTER 18

"**S**urprise!" A chorus of voices greeted me as the kitchen overhead light blazed on. Helium-filled balloons floated toward the ceiling. The round table was piled high with wrapped gifts and on the counter, white and silver wedding bells topped a tiered cake surrounded by plates and platters of food. Several bottles of champagne chilled in an ice-filled aluminum bucket.

My aunt stepped forward and hugged me. "It's your wedding shower. Did we surprise you?"

I sat in the nearest captain's chair. "Surprised me for sure," I said, heartbeat still pounding in my ears. "What was the crash?"

"Marty dropped her deviled eggs," Wanda offered, "but it's okay. We have more."

The room was full of friends. The Angels, Betsy Leavitt and Louisa Abney-Babcock were there, along with

Marty, Rhonda, Shannon Berman, Francine, Carla Roell, Pete's sister Marie and his mom Mary Catherine, Buffy Doan, Therese Della Monica, River North, camera-ready for her late show in gold embroidered red silk, along with several high school and college friends.

The day's delaying tactics suddenly made sense—the aisle-by-aisle tour of the market, the paper goods inventory at the station. They'd needed to keep me distracted for as long as it took for all of the WICH-TV crew to get to the Winter Street house with their gifts and goodies ahead of me.

Once my heart had stopped pounding and I'd been ceremoniously seated in a specially decorated chair and been presented with a bouquet of pink roses from Pete, the party got down to business. Lots of lovely lacy lingerie, sweet-smelling soaps and lotions, three cookbooks—one from Wanda, one from Aunt Ibby and one from Pete's mom, a king-sized purple-satin sheet set from Buffy Doan, a beautiful Dakota Berman seascape painting from Shannon, a copy of *Feng Shui: Arranging Your Home for Health and Happiness* from River—I'd have lots of thank-you notes to write! After the gift-opening festivities we enjoyed champagne and the delicious treats everyone had contributed, followed by cake and ice cream—both chocolate in honor of me, the bride-to-be. I can safely say a good time was had by all. The party ended at a reasonable hour—most of us had to work in the morning. Marty and Therese headed back to the station to get River's set, film and phone lines ready for the midnight show. River was already dressed and made up so, with one of my aunt's big aprons covering the red silk gown, she stayed to help Aunt Ibby and me with the cleanup.

Dishes washed, leftovers put away and wrapping paper recycled, we three sat down for decaf coffee and a few of Marie's butterfinger cookies. O'Ryan chose a chair next to River and looked from side to side, as though sizing all of us up. I decided to share with these two most trusted women—and one interested cat—what had happened to me in Rhonda's office.

"The sight of that cliff across the water from Pirate's Island made me feel faint," I explained. "I had to sit down." I looked at my aunt. "Aunt Ibby, it was as if that vision I had in my patent leather shoes had come back. I'm sure it's the same cliff. I'm sure it's the place where they died." River and my aunt nodded in silent unison. "I'm thinking that maybe when Pete and I go to Maine," I continued, watching their faces, "I might put some flowers or a wreath or something there, beside that cliff. Rhonda thinks it might give me the closure that's been missing all these years."

I saw tears in Aunt Ibby's eyes. "I'm so sorry you had to experience that again, Maralee. But yes, I believe Rhonda may be right."

"It won't be easy," River said. "It will be painful. But Pete will be there with you. I think you can do it. Should do it. I brought my cards. Want to see what they have to say?"

"Couldn't hurt," I said. River reached into her velvet bag and withdrew the familiar box.

Placing the stack of cards facedown on the table, River bowed her head. Aunt Ibby and I did the same. I peeked at O'Ryan. The cat's golden eyes were downcast too. "I consecrate this deck to bring light wherever there is darkness," River said, "and I dedicate this deck for guidance and wisdom for myself and others for the highest good for all concerned."

She began to shuffle the cards. "This will be another short reading. I'm going to use a six-card method, Lee, because for now we just want an answer to one question: Will a visit to the site of her parents' death be beneficial to Lee?" She cut the cards into three piles, then turned the piles faceup. "These are your first three cards." She took the bottom card from each pile and placed each one faceup just above the pile she'd taken it from. "The remaining three. Here we go." She pointed to the two cards at the right. "These two cards are the past," she said, then pointed to the two on the left. "These are the future. The two in the middle are important. They represent your own present attitude about the question."

I'd never seen River use this particular layout before. I leaned forward and inspected the two cards on the right. "The two of wands," I said, "and the queen of cups. What do they mean?"

"They represent the past, so I believe they may signify your parents." She tapped the two of wands. "Here is a man of property looking out to sea. He's hoping his ships will come in fully loaded with goods. He's kind and creative and has an interest in things scientific." She looked at me.

"My dad was an engineer," I said. "All the rest of it fits too."

"Good." She moved her finger to the cards on the left. The queen of cups. "A woman with light hair and hazel eyes?"

Aunt Ibby nodded. "Carrie had red hair like Maralee's, and green eyes. Close enough."

River continued. "She is a good wife and a loving mother. She is poetic and quite beautiful. Her card shows her looking into the cup of her imagination, but it is closed. She keeps her dreamlike thoughts to herself."

"Yes," Aunt Ibby said. "I know she wrote poetry but she rarely showed it to anyone."

I understand her. I usually keep my dreamlike thoughts to myself too. I have to. I wonder if she saw visions too? River moved on to the cards on the left. Cards of the future.

"Here we have some people you don't know yet but who have an effect on you. Here's the five of swords and the high priestess." She twisted her long braid, making the little gold stars shimmer. I've seen her do that on TV when she's reading something she doesn't want to tell the caller and is trying to think of a nice way to frame it. O'Ryan seemed particularly interested in the five of swords. He even reached out a furry paw and touched it briefly.

"Not great, huh?" I asked.

"You're getting too good at this," she said. "But no, it's not really bad, just maybe asks more questions than it answers. Like, for instance, the five of swords. O'Ryan is wondering about that one too."

"What do you think it means?" my aunt asked. "And you know I take all this with a grain of salt."

"As you should," River said. "You see that the fellow with the swords looks pretty unpleasant. There are storm clouds behind him too. In general, the card signifies winning by being unfair."

"Cheating?" my aunt asked.

"Pretty much. If I was reading this card for a stranger I wouldn't know whether he was the cheater or the cheatee."

"Maralee isn't a cheater."

"Of course not. But will someone try to cheat her? In this layout, a lot depends on the card next to it."

"The high priestess," I said. "And she's upside down."

"You see, she can represent the things hidden in the depths of our consciousness. Sort of like the things that show up in your visions, Lee. But the fact that she's reversed can tell you that a conceited, selfish woman is mixed up somehow in the answer to the question."

"Not too clear," I said.

"Sorry. It is what it is. Let's move on to the middle two cards. Your attitude about what's going on." She smiled. "I guess you recognize one of them."

"Pete's card. The knight of swords. I'm so glad to see it," I said. "Even relieved to see it."

"Me too. See how Pete—I mean, the knight—charges ahead to get rid of those storm clouds?" She touched the card. "He'll be really important in this visit to that cliff having a good outcome for you." She moved her hand slightly and touched the ten of pentacles. "Our last card shows us a grandfather surrounded by his family and even his dogs. This, combined with Pete's card, is good news, Lee. It tells us that family matters will be straightened out. Sometimes it has to do with property, so the fact that the island belongs to your relative can be important. All in all, I'd say yes, this trip—this pilgrimage—to see that cliff is a good idea on so many levels. Rhonda is probably right too, about it bringing you some needed closure." She stood, picked up the cards and put them into the box. "Now the tarot and I are off to entertain our *Tarot Time* audience.

"I've made up a little package of goodies for you to share with your coworkers tonight, River," Aunt Ibby said. "Maybe I'll stay awake and watch the movie. What is it?"

"A good one." River shed the apron and accepted the ribbon-tied box. "*The Lighthouse*. Willem Dafoe. I don't think I've ever seen it."

"I have," my aunt said, "and I'll skip it. Way too creepy for me."

CHAPTER 19

O'Ryan and I were soon in bed. I wanted to call
Pete—to thank him for the roses and just to hear his
voice—and I wanted to tell him about the episode in
Rhonda's office, but it was 11:30 and maybe he'd be
asleep.

I didn't have to make the decision. He called me.
"Shower festivities over?" he asked. "Were you surprised?"

"Totally surprised," I said truthfully. "It was wonderful. Thank you for the roses. How did so many of you
manage to keep it a secret?"

"Amazing, isn't it? Your aunt coordinated everything—right down to pacing out the number of timed
steps in your shopping trip."

"With me cussing under my breath the whole way," I
said. "Then getting scared to death in the pitch-dark

house. But it was worth it. What good friends and family I have."

"Just a few more days and I'll be family too." He spoke softly.

"And we'll be in our own house. Mr. and Mrs. You and Me. Together forever."

"Forever," he agreed. "Are your movers all set to put your stuff in? Mine are going to bring the rest of my furniture over there tomorrow morning. Joanne will be there to let them in."

"Mine too. Hope they won't bump into each other."

"Never happen. I'm sure Aunt Ibby has all that coordinated too." He laughed.

"Pete, something happened today I want to tell you about."

"What happened, sweetheart? Are you okay?"

"I'm fine," I assured him. "It was only something—strange. You remember how you showed me the Google Earth picture of my dad's sister's island up in Maine?"

"Sure."

"Well, today Rhonda pulled up the same picture. We could see the airstrip and the lighthouse and everything," I told him.

"Yeah. Quite a ranch," he said.

"She expanded the view," I recalled, "so that we could see the shoreline nearby."

"The island is just a short boat ride from the mainland, I understand," he said. "I guess we'll hire a boat to go out there."

"I could see cliffs at the edge of the water," I explained. "Tall, raggedy-looking cliffs. I recognized one of them. I remembered it. I felt as if I was going to faint, Pete. It was the cliff I saw in that vision when I was a little girl. The picture in my Mary Janes. It's the cliff where the plane crashed."

"Oh, Lee. I'm so sorry. That must have been awful for you."

"It was. But Pete, I need to go there. To see it. To face it. We'll leave some flowers like people do in cemeteries on Memorial Day."

"It will be some kind of closure for you, won't it? Doing that?"

"That's what Rhonda said. I hope so."

"We'll do it. I promise. Now think about good things. Think about our wedding. Go to sleep. Skip the late movie. Sweet dreams."

"I will. Good night. I love you."

I tried to do as he suggested. I thought about the wedding. Had I done the right thing in making Mama's dress strapless and trainless? Would the Fabulous Fabio deliver the cake on time? Should I have hired a DJ instead of the band that played at Shannon and Dakota's wedding? Questions—some important, some silly, but none sleep-inducing—danced like misbehaving sugarplums through my head. I gave up after an hour or so and turned the TV on. O'Ryan, eyes closed, cuddled close to me.

Crashing waves, screaming seagulls, pounding rain. Two men fighting on a spiral staircase in a lighthouse. In the dim, gray light, one man bashes the other one with a shovel. Not the stuff sweet dreams are made of. Should have listened to Aunt Ibby. I turned it off, hugged my cat and wished Pete was there.

The movers arrived early. I woke to the *bump-bump-bump* of heavy articles being muscled down a couple of flights of stairs. I tossed on a robe and watched over the railing as my bedroom bureau, partly covered in a khaki quilt, started on its journey to a new home. O'Ryan, with his head poked between the balusters, watched beside me.

The two burly men in charge of my worldly goods approached the front-door exit. Resting their burden for a second, one of them reached for the doorknob, just as the doorbell chimed "The Impossible Dream."

"I'll get it." I heard my aunt's voice. "I'm expecting someone." She wedged herself between bureau and door, pulling on the knob and admitting her early-morning caller. It was Michael Martell—with a great-looking pair of 1960s Danish modern brass and teak table lamps—one in each hand.

"Good morning, Ms. Russell—Ibby," he said. "I stopped at an antiques store and bought these for the apartment. Old habits die hard. Salem has some wonderful shops. Hope it's not inconvenient for you."

The movers rested the bureau on its sturdy base, each leaning on the quilt-covered top, looking back and forth between the two speakers. "Not at all. Come along with me Michael," my aunt directed. "We'll use the back entrance. As you can see, Maralee's movers are here for her things." She motioned for the man to follow her through the living room, turned and faced my guys. "Carry on," she said. "We'll be out of your way."

I ducked back into my room, while O'Ryan, ever curious, darted down the stairs toward whatever was going on down there. I fully intended to follow his lead. I dressed hurriedly for work, jeans and lightweight turquoise sweater, waited while my movers returned to the attic for their next burden, and was downstairs before they reappeared.

I followed the sound of their voices from the kitchen. Their owner of the lamps—which now rested on the kitchen counter—sat in one of the captain's chairs and faced my aunt across steaming mugs of coffee and a plate full of cinnamon rolls. O'Ryan sat in the chair beside Martell's, watching the two humans and ignoring his red bowl.

"Good morning, Maralee." Aunt Ibby greeted me with a smile. "Dr. Martell stopped by to drop off a few personal touches for his apartment. I'm offering him a sample of the breakfast part of our little bed-and-breakfast venture. Simple fare. Nothing fancy. Please join us."

"Thanks. I will." I selected a mug, poured myself a coffee, and sat beside the cat. "So, Dr. Martell, will you be moving in right away?"

"This very afternoon," he said. "As soon as my classes are over for the day."

O'Ryan leaned away from me, edged a little closer to the man, and snaking out one big yellow paw, touched Martell's arm.

"For goodness sake, look at that," my aunt said. "O'Ryan has taken a liking to you, Michael. You might want to block the cat door in your apartment before he takes to visiting you uninvited."

Martell stroked the cat's head. O'Ryan closed his eyes and leaned closer. "I'm fond of cats, Ibby. We always had them around when I was a kid. I even had one in my antiques shop. A calico named Prudence. That was the inspiration for my Antiques Alley Mystery series."

"I thought as much," Aunt Ibby said. "Two of my best friends are big mystery fans. In fact, they join me every week to watch *Midsomer Murders*. Perhaps once you get settled you might like to join us sometimes."

"I'd like that very much." By this time the cat had moved into his lap.

"Good. We have some snacks and a little wine and discuss the plot and detection methods and the like." Aunt Ibby refilled his coffee mug.

"No wine for me." He held up the hand not involved in petting the cat. "I never took another drop of alcohol after—you know."

We knew. There was an awkward silence. I broke it. "I have to get started for work," I said. "I'll get the real estate agent's card for you, Dr. Martell. She's awfully good." I hurried out of the room and up the stairs, passing the movers carrying O'Ryan's favorite zebra-print wing chair. I grabbed my purse and briefcase from my room. My antique writing desk and chair, properly swathed in khaki quilts, were on their way out the door when I paused once again to deliver the promised business card and to thank my aunt once again for the shower.

Dr. Martell didn't seem to be in any hurry to get to the Tabby. *None of my business.* I left by the kitchen door and the back hall. O'Ryan, a bit reluctantly, I thought, followed me out to the garage, watching as I backed the Jeep out and headed to my job.

I was greeted with excited chatter from my friends who'd attended the festivities. My name was on Rhonda's whiteboard. *Lee. See Mr. Doan.*

"Anything wrong?" I asked her.

"Nope. He wants you to take a camera to Maine. Grab some footage for that documentary he's planning on New England vacations."

"I'll be on my *honeymoon*, for God's sake! And he wants me to work?"

"Sure. I'm afraid it might be a little bit my fault," she said. "I told him about your relative owning that Pirate's

Island. Seems he'd heard of it. It's quite the tourist attraction. They let people dig for pirate treasure out there."

"I didn't know that." I was surprised. Aunt Ibby hadn't mentioned anything about treasure hunters on Aunt Doris's island. "I wonder if anybody ever finds anything."

"They do." Rhonda's smile was broad. "Gold coins, mostly, and somebody found a gold chain a couple of years ago."

"No kidding. Well, I'd better go in and see what Mr. Doan has in mind."

"I didn't tell him about you kind of freaking out about those cliffs on shore."

"Thanks. I won't tell him either."

CHAPTER 20

I tapped on the door marked MANAGER, then pushed it open. "You wanted to see me, sir?"

"Ms. Barrett, please sit down. I understand you'll be visiting within the New England states on your upcoming *paid* vacation," he said.

I sat. "My upcoming honeymoon," I corrected. "Yes. New Hampshire and Maine."

"Good choices," he said. "I'm particularly interested in a place called Pirate's Island. I've heard that you plan to spend some of your *paid* vacation time there."

Oh-oh. He's making a big deal out of the paid part. Sure sign he wants something extra for his money.

"I have relatives there. We plan to visit them but we have no plans to stay on the island." I shook my head. "None at all. With such a *short* . . . um—vacation, we plan to see as much of Maine as we can. Boothbay Harbor, Kennebunkport, maybe even all the way up to Mount Desert to catch the country's earliest sunrise."

"Pirate's Island is the part the station is interested in." He reached below his desk and produced a camcorder small enough to fit in my handbag. I knew that because I'd used it before. "Here you go. Top-of-the-line HD camcorder with surround sound. Shouldn't take you too long to get what we need. You could probably get it all done in a day or two. Get somebody to talk about the pirate history of the place. Climb up into the old lighthouse. Get some pictures of those gold coins the tourists keep finding. Listen, your relatives will appreciate the free publicity."

I hesitated. It was true that Aunt Doris and Uncle Bill— I was already beginning to think of them that way— would without doubt enjoy the TV exposure. Mr. Doan pushed the camcorder toward me. "We'll pay you extra, naturally. Just keep track of your hours. It'll be fun. You might even dig up some treasure for yourself. Why not? Other people have."

I felt my resolve weakening. Maybe it *would* be fun to work on a documentary. "I'll ask Pete what he thinks about it," I promised, "but I have no idea whether my aunt and uncle would even invite us to stay overnight."

"Okay. Think it over." He nudged the camera a little closer to me. "Why don't you take this along, anyway. Practice a little with it."

"All right. But I'm not making any promises. It is my honeymoon, after all." I eased the camcorder into the hobo bag. It fit easily.

"Understood. Hurry up and decide though. I sure don't want to have to fly Palmer up there." He gave a big, fake sigh. "You'll do a much better job, being family and all."

Understood. And you don't have to pay airfare or hotel for me.

The threat to give the assignment to Scott had the desired effect. How much time could it take, anyway? I'd do some footage of the island and interview my aunt—or uncle—or both for the history of the island. The Visitors and Convention Bureau would probably have enough information to get me started before we even left Salem. I'd have to run the idea by Pete, but I was pretty sure he'd go along with it.

"I'll get back to you as soon as I can," I told Bruce Doan, slung the hobo over my shoulder, left the manager's office and headed to my own—with a lot on my mind.

My thoughts that morning were, I admit, quite a bit muddled. The camcorder weighed on both my handbag and my mind. Should I or shouldn't I? I hadn't stopped thinking about Aunt Ibby's morning kaffeeklatsch with Dr. Martell—or Fenton Bishop—as the case may be. Should she, or shouldn't she? Not my call. Thoughts about my upcoming wedding, though, were uppermost in my mind and the recent conversations about Aunt Doris and Uncle Bill had brought thoughts of family to the forefront. Doris Raymond was my father's sister—just as close a blood relative on that side of the family tree as Aunt Ibby was on my mother's side. I thought again about how fortunate Pete was to have so much family nearby—and at our wedding ceremony. I felt tears welling up and turned away from the window separating me from the newsroom.

I don't have my dad, or even any male relative to walk me down the aisle. Aunt Ibby would walk with me, would give me away. *Not the same as having a dad. Not at all.*

I'll wear my mom's wedding dress, but she won't be there to see me in it. I'd loved every minute of the fittings. The feel of the satin on my skin had made me feel close to her. *Not fair. Not fair at all.*

I brushed a hand across my eyes. Told myself how lucky I was to have Aunt Ibby and Pete and my many friends. But the bridge of my nose still ached from unshed tears—the pain of that long-ago loss was still there. *You can cry later*, I told myself. *Not on company time.* The self-reprimand worked—at least for the time being. I pulled the camcorder from the bag and put it on my desk. "Get somebody to talk to you about the pirate history of the place," Doan had said. If it was as much of a tourist attraction as he thought it was, there must be plenty of information on it online.

I typed *Pirate's Island Maine*. He was right. Most of it was advertising, pitching the day trips to the island. Fares for the basic tour included a boat ride to the island and back and a guided group tour of the island. Visitors could upgrade packages to include a visit to the lighthouse, rental of a metal detector and a map showing where gold coins had been found. The most expensive day trip, at $100 per person, offered a boat ride to a cave only accessible at low tide, where legend says that pirates visited in the 1700s and left an X carved into rocky cave walls. There was a deluxe overnight stay in the lighthouse keeper's cottage too, including all of the above extras for $500 a person. Cool! How could I pass this up? And as Doan had said, it shouldn't take more than one or two days and besides—it would be fun. I could hardly wait to tell Pete about the assignment—and hoped he'd approve of my doing it.

Maybe I could dream up a Ranger Rob pirate-themed

show. Why not? Eye patches for all the little buckaroos and pirate toys from the toy trawler. I could use footage from the island for the intro. Glad that my mind was back on the program director track and away from the pity party I'd been heading for, I pulled up the two weather reports Wanda had done in her new persona, along with the one from the previous day's cooking show. With just a few edits these would work for her application to the *Hometown Cooks* audition. I decided that Wanda looked about as "hometown" in both as she was ever going to. I filled out the online application, attached the videos and hit *send*. Done. I worked straight through lunch—a granola bar and a Pepsi—then made sure the business-hour guy would have his new paper shredder by showtime on Saturday.

I was aware of a motion behind me in the newsroom and spun my chair around. Scott Palmer again. He pointed to the camcorder still on my desk. *What's up?* he mouthed, frowning. Great. Now I'd have to explain the Maine assignment before it was even confirmed. Otherwise he'd be sure I was trying to go back to reporting, upstaging him somehow—which I had absolutely no intention of doing. I motioned for him to come around to my door.

"Something new has been added?" He pointed to my desk again. "Special assignment?"

"Not really," I said. "You know how Doan likes to get as many jobs out of all of us as he can? He heard that Pete and I are going to Maine and he's planning some kind of New England documentary. Wants me to grab some pretty footage of the Vacation Land State he can add to the stuff he got for free from the Visitors and Convention Bureau up there."

"Jeez, Moon. On your honeymoon?"

"Yep. I'm not even sure Pete's going to go for it. Don't worry. Your time will come. Where are you going on your next vacation?"

"My next one is in January. Probably Vermont. Skiing."

"See? There you go. The trusty camcorder will be in your backpack, wanna bet?"

That brought a smile. "Nope, I'm sure you're right. Anything else interesting going on in your world that I should know about?"

"Wedding stuff," I said. "A lot of wedding stuff. You plan to be there?"

"Of course. Do I need to send back that little card? I don't know what I did with it." He looked really worried.

"No problem. I'll put you on the acceptance list."

"Great. Well, I'm off. Francine and I are covering a Salem High School sixtieth class reunion. Sounds pretty tame."

"You never know," I said, remembering Aunt Ibby's forty-fifth high school reunion, which had been *anything* but tame. "Have fun."

Pete and I had agreed to meet at the new house after work. I left my office at five, anxious to see how the movers, with Aunt Ibby's input, had placed our belongings in their new surroundings. Pete couldn't get away from the police station until nearly six, so he met me at Aunt Ibby's. I dropped off the hobo bag with its weighty new acquisition in my bedroom—plenty of time to discuss that later—and together we walked down Winter Street, enjoying the early-evening activities of our neighborhood: Kids on bikes, people walking dogs, the happy *ding-a-ling* of the ice cream truck. I squeezed Pete's hand. "This is a good place for us."

He squeezed mine back. "I know."

It's one thing to walk through an empty series of rooms—admiring floorboards, brickwork, and fireplaces. It's quite another experience when the spaces are filled with your own familiar belongings, the walls accented with paintings, prints, and objects you both love.

In the living room, Pete's gray three-piece sectional faced the fireplace, brightened by red throw pillows that used to be on my bentwood bench. O'Ryan's favorite black-and-white zebra-print wing chair and one of my black leather club chairs were arranged beneath the front windows, separated by an antique tip-top table rescued from the attic. An Edward Hill painting of the White Mountains hung over the fireplace, and a glass-topped coffee table with a gray driftwood base held a handsome potted jade plant from Joanne.

In the nearby kitchen, my Lucite table and chairs looked just as perfect as I'd thought they would and my much-loved Kit-Cat Klock on the wall rolled googly eyes and ticktocked time with his tail. Colorful fiesta ware, jadeite, and my collection of cookie jars looked perfect displayed in glass-fronted cabinets

A few more homey pieces from both of our apartments had been added to the den, and the sunroom still looked fine with the addition of an area rug and some assorted-sized baskets holding magazines, potting tools, and cat toys.

Happy with it all, we climbed the stairs to the master suite. My king-sized bed with the snowy-white woven spread faced the window looking up Winter Street through the branches of a fine old chestnut tree. The graceful old "ladies desk" that had been crowded into my narrow apartment bedroom had the space it deserved to show off its lines and my oval-framed full-length mirror looked at home between his-and-her closets. The multi–secret-compartment bureau stood against a wall surrounded by a family gallery of framed photos. Pete's grandparents, parents, his sister Marie and brother-in-law Donnie were all represented in studio portraits, along with action shots of the two nephews in their hockey uniforms. There was a publicity headshot of me and a picture of Aunt Ibby and my mother sitting on the same bentwood bench that was now in our sunroom. There was a wedding photo of my parents too—my mother, happy and excited in the champagne satin gown I'd be wearing in a few days; my dad, his love for her showing in his eyes.

I lingered for a moment, reaching out to touch the flat likenesses of my parents, trying to recall their dear faces. "I never even got to know them," I murmured. "And they didn't know me." *Not fair. So not fair.*

Pete didn't say anything. He didn't need to. He just held me close and the tears I'd been holding back all day flowed.

CHAPTER 21

After a while, the crying passed. I wiped my eyes, gratefully accepted Pete's willing shoulder to lean on and actually felt better.

"The family part of this is hard for you, isn't it?" he whispered. "Heck, I even have grandparents, let alone sibling and parents and in-laws and all."

"I know. It's nobody's fault. I can't be unique. There are plenty of people with small families. It just hit me today, though—the part about not having Daddy walking me down the aisle, or my mom seeing me wearing her wedding dress."

He gave me an awkward pat on the back and smiled. "But hey, babe, *mi family su family*. After Sunday my people are your people and your people are my people. And besides, we're going to get acquainted with your aunt and uncle from Maine. Maybe you even have some long-lost cousins up there." He tipped my face up and gave me a kiss. "And maybe you and I will be making an addition or two to the family tree before too long. Please don't cry."

The tears slowly dissolved into sniffles, then to hiccups and finally went away. Pete and I sat in our pretty sunroom for a while, and Pete measured the glass pane, soon to be replaced with a cat door. We did a final walk-through, turning off lights, locking doors. We stepped back outside onto a quiet Winter Street and walked together back to Aunt Ibby's house.

I wished Pete a good night as he climbed into his car, waved as he drove toward the common, then unlocked the front door. O'Ryan greeted me with enthusiastic *mrrows* and purrs. I picked him up and started up the stairs to my room.

"Maralee? Is that you?" Aunt Ibby called from her office. "How does the house look?"

"Marvelous. Better than we dreamed. I recognized your handiwork everywhere." I followed the sound of her voice and approached the office doorway. "You're busy. I can tell," I said. "I'll tell you all about it in the morning."

She pushed reading glasses up onto her forehead. "Nonsense. It's nothing important. Come on in here and sit down." She stood, frowning, and faced me. "You've been crying, child. Whatever is wrong?"

"You know me too well," I said. "I didn't want you see my red eyes. Just feeling sorry for myself about Daddy not being here to walk me down the aisle. Mummy not seeing how I look in her dress." The bridge of my nose started to ache again. "Pete understood. I had a good cry and I'm over it. Truly. I'm fine." I stood up straight. Shoulders back. Brave soldier. "Fine," I said again.

"No, you're not. Come in and sit down and we'll talk about it." I did as I was told. Sat in the cherrywood chair with O'Ryan on my lap.

"I expect it was the picture wall in the bedroom," she said. "Was that it?"

"Partly," I admitted. "But I've been feeling sad all day."

"You have reason," she said, "but more reason to be happy."

"I know that. I have you and Pete and plenty of friends." The cat looked up at me. "And O'Ryan," I added. "I have an aunt and uncle in Maine that I'm going to see and get to know—and as Pete says, we may be adding to the family tree before too long. There'll be lots more pictures for that wall."

"Of course there will. Let me tell you a little about your aunt Doris and your uncle Bill. I've only met them a few times—Uncle Bill only once, actually, and that was at the funeral." She returned to her desk chair. "Doris is your father's only sibling. She was quite a lot older than he. Ten, maybe fifteen years. She was married once before she met Bill. Widowed young, like you. Her husband died in the war. Vietnam. He was from a fine old Maine family. That's where the island came from. She inherited it. Of course, it wasn't called Pirate's Island then. The name came later—sometime after your parents' accident."

"Interesting. Did my mother like her? I mean—were they friends?"

"Oh, yes indeed. Carrie and Doris were great friends. Your folks went up to visit them often. I don't remember that Doris and Bill came here, but maybe once or twice. She doesn't like to travel. The note on last year's Christmas card said that she actually doesn't like to leave the island at all anymore if she can avoid it."

"I'm glad they were friends. Maybe Aunt Doris can tell me some stories about Carrie from before she was my mom."

"I'm sure she can. Being on the island might be an adventure for you," she said. "Speaking of pictures, take plenty of them. I've never been there."

"Pictures! Oh, wow. I forgot to tell Pete. Mr. Doan gave me a camcorder to use. He wants me to shoot some footage of the island and to get somebody to talk about the pirate legend."

"Back to being a reporter for a little while? What fun."

"I wasn't too crazy about the idea when Mr. Doan first brought it up," I admitted, "but now I'm looking forward to it. I hope Pete approves."

"I'll bet he will," she said.

"We're putting the cart before the horse, though, aren't we?" I worried. "Maybe they won't invite us to their island at all."

She wore her thoughtful, wise-old-owl face. "It seems to me it would be a good idea to call them. There's a phone number in all of their ads."

"I will," I promised.

"I can't possibly imagine that they wouldn't be delighted to see you both. After all, Doris is your father's only sister," she said, "and certainly one of the last people to see your parents before they got into that little plane of theirs. I still find it hard to accept what happened to them." She looked down at her lap. "'Pilot error' they said. And your father was such a careful person." She made a sad *tsk-tsk* sound.

"I'll call them tonight," I said, "and see what they say.

No point in telling Pete about Mr. Doan's big idea if we aren't invited anyway." I tried to smile as I spoke, but the thought of the last people on earth to see my parents alive not wanting to meet me was impossible to consider.

Aunt Ibby must have sensed my sadness. "It'll be fine. You'll see." She stood up again. "Come upstairs with me. I have something for you. Call it an early wedding present."

I followed dutifully, climbing the front stairs behind her with O'Ryan at my heels. She opened the door to her room and motioned me inside. O'Ryan ran ahead and launched himself onto her bed. I sat in a Boston rocker and waited for whatever was going to happen next. *An early wedding present?*

She approached her bureau and reached for her jewelry box. My aunt doesn't wear much jewelry. Never has, in my memory. But there are a few choice things that she wears on special occasions. She doesn't even have a proper jewelry box either, although I've offered to buy her one. As far back as I can remember she's kept her jewelry in a miniature wooden cedar chest. Grandmother Forbes's gold wristwatch was in there—the kind you have to wind. Six o'clock and twelve o'clock were marked with diamonds. I knew that some of my mother's jewelry was in the box too. Aunt Ibby had often told me that the contents of the chest would someday be mine.

"I want to give you something of your mother's." She held up a small, square white box. "I was going to give you this on your wedding day for the 'something old.' You know? But I think she'd like you to have it now. She was wearing it when she died. I'd never seen it before, so they must have bought it while they were in Maine." She handed me the box.

The ring inside was beautiful in its simplicity. A round, brilliant green stone was centered on the plain gold band. "Look inside," my aunt said. "It's engraved."

I held the ring close to my eye. The word *Forever* was engraved in tiny script.

The sadness closed in again. "But they didn't *have* forever. They had hardly any time at all." *Not fair. So not fair.*

"They had *their* forever. You and Pete will have *your* forever." She smiled. "Maybe someday you'll have a daughter and you'll pass the ring on to her. For *her* forever. Time is what it is. Live in the moments you have."

I slipped the ring onto my right ring finger. "It's beautiful. I love it. Thank you."

"Does it fit?"

"It's a tiny bit loose."

"Take it to a jeweler as soon as you can. They can put one of those ring size-adjuster gadgets on while you wait."

"I will," I said. "It makes me feel close to her. I'll wear it for all of my forever." I held my hand out, admiring the fiery green of the emerald, the glint of the gold band. "I love it," I said again, feeling my mother's approval.

"I'm glad." She closed the jewelry box. "Come on back down to the kitchen. I have some chocolate ice cream in the freezer that's calling your name."

I cupped my right hand over my ear. "I hear it too. Let's go." O'Ryan was out the door and into the hall ahead of us. We followed him downstairs and into the foyer. I heard a knocking sound. Stopped walking and listened. "Is that someone knocking on your kitchen door?"

"I think it is. It's probably Michael. He moved into his apartment today, remember?" She stepped ahead of me. "I'm coming," she called.

CHAPTER 22

O'Ryan and I followed my aunt, fluffing her hair and smoothing her skirt as she walked toward the kitchen. "Coming," she called again, turning the lock. *At least she didn't leave it unlocked for him.*

Michael Martell ambled into the kitchen, smiled and nodded to both of us. "Hello. Lovely evening." He waved a single sheet of paper in the air. "Ibby, I picked up a copy of my class schedule you asked for. I appreciate your offer to post it in the library."

My aunt accepted the paper. "Thank you, Michael. I'm sure there'll be a lot of interest in your session on 'how to write today's murder mystery.'"

I pulled out one of the captain's chairs and sat. "Hi, Dr. Martell. How did the new lamps work out?"

"Perfectly. I already had a pair of mid-century fiberglass lampshades—you know the kind, with atomic designs," he said.

I knew exactly what he meant. I love those lampshades and I knew they were perfect for the lamps he'd shown us earlier. "I'll bet you miss being in the antiques business."

"Sometimes. But my Antique Alley Mystery books have given me an imaginary shop." He squinted a bit and leaned toward me. "That's an unusual ring."

"Thank you," I said, holding my hand up so he could get a better look at it. "It belonged to my mother. Aunt Ibby just gave it to me today. It will be the 'something old' for my wedding."

"It certainly appears to have some significant age to it," he agreed. "May I take a closer look?" He pulled a small circular gadget from his shirt pocket. "My jeweler's loupe," he said. "I never know when something that needs close inspection might show up." He held out an expectant hand. "May I?"

I handed him the ring. He sat across from me and put the glass to his right eye. O'Ryan once again chose to sit in the man's lap. Martell turned the ring from side to side, peering at the inscription inside and at the stone in the center. He hummed a soft "um-huh" and whispered "my, my," and finally whistled a long, low whistle. "Where did your mom get this, if you don't mind my asking?"

"In Maine," my aunt put in. "That is, we're pretty sure that's where she got it."

"I don't pretend to be an expert on this sort of thing," he said, "but I'd guess this ring was crafted sometime in the early 1700s."

"That old?" I was surprised.

"The engraving is modern. The band isn't marked but

it appears to be at least eighteen-karat gold. The stone is a fine emerald—maybe Colombian" He put the loupe back into his pocket and handed my ring back. He stood, gently dislodging the cat. "I'll tell you where I've seen a similar piece."

I slipped the ring back onto my finger. "Where's that?"

"Key West. In Mel Fisher's museum. Ever been there?"

Of course I'd been there. When Johnny and I lived in Florida we'd made several trips to the Keys. I even had a necklace with a gold coin from the *Atocha* on it That's the pirate ship Fisher discovered. "Youi think my ring is pirate treasure?" The words slipped out.

Martell didn't laugh at the question. "Possibly," he said. "Do you know *where* she was in Maine when she got it? Big state."

She was in a place called Pirate's Island.

I thought it, but didn't say it. A look passed between me and Aunt Ibby. She didn't say it either.

"They were on vacation," I said. "They may have visited any number of places. Antiques shops all over the place up there." That was true.

"Well, it's a really nice piece. I'm sure you'll enjoy wearing it on your wedding day. I won't bother you ladies any longer. Thanks again for posting my schedule in the library. And Ibby, I'll look forward to seeing you in the morning."

What?

"Blueberry pancakes," my aunt said. "Picked the berries myself."

Oh yeah. Bed-and-breakfast. I'd almost forgotten. "Good night, Dr. Martell," I said.

"Good night, Ms. Barrett."

He went out the back door. I locked it behind him and

listened as he climbed the twisty staircase to his apartment. I returned to the table where O'Ryan and Aunt Ibby waited. I held my right hand out, staring once again at my ring. "The 1700s," I said. "Do you believe it?"

"When we get a chance, perhaps we should have it appraised by somebody knowledgeable about such things," she said. "After all, Michael admits he's not an expert. It may be a clever reproduction."

"They'd been on Pirate's Island," I said. "If Dr. Martell is right about the age of my ring, maybe they dug it up when they were there. That's so romantic." Again, I held out my hand, admiring the ring. "They must have been so thrilled. I'll bet Aunt Doris and Uncle Bill will be excited to see it again after all these years. I'm going to call them tonight. I can hardly wait to talk to them both."

"Chocolate ice cream first?" She opened the freezer door.

"Naturally." I selected bowls and spoons while she manned the ice cream scoop. "I'm getting nervous about calling them. What should I say? I mean, it's been over thirty years and they've never tried to get in touch with me. They know I'm here. They know I'm their niece."

"It's possible that they think you should have contacted them." She put an extra scoop of chocolate into my bowl. "It's my fault. Your parents dying the way they did—it affected you so deeply—I wanted to shield you from the reminders of it all. I never talked to you about Doris or that island or the cliff where they crashed. I almost wish I hadn't put them on the wedding invitation list. That I'd left things the way they were."

I saw what she meant. "That way I would never have seen that cliff and recognized it from the picture in my shoe. I wouldn't have relived that awful moment."

"Then you understand."

"Of course. Rhonda thinks I may have been dealing with some kind of post-traumatic stress all this time."

She stiffened her back. "Maybe. But it is what it is. Now is the time to deal with it. Whatever Doris and Bill think or say, you deserve the closure that visiting that place can give you. Pete will be there to support you. You'll be fine. You make that call."

I looked at my watch. "You don't think it's too late?"

"Not even nine o'clock yet," she said. "Get it over with. Got the number?"

"I wrote down the number that's in their Pirate's Island ads. It's the only one I have."

"That's the one I have too. I believe they run the business from their home. Scoot, now. Go upstairs and make the call. I'll clear up these dishes."

I gave her a hug and followed O'Ryan to the foyer. He paused in front of the hall tree, then jumped up onto the seat, facing the mirror. Could the cat see the same flashing lights and swirling colors that I was seeing?

I wanted to look away. I knew as soon as the thing started to take shape that I didn't want to see it. I stood there in the front hall of the house where I was raised, put my hand on O'Ryan's head—taking comfort from soft, warm fur—watching a man's hand holding what appeared to be a fuel nozzle. The view shifted slightly. The fuel was being pumped into something yellow. I knew my dad drove a yellow Corvette convertible. I remembered riding in it. What fun! A happy memory.

The view shifted again. Not the Corvette. The plane. It was yellow too. Someone—my dad?—was fueling a yellow plane. The picture blinked away. "Good," I said to the cat. "It's gone. Let's go upstairs." The picture blinked back on. This time the man's hand held a gasoline pump hose, a stream of liquid pouring onto a patch of daisies. I waited. The picture blinked off. The hall tree mirror reflected a large yellow cat and a distraught-looking redhead.

O'Ryan leaned into my hand for a brief moment, then hopped to the floor, turned and started up the stairs. I followed. "Never mind what's in the mirror," I told myself. "Concentrate on the phone call to Pirate's Island." O'Ryan looked up at me as we reached my bedroom. "Darned visions don't make the least bit of sense anyway," I told him and pushed the door open.

The cat and I climbed onto my bed. I fished my phone from my hobo bag, pushing the camcorder aside. I'd already programmed the phone number for Pirate's Island into the memory. I tapped it and I heard a phone ring.

A man answered.

"Pirate's Island," he said. "Fun for the whole family. How may I direct your call?"

"This is Maralee Kowalski Barrett," I said. "I'd like to speak to Doris or Bill, please."

"Bill Raymond here," he said. "Who did you say you are?"

"Maralee Kowalski," I said, leaving off the Barrett for the moment. "Doris is my father's sister. My aunt."

"Oh sure. You're Carrie and Jack's kid. You're getting married. Congratulations. Wait a sec. I'll get Doris." A pause with sounds of music and muffled conversation in the background. A shouted, "Hey, Doris. Pick up the office phone. It's for you."

My Aunt Doris answered with a timid "Hello?"

"Hi," I said. "This is Maralee Kowalski." Then, borrowing from her husband's words, I added, "Carrie and Jack's daughter."

"Are you really? Oh, my goodness. What a surprise," she said. "Well now, you must be all grown up. I hear you're getting married."

I'm thirty-five. I hope I'm grown up enough to get married.

"Yes, that's true," I said. "The wedding is next Sunday. I'm sorry you and Mr. Raymond can't be there, but Pete and I will be honeymooning in Maine and we'd like very much to see you two while we're in the area." *Might as well get to the point. The most she can say is no.* She didn't reply right away. I pushed my luck. "Maybe we could even spend a day or two on your island and get acquainted."

"Why, sure," she answered brightly. "I guess you'll be wanting the deluxe package, then?"

CHAPTER 23

"Uh, yeah, well . . . sure—that sounds good," I stammered. "We plan to spend some time in New Hampshire on the way up, so our plans aren't firm yet, Aunt Doris. Can I call back later and let you know the dates we have in mind?"

"Sure thing, hon. Not too busy this time of year. It really gets crazy in another month or so. It'll be good to see you, Maralee. It's been a long time."

"We're looking forward to it," I said, and that's the way we left it. Once I thought about it, her response made perfect sense. Even though we're blood relatives, we hadn't seen or spoken to one another for thirty years. She and her husband ran a vacation attraction. Why would I expect an open-arms welcome and invitation to stay with them? Pete had had the right idea when he suggested we just hire a boat for a ride to the island and back. We'd visit with my aunt and uncle, then we could go to the cliff site with our flowers and continue on up to Mount Desert to catch the sunrise. Somehow Aunt Ibby and I had built this island visit into something more than it needed to be.

O'Ryan reached a lazy paw toward the camcorder, hooking it by the strap and pulling it toward me. Using both paws and his nose, he nudged the thing into my hand. "You're right, smart cat," I told him. "On the other hand, Doan wants pictures of the island and I'm sure the station would pay for the deluxe package. Let's call Pete and run the whole idea past him."

That's what I did. I explained Mr. Doan's proposal, Aunt Ibby's thoughts about my getting to know my paternal relatives, and Doris Raymond's businesslike solution to the idea of our visit to her island. Pete came up with a sensible compromise plan immediately.

"Let's take the day trip boat over, do the tour, you shoot some video for Doan, we introduce ourselves and if it looks like something you want to continue, we'll buy the deluxe package."

"Perfect," I said. "Guess I was overcomplicating things."

"Yep. Don't worry about it. Everything will be fine. We all set for the rehearsal dinner?"

"I think so." Our casual-dress rehearsal on Saturday evening would be held at the Old Town Hall—same place as the wedding. Mr. Pennington would officiate. Marty McCarthy would take pictures. Afterward, the wedding party, along with parents, grandparents, siblings, aunts, and uncles would gather outside in a reserved picnic table area. We'd prepaid for several food trucks (all WICH-TV advertisers) to gather nearby, offering American, Mexican, and Chinese menus along with an ice cream vendor so that we could offer plenty of choices. I was pretty sure everyone would love it.

"I feel better now," I told him. "Thanks for making sense out of all this."

"That's what I'm here for. Love you," he said.

"Love you too," I told him, knowing I hadn't shared the latest vision: fuel and a patch of daisies—which didn't make the least bit of sense anyway. I'd tell River about it later, although she'd already told me that reading my visions was sort of like reading dreams—not at all like reading the cards. O'Ryan moved closer to me and stretched a paw toward my right hand. "And Pete, I have something to show you. Aunt Ibby gave me an early wedding present. Something old."

"What is it?"

"Describing doesn't do it justice. I'll show you tomorrow."

"I hope it's not that darned thing in her front hall with the mirror on it," he said.

I laughed at that idea. "I'd turn it down. This is much smaller and prettier. Good night."

Feeling better about meeting the Raymonds, and happy about the way the wedding plans were progressing, I opened the box of note cards marked *Mr. and Mrs. Peter Mondello*, consulted the neatly typed list of names and addresses and gift descriptions my aunt had prepared, and began writing our thank-you notes.

In the morning I put "Love" stamps on each of the envelopes I'd stayed up after midnight to address, and started downstairs to Aunt Ibby's. O'Ryan had already left. "Aunt Ibby, it's me," I called as usual when I entered her living room. I heard voices from the kitchen and assumed that the breakfast part of the B and B was already in progress. I was correct. Michael Martell was seated at the round table, neatly dressed for his teaching job, coffee mug and muffin before him—and sitting in my usual chair. Brushing aside a tiny flash of annoyance—after all, my name isn't on the chair—I wished my aunt and the boarder a good morning. *At least the cat isn't sitting in his lap.*

"Good morning to you, Ms. Barrett." Martell wore a morning-person smile. "I was just telling Ibby here that I couldn't stop thinking about your mother's ring—and about her probably acquiring it somewhere in the state of Maine. So I did a bit of research." He pulled a small notebook from his jacket pocket. "I hope you don't mind. That you don't think I'm being nosy."

"Of course I don't mind." I tried for polite enthusiasm and sat in the chair opposite his. "I appreciate your interest." Which, in a way, I did.

Aunt Ibby wore her regular morning-person smile. "I can hardly wait to hear what you've found, Michael." She poured a mug of coffee for me and one for herself and joined us at the table. "I'll be working a half-day at the library today, but I have time for coffee."

"I mentioned last evening that your ring reminded me of one I'd seen at Mel Fisher's museum in Key West," he began. "The ring Fisher found on the *Atocha* comes from what is generally accepted as pirate treasure."

"Yes," I agreed. "I've been to the museum. They have some amazing things."

"So I began to research the possibility that there may have been pirates lurking around in Maine too." He held the notebook up and gave it a little shake. "Found two of 'em!"

"That's funny. I did the same thing," my aunt said. "I'll bet one of them is Dixie Bull."

"Right you are, Ibby," he said. "Back in Maine they called him 'the Dread Pirate.'"

"An Englishman," my aunt said. "Fur trader. Burned down the whole darned town of Pemaquid."

A frown crossed Martell's face briefly. "The other one is Black Sam Bellamy, captain of the infamous *Whydah*."

"Wealthiest pirate in recorded history," Aunt Ibby put in.

"Some say he buried some of his treasure on islands off the coast of Maine."

"Casco Bay," my aunt said. "Damariscove and Cushing Island."

It was a lot like listening to Aunt Ibby and Mr. Pennington trading famous movie quotes, each trying to one-up the other.

"Black Sam had a sort of Robin Hood reputation." Martell reached for another muffin. "He was called 'Prince of Pirates.'" He smiled at my aunt.

She smiled back. "He was called Black Sam because he had long, flowing black hair. He tied it back with a black bow."

There was a long moment of silence. *Have they called some kind of mutual truce on pirate history?* Martell consulted his notes. He pointed to the ring on my hand. "I'm wondering if your ring came from lost treasure from one of those pirates."

Aunt Ibby and I looked at each other. *Should we tell him about Pirate's Island?* She spoke first. "Oddly enough, Michael, Maralee and Pete are planning to visit the same Maine island where her parents were guests just before they died. It's known as Pirate's Island."

CHAPTER 24

I decided to let Aunt Ibby tell the story. I wasn't the least bit reluctant to excuse myself from breakfast and leave for work. Given the subject matter—Pirate's Island—the verbal sword fighting might resume any minute. Anyway, she knew as much as I did about the place.

"This is all so interesting," I said, "but I need to get going. Busy day ahead." I put my dishes in the sink and with O'Ryan following me, went back up to my room. I gave hair and makeup a quick check, stuffed the camcorder into one of the secret compartments in my bureau—it was, after all, valuable station property—picked up the handbag, and—leaving my door open for the cat's convenience—I started down the stairs.

There was still a hum of conversation issuing from the kitchen. I couldn't make out the words—even though I admit I tried. My car was in the garage behind the house.

If Aunt Ibby had been alone I would have walked through her living room into the kitchen and out the back door. Simple. Now I'd have to use the Winter Street exit, cut through the iron gate, pass by the house and the garden and follow the flagstone path out to Oliver Street. Feeling vaguely grumpy, I unlocked the garage and backed the Jeep out onto the street.

On the way to the station, grasping the steering wheel, I couldn't help admiring the rings on each of my hands— both of them sparking in the morning sun. Had my mother's emerald ring been part of a legendary pirate's hoard? Had it been submerged beneath Maine's cold water for hundreds of years? I liked the romantic idea. Had it perhaps even passed through the hands of Dixie Bull or Black Sam Bellamy? The idea of visiting Pirate's Island grew more attractive by the minute. Meanwhile, having a ring with a possible *real* pirate history to show off to Pete and my WICH-TV friends was going to be fun too.

Rhonda spotted the ring before I'd had a chance to say a word about it. "That's new. Is it a real emerald? It's gorgeous. Where did you get it?"

"Aunt Ibby gave it to me last night. It belonged to my mother." I moved my right hand closer, to give her a better look. "She was wearing it when she died, but she didn't have it before they went to Maine. So we figure it must have come from up there."

"The emerald has such depth," she said. "I've never seen anything quite like it before."

"Dr. Martell thinks it's very old. Maybe all the way back to the 1700s," I told her.

"Dr. Martell? The wife killer?" She was clearly surprised. "Where did you see him?"

"At my house," I admitted. "In Aunt Ibby's kitchen. He moved into one of her B and B apartments yesterday."

Her eyes widened and then she squinted. "And Pete's okay with that?"

"He says the man has served his time. Was a model prisoner. Pete is in touch with Martell's parole officer."

"If Pete says he's okay . . ." She frowned, then finished the thought. "He must be okay."

I sure hope so. I moved past the reception counter and took a quick look at Rhonda's whiteboard. "Anything interesting for me? What does 'General Tso's chicken' mean?"

"That's what you're supposed to find out. It's on the Chinese food truck menu for the rehearsal dinner Saturday," she explained. "Pete's grandma wants to know what's in it. She's on a new diet."

"Okay. First I'll ask Wanda. If she doesn't know, I'll call the Chinese food truck guy."

"Good idea. Is he nice?"

"The Chinese food truck guy?"

"No, silly. The wife killer."

"Very polite. Considerate. Smart. Aunt Ibby seems to like him. So does O'Ryan."

Rhonda tipped her head to one side and gave me that "seeing right through me" look she does so well. "But you're not sure about him?"

What could I say? I had no reason to distrust Michael Martell. In fact, he'd gone out of his way to help me learn about my ring. I dodged the question. "I've barely met the man. Too soon to have an opinion one way or the other." I pointed to the whiteboard. "Anything else in the works for me today?"

"Not officially. Scott's been asking when you'd be in, but didn't say why. He's probably lurking around your office by now."

"That's where I'm headed."

She was right. Scott had pulled his chair so close to the transparent wall separating our spaces that his breath had steamed up a spot on the glass. As soon as I entered my office, I saw his knuckles rap—soundlessly of course—as he mouthed *Hey, Moon!* It was pointless to pretend I couldn't see the commotion. I knew my phone would ring. I put it on speaker. "What do you want, Scott?"

"You're not planning to mess up your honeymoon by doing that Pirate's Island gig, are you?" One thing about Scott, he gets right to the point. No small talk.

"Thinking about it," I told him. "Why?" I already knew the answer to that. Paid vacation in Maine and credits on a documentary. The same benefits I'd get.

"So you haven't told Doan you'd do it?"

"No," I admitted. "I'm not sure the island owners would even welcome a reporter."

"Imagine that. Somebody owning a whole island. They must be rolling in dough."

That somebody is my closest relative besides Aunt Ibby. "Guess so," I said.

"Don't worry. They'll love having a reporter there. I looked 'em up. It's a regular tourist trap." Big smile. "They get people out there by boat and sell them a bunch of phony pirate crap. Listen, Moon. I'll take this one off your hands. You and Pete just have yourselves a nice romantic honeymoon and forget about Doan and the station and your job for a while. What do you say?"

"You looked them up?"

"Sure. I'm a professional, remember?"

"I know you are. What did you find out?" I was interested. Aunt Ibby and Dr. Martell had looked up area pirate history and I'd looked at some of the island's advertising. I knew that Scott liked to dig for dirt. Had he found anything I didn't know about my newfound relatives?

"Enough that I'm sure I can get more than some documentary footage of a broken-down old lighthouse and some harbor seals sleeping on rocks." He did the long look. "I don't mind climbing around on rocks and getting my hands dirty. Give me this one, Moon."

I was tempted. I liked Pete's plan. Take the boat ride. Meet the fam. Do our memorial for my parents and leave.

"I'll think about it. Now go away. I have work to do." I hung up the phone, turned my back, opened a random desk drawer and pretended to be busy. It worked. When I peeked at the newsroom after a few minutes, he was at his desk, talking with Francine. Probably, I thought, the two of them were getting ready to climb into the mobile unit to chase a news story. Once again, I felt a tiny wave of regret that *I* was no longer the one with the mic covering the ever-changing field reports.

With only the faintest little sigh, I turned on my laptop and pulled up the folder marked *Hometown Cooks*, renewing my determination to make sure Wanda would be among the next season's winners.

My intercom buzzer sounded. "Yes, Rhonda?"

"I have a call for you on the studio line from a William Raymond. Do you want to take it?"

William Raymond? My uncle from Pirate's Island? "Sure. Put him on."

"Hello, Maralee? This is your Uncle Billy. We spoke yesterday."

"Yes. Good to hear from you, sir." I wasn't quite ready for the "Uncle Billy" title.

"I didn't realize at first when you called that Maralee Kowalski was Lee Barrett—the TV personality." A hearty chuckle. "Doris and I didn't put it together until we remembered the name on the wedding invitation. Lee Barrett. I guess Doris and your aunt still exchange Christmas cards, but all these years Ibby always just signed them Ibby and Maralee. Heck, we used to watch you on that network shopping channel out of Miami and never knew you were family. Found you right away with Google. WICH-TV, huh?"

"That's right," I said. "I came home to Salem right after my husband died."

"Right. Johnny Barrett. Hell of a driver. Sorry we lost him." Soft sigh. "But, hey, you're getting married again. That's wonderful. Doris and I are looking forward to hosting you and the mister. Maybe you'll even want to tell the folks in Salem about our little island. When can we expect to see you?"

Now conflicting thoughts began to converge. Did I want us to be "hosted" while we were on our honeymoon? My newfound uncle clearly wanted some publicity for Pirate's Island. Did I want to be responsible for producing usable footage for Doan's documentary project? What if it rains? Do I have to stay until the weather clears? Pete and I had purposely planned an unstructured road trip. Except for the New Hampshire Raceway event, and more recently the idea of visiting the site of my parents' death, we would just be happy wanderers, going wherever the mood took us. Maybe we'd stop and see if that trained bear was still at Clark's Trading Post. Maybe we'd catch that first sunrise. Maybe not. William Raymond waited for an answer. I gave him one.

"I appreciate your kindness, but our honeymoon plans are pretty loose at this point. We do want to meet with you and Aunt Doris, of course, but can't set a firm date. How about we call you from the mainland when we get in the neighborhood? If it's a convenient time for you we'll hop on one of the tour boats and look forward to seeing you both."

There was a pause. I didn't know whether my uncle would like my decision, but I was pretty sure Scott Palmer would. I actually hoped that Mr. Doan would hand the Pirate's Island assignment over to him.

"That'll be just fine, sweetheart," William Raymond assured me after a moment. "Whatever works for you two. Your Aunt Doris is really looking forward to your visit. Nice talking with you. Bye for now." *Click.* He was gone.

I was pleased with my decision—sure Pete would be; hoped Mr. Doan would be; wondered if Aunt Doris and Uncle Billy would be. Anyway, it was a decision and that in itself was a good thing. I returned to my *Hometown Cooks* file, ready to give it my full attention. Within a couple of hours I'd done a promotional piece pitching Wanda's cookbook, sent photos of the "new Wanda" along with a press release to all of the newspapers within our broadcast range, and submitted a follow-up letter to the director of the popular network show. That task completed, I still had plenty of time to tell Mr. Doan that I'd decided not to spend any of my honeymoon working on his documentary.

I went back to Rhonda's office where the TV was

tuned to WICH-TV—meaning the station manager was in. "Would you see if Mr. Doan has a minute to see me?" I asked.

She looked up from her *People* magazine. "Sure. Everything okay?"

"Just a teensy change of plans," I said. "No big deal."

"That's good." She tapped on the console. "Mr. Doan? Got a minute to spare for Lee Barrett?" She nodded to me. "He says go right on in."

I thanked Rhonda, and shoulders back, head high, smile in place, tapped on the manager's door, then pushed it open. "Yes, come in, Ms. Barrett. Plans all made for your little side trip to the Pirate's Island?"

"Not exactly, sir."

He frowned. "Why? What's wrong? I thought we had a deal."

No, we didn't. "It was a good idea, a good offer, Mr. Doan, but it's just not going to fit in with the rest of our honeymoon plans." I tried to look disappointed. "But I talked with Scott a while ago and I'll bet he'd be happy to work on the documentary."

"I expect he would." The word *grumble* accurately describes the way Bruce Doan's voice sounds when he's displeased. And he was displeased at that moment. With me. He leaned to one side as though trying to see if I was hiding something behind my back. "Where's my fancy camera?"

"I left it at home, sir," I said. "It's perfectly safe. I'll bring it back first thing tomorrow morning."

"Well, maybe you could just scoot home now and grab my camera," he said. "I'd like to get Scott started on this right away and he might as well have all the tools he's going to need. Have you got any notes on the place to hand over?—since you won't be needing them for anything."

I was ashamed to admit it, but Scott and Rhonda had already done more research on Pirate's Island than I had. "I'll give him everything I have so far," I promised. At least I'd be able to offer some history of Maine coast pirates in general—thanks to Aunt Ibby's and Michael Martell's interest in the subject. I wouldn't dare to ask for Martell's little notebook, but I was pretty sure my aunt— with a librarian's zeal—would have documented whatever she'd learned about Dixie Bull and Black Sam, and would be happy to share it with me.

I phoned my aunt from the parking lot, telling her I'd decided a working honeymoon was a bad idea and that I was on my way home to pick up the camcorder. I asked for the pirate lore she'd collected and she sent it immediately, complete with maps and artists' depictions of the two long-ago pirates. I felt as guilty as though I'd copied somebody's homework, but gratefully accepted anyway. When I pulled up in front of the house on Winter Street, the vintage Lincoln was already there.

He left for work when I did just a few hours ago. Did he get fired already?

O'Ryan greeted me with happy tail wagging and silent meows from the front hall window. I unlocked the door and accepted his enthusiastic greeting. "I love you too," I told him and began to climb the stairs. The door to my bedroom was still ajar and the cat got there before I did. I followed him inside, pulling the door partway shut behind me. He was already curled up on my bed, pretending to be asleep. I tiptoed past him, pulled open a small drawer, pressed a carved curlicue that released the large panel on the side of the bureau. "I know you're awake, cat," I told O'Ryan as I pulled the camera from its hiding place. "Get up. We're going back downstairs."

"Hello? Is somebody here?" The male voice came from the hallway just outside my room. "Ibby? Is that you?" The door began to swing open.

"Michael!" I practically screamed his name. "What are you doing here? You scared me half to death."

"I heard voices in there. I knew you were at work and Ibby is at the library. I didn't think anyone was home. I'm sorry." His voice was calm, reasonable. I was pretty sure mine wasn't.

"What are you doing here?" I demanded again. Heart pounding, I pushed the panel on the side of the bureau shut. It closed with a satisfying *click*.

"Ibby said I could look at the larger apartment." He held up a key. "To see if I liked it better than mine. I didn't. I was just leaving." He stared at the bureau. "That's the dresser with six secret compartments. I saw it once in an auction catalog. Famous Salem maker. There are only three of them known to exist."

"Two, actually," I said, my heart resuming a normal rhythm. "The other one burned in a house fire."

"What a shame." His tone was sincere. "You're amazingly lucky to have one."

"I had two of them," I admitted. "The house fire was here. Our whole top floor. You're right about me being lucky, though. I found this one in a Salem antiques store."

"Cost the earth?" He grinned, bent to pick up O'Ryan, who was by then circling his right ankle, purring loudly.

"Yep," I said. "Worth it to me. My grandma gave me

the first one. Taught me how to open all the compartments."

He lifted the cat, who'd caught a claw in the hem of Martell's slacks. He adjusted the pant leg quickly, but not before I caught a glimpse of the bulky leather ankle monitor. Not entirely surprisingly, my aunt's new boarder was under house arrest—in our house.

CHAPTER 25

I made it back to the station in record time—with camcorder safely stashed in the hobo. I'd said a quick "see ya later" to Martell, making sure he left the house ahead of me, and watched in my rearview mirror until the Lincoln had pulled away from the curb. Mr. Doan seemed happy to get his camera back and I was relieved to turn it over to him. Through the glass wall of my office I saw that Scott's desk was still empty. I was reasonably sure that he'd be getting the Pirate's Island assignment as soon as he got back to the station. Good for him.

With Aunt Ibby's carefully researched Pirate's Island lore safely stored, it occurred to me that it would be a good idea for me to pay more attention to the rugged land across from the island—the place where my parents had died. I'd never looked up any of the newspaper accounts of the accident and Aunt Ibby had carefully avoided the

subject all my life. And why wouldn't she? My reaction
to what I'd seen in my shoe had been terrifying to me, but
also to my aunt. I knew they'd both died instantly—a
blessing, considering the violence of the crash—and that
the event had been caused by "pilot error"—whatever
that means. I'd never felt it necessary to inquire further
into the details of their deaths. I still didn't—but if we
were going to actually stand at that site, place a memorial
token at that spot, I needed to know more about what had
happened that sad day to the small yellow plane and the
two most important people in my life.

The search didn't take long. Both Maine and Massachusetts papers had covered the tragic story. I simply ref-
erenced the archives, typed in the date of the crash and
each of their names. A microfiche copy of the *Maine
Times-Record* popped up immediately. It gave the date
and the time of day. It said that a Piper J-3 was destroyed
during a collision with terrain and a post-impact fire. Witnesses reported that the small yellow airplane was on initial climb out after departing from a grass runway on a
Ruby Light Island. *So that was its name before it was Pirate's Island?* At approximately 250 feet, according to
witnesses, the airplane banked sharply and descended
into the terrain. Both people on board were fatally in-
jured.

I looked away from the screen. This wasn't going to be
easy. I skipped over some meteorological information.
*The airplane wreckage path followed a magnetic heading
of approximately 125 degrees*, I read. What did that
mean? *From the first ground scar mark to the location
where the engine came to rest was measured at 29 feet
four inches*. I could visualize that distance. The plane
must have tumbled, I thought. I read on. *The wingspan of*

a standard J-3 Cub is listed at 35 feet, two inches. The fuselage was buckled over approximately 90 degrees toward the right side of the airplane.

I'd read far enough to know that this had been a horrendous wreck—that no one could have survived in the twisted, burning remains of that cute yellow plane. I looked away from the screen. *Why had it happened? Why had they died in this horrible way?*

"Pilot error," someone had said. But how could that be? I'd always heard that my brilliant engineer father was meticulous about details. What pilot error could he have made that would have resulted in such a tragedy? I scrolled past terms I didn't understand. *Horizontal stabilizer. Jackscrew mount. Gascolator bowl.* The report stated that toxicological testing was done on both victims and all tests were negative. So alcohol or drugs were not to blame. I read on. No fuel samples could be taken from the airplane wreckage. The fuel valve was found in the *off* position.

The investigator had contacted my father's regular mechanic at Beverly Airport, where the plane was kept, to discuss the positioning of the fuel valve. The mechanic stated that the fuel valve handle on Daddy's plane was *always* left in the *on* position.

I skipped to the bottom of the page, to a paragraph headed *NTSB Probable Cause*. The National Transportation Safety Board had released a statement. *The failure of the pilot to ensure that the fuel selector was properly positioned to the full "on" position before takeoff resulted in a loss of engine power due to fuel starvation during the initial takeoff and the pilot's failure to maintain control of the aircraft.*

So that was the final word on the subject. Pilot error. I

reread the article—pausing to look up definitions of unfamiliar words. Apparently, my brilliant father had somehow moved a simple switch from its normal *on* to *off*. I found this very hard to believe.

Soon Pete and I would spend time on the island that had been the last place my parents had been—and not far away from the spot where, on that same day, they'd died. I wondered what memories my father's sister and her husband could share with me about their last days and moments on Ruby Light Island. Would they be willing to talk to me? To help me understand what had happened? In my search for answers I'd come away with more questions.

A brisk tap on my office door drew my attention away from the screen. I motioned for a smiling Marty McCarthy to join me. "Thought you might be ready for a coffee break." She put a purple WICH-TV coffee mug on my desk. "Three creams, no sugar, right?"

"Right," I said, "and a break is just what I need."

"Thought so. You must be up to your neck in last-minute wedding plans. Only a few days left before the big day."

Last-minute wedding plans was exactly what I should be thinking about—not sad, probably unanswerable questions about how my parents had died. Marty glanced around the office. "Anything at all I can help with? Need any errands run? Phone calls made?"

I shook away the lingering mental image of the distorted yellow plane. I pulled the three colorful food truck menus from my top drawer. "Take a look at these, will you? Is this enough variety for everybody? There'll be the traditional ice cream truck too."

"Are you kidding? Everybody is looking forward to

this. No rubber chicken and wilted salad for you, Moon." Big smile. "It will be perfect. So will the wedding. And," she added softly, "you and Pete will live happily ever after. Heard you found a house."

"We did." I was glad she approved of the menus. I was actually feeling good about the plans and preparations we'd made and couldn't think of any errands that needed running or phone calls that needed to be made. "We've even put most of the furniture in place. It's move-in ready at this minute."

"Aww. You two are so cute. I guess he'll carry you over the threshold."

I might have blushed. "Already did that."

"I'll let you get back to work. Just put the empty cup in the break room when you're done." She stood, preparing to leave. "Remember, I've been around Salem forever. I know lots of people. Plenty of contacts. You need anything at all, Moon, you call me."

"I will," I promised, wondering if she had any contacts on the National Transportation Safety Board.

As Marty had reminded me, I returned the purple mug to the break room, rinsed it in the sink, dried it and hung it on a peg. I accomplished all this as silently as I could, determined not to wake the snoozing, and softly snoring, field reporter, comfortably sleeping in an aged purple recliner. I was about to tiptoe from the room when Scott woke up. "What? Who? Oh, hi, Moon. What's up?"

"Nothing much new. Where did you and Francine go? I didn't catch the news."

"Good one. You would have liked it, Moon. We covered an interview with that mystery writer—Fenton Bishop. Seems some students were upset about him teaching there—what with him being a wife-killer and all, so Pennington called a surprise Q and A meeting this afternoon—invited the complainers so they could see for themselves that he's completely rehabbed.

"Wish I'd caught it," I said, meaning it. "How did he do?"

"Convinced me," Scott said. "Quite a charmer. Had the rabble-rousers eating out of his hand in about two minutes."

"So you think he's okay? Safe to be around, I mean?"

"Safe for your aunt to rent a room to, you mean?" he asked. "I heard he's already moved in. That right?"

"Word gets around fast in Salem," I said. "Yes. He's the first tenant in her B and B. He was there for breakfast this morning. Seems pleasant enough. So you don't still think he's left a trail of bodies behind somewhere?"

"Nah. I never really did think so. Just a shtick. It got me an investigative spot, didn't it?" Big smile. "And about word getting around, did the word get to you yet that Doan handed me that Pirate's Island gig. Handed me your camcorder too. What do you bet I'll get another late-night news feature out of that one too?"

"I wouldn't be one bit surprised," I told him, meaning it. "Maybe we'll see you there."

"Count on it," he said.

CHAPTER 26

I hoped, as I pulled into the garage, that I'd be able to talk with Aunt Ibby without interruption from the new houseguest. The Buick was in the garage and I didn't see the Lincoln anywhere around, so maybe the coast was clear. I approached the back door, remembering once again that I no longer had a key. *There's no reason for my not having a key*, I thought. *It's not as though I'm going to intrude on the upstairs tenants.*

O'Ryan's fuzzy head appeared from the cat door. He looked from left to right, then ran toward me. "Makes no sense," I told the cat, "that you can come and go as you please, but I can't." I picked the cat up. "Maybe it's unlocked." I jiggled the knob. Sure enough, it was open. I stepped inside, put the cat down, and tapped on my aunt's kitchen door. "Aunt Ibby? It's me."

Two clicks sounded. She'd secured both the regular lock *and* the dead bolt. Unusual.

"Hello, Maralee," she greeted me with a smile. "A lovely evening, isn't it?"

"Sure is," I agreed. "I hope this weather holds for our outdoor wedding rehearsal dinner."

"It will," she assured me. "Wanda says there's no rain in the forecast until next week sometime. By the way, she was back to the old Wanda—shorts and tiny tops."

"I know," I said. "No decision there, I guess. She looks great no matter what she wears—or doesn't wear." I tossed my handbag over the back of one of the captain's chairs and sat down. "What's up with the double-lock on your door and the back hall being wide open?"

"Oh, that. Michael left it unlocked. I thought maybe he'd misplaced his key so I didn't lock it. That meant any old body could just walk in, so I double-locked mine." Sly grin. "Pete would be proud of me."

"He would," I agreed. "But I think I need my back door key back—in case of emergency, you know."

"Yes. You're right. I got a new one for you this morning. It was just that you had the only spare key and Michael needed one of his own in a hurry." She pulled a shiny key from the apple-shaped key rack I'd made when I was a Girl Scout. "Here you go."

I attached it to my key ring immediately, alongside the ones to the new house. "I hope the new tenant hasn't misplaced his key. We wouldn't want it to get into the wrong hands," I said. "Maybe he just forgot to lock the door when he left." *As if that isn't bad enough.*

"Maralee, you have misgivings about Michael, don't you? Could you tell me why?"

It was a tough question for me to answer. I didn't *know*

why. Everyone else—my aunt, Pete, Mr. Pennington, the parole office, the Tabby students, even Scott Palmer—were willing to accept the man at face value. He'd repented his crime, served his sentence, and deserved to build a future, to enjoy his rights to life, liberty and the pursuit of happiness.

I admitted it. "I don't know. Pete thinks I'm being overprotective of you. Maybe that's it. Michael has been perfectly polite and helpful and gentlemanly. I have no good reason to distrust him." *Other than that, he's a confessed murderer and is still wearing an ankle bracelet.* "I'll try to be fair," I promised. "Pete's probably right. He usually is. I worry about you too much."

"And I you." She reached for my hand. "We have been everything to one another for so long it's hard to let go."

"You're worried about me? About me marrying Pete and moving away?"

"Oh course I am. Did you think I wasn't worried when you moved to Florida? When you married Johnny?" She squeezed my hand. "I did not give birth to you, but I feel that in so many ways I am your mother. I think about dear Carrie and your father. Would they approve of the way I've raised you? I don't know. They were so young. They didn't get to see you grow up in a changing world. Would they have done things differently? Would you have been a different person if they'd raised you?" Again she said, "I don't know."

"I've been thinking about them too," I said. "I looked up some information on the plane crash."

"Oh, dear. Was that a good idea?"

"It was mostly about what they learned from examining the wreckage. It was a terrible accident. They didn't have a chance of surviving. Picturing it was awful."

"They loved that little plane. They both enjoyed many good times in it. Would you like to see some pictures of happier days—to replace the pictures you have in your mind right now?"

"Yes, please," I said, thinking again about the fuselage buckled over 90 degrees—about how the plane might have tumbled the length of a football field—and about the fire. My aunt left the room and returned carrying one of her many photo albums. She sat beside me and opened the book, pointing to a photo of my smiling parents beside the yellow plane that I now knew was a Piper J-3. "I need a closer look," I told her. I stood and pulled open the junk drawer where we kept odds and ends—rubber bands, paper clips, a corkscrew, a large magnifying glass. "I used to use this when I played Nancy Drew," I remembered and held the glass over the photo.

"You were always looking for clues," Aunt Ibby said.

"What's the picture painted on the plane just behind my mother?"

"It was your daddy's favorite cartoon character. She was on the front page of the Sunday funny papers back when he was a kid." The painting, bright against the yellow background, showed a beautiful, big-eyed buxom blonde with an off-the-shoulder polka-dotted blouse and tiny shorts. "He named the plane after her and had her picture painted on it."

I looked closer. "She's really cute. I think Wanda has that same costume."

"She does. She wears it on Sadie Hawkins Day every November. That's when the girls can ask the boys for a date. Don't you remember?"

"Sure. I remember Sadie Hawkins Day. I just don't

know who the blonde is. What's her name? What was the name of the plane?"

"Daisy Mae," my aunt said. "He called the plane *Daisy Mae*."

Daisy Mae. Daisies. Like a field of daisies in my vision. Gasoline poured on daisies.

I knew that the yellow plane ran on gasoline. So what? Was I getting close to what the vision was trying to tell me? I needed to learn more about what had happened to my parents. I needed to know exactly what had happened to the plane named *Daisy Mae*—and I had a feeling that the answers must be somewhere on Pirate's Island.

"Aunt Ibby, I learned today that Pirate's Island used to be called Ruby Light Island. Did you know that?"

"Sure. That was its name when your parents went to visit that sad weekend. There's an automated lighthouse there now," she said. "The Coast Guard takes care of it. But the old lighthouse is still there too. It used to be attended to by a lighthouse keeper who made sure the light could be seen—warning mariners away from the rocky shoreline. Doris and her husband live in the main section of the old lighthouse keeper's cottage on the island and they give tours of the old lighthouse. Of course, the cottage is completely updated, I understand."

"When did the island's name change happen?" I wondered.

"It wasn't too long after your parents' accident that they started calling it Pirate's Island," she recalled. "But the pirate story about the treasure buried on the island has been around for as long as I can remember."

"They tell that story in their advertising," I remembered. "Something about a report of pirates coming ashore with a chest and hiding it there. Do you think those pirates—the ones that buried the treasure—were connected to Dixie Bull or Black Sam Bellamy?"

"Of course, I've never actually seen the log," she admitted, "but I'd guess from the time period involved— 1717 or thereabouts—it would have to be men from Black Sam's crew."

"The wealthiest pirate in recorded history," I said, remembering her back-and-forth with Michael Martell.

"So they say," she said. "At least the log seems to be real. Perhaps your aunt Doris will show it to you when you're out there. There wasn't an actual lighthouse on the island back in Black Sam's time. That came later. Mariners depended on fires built on hilltops or islands to mark the entrances to ports. The story is that the lightkeeper lived in a house on the island. He maintained the fires and kept a log."

"Scott Palmer is going to have a ball with this assignment," I said. "Real pirates and real treasure. I'm almost sorry I gave the story away."

"It's your honeymoon, Maralee," she said. "There'll be plenty of time for storytelling later. This time is for you and Pete to enjoy together." She closed the photo album. "Shall we have a glass of wine and talk about your happy days ahead?"

I knew she was right. I pulled two stemmed glasses from the cabinet while she opened a nicely chilled bottle of rosé. And with our favorite cat looking on—making the occasional cat-comment—we chatted about me wearing my mom's wedding dress. About the fun we'd have at the outdoor rehearsal dinner. About arranging our wedding gifts in the new house. About our simple, beautiful wedding ceremony. About our vows to each other. And about our happily ever after.

It was nearly midnight when we climbed the stairs to our respective second-floor bedrooms. I dreamed of Wanda in her Daisy Mae outfit accepting an Emmy award for the *Hometown Cooks* program.

CHAPTER 27

With a clear conscience—wedding plans perfected, work issues settled and programs set to go as scheduled—I set out for the beauty shop for manicure, pedicure, shampoo and blow-dry in preparation for our evening rehearsal dinner. A new outfit hung on my bedroom door, matching shoes lined up neatly on the floor below the skirt. My wedding dress in Aunt Ibby's room was encased in a zippered bag, ready for transport to the dressing room at Old Town Hall in the morning. I'd already talked/texted all of the bridal party—double-checking every little thing.

My feet were submerged in warm water smelling vaguely of honeysuckle and both hands—slathered in almond lotion—rested on a pillow on my lap when Pete called. "Are you still getting worked on? Not that you need it," he said.

"Hands and feet getting done now," I told him, holding the phone gingerly with two fingers. "Hair next."

"Chief gave me the day off too," he said. "After you're through there, want to go to lunch with me? Something has come up I want to talk to you about."

"Is something wrong? I was just sitting here thinking of how perfect everything is."

"No, love. Nothing wrong at all. Just something interesting," he said. "Chief says it's okay if I tell you about it."

That made me feel good. Maybe being married would mean that we could share more job-related happenings—especially now that I wasn't doing news anymore. "I'll call you the minute I'm through here," I told him. "Where shall we meet?"

"The Willows? Some of the food stands are open."

"Perfect," I said. "But I'll probably pass on lunch—we have all those food trucks lined up for tonight. I still have to fit into that dress. My mother was a size eight."

"Meet me by the mini-golf," he said. "We'll get some exercise before we eat the chop suey sandwiches."

"Troublemaker! I'll see you later." I relaxed, closing my eyes, enjoying the pampering and wondering what police business Chief Whaley had okayed for my ears. I'm not one of his favorite people in the first place, so the fact that he'd given Pete permission to share anything with me was a big surprise. I could hardly wait to learn what it was.

With sparkly pink toenails, neatly trimmed and tapered natural fingernails and professionally tamed too-curly red hair, I met Pete at the designated place. "You look delicious," he said. "Will you marry me?"

"I will," I said. "Right after I beat your socks off at this golf game."

I did win—with a little cheating—and we headed up to the boardwalk for the promised chop suey sandwiches, then to a park bench overlooking the water. "So tell me about the chief's change of heart."

"Okay. You remember I told you about the chief wanting to look into the Martell guy."

"Sure."

"Seems that the chief's wife is a big fan of those Fenton Bishop books—the ones he writes about the antique shop owner who helps the police solve crimes," he explained.

"Antique Alley Mysteries," I said. "Aunt Ibby and the Angels are planning to read the whole series."

"Mrs. Whaley suggested to the chief that maybe Fenton Bishop could help our department solve a few things—like fakes and forgeries."

"A writer—solving *real* crimes? Did he go for the idea?"

"He did. You'd be surprised how common forgeries are, especially in a place like Salem with all kinds of important museums and art galleries. Chief says he's never heard of a major collection that didn't have a load of fakes."

"No kidding? I never thought about it."

"Oh, yeah. Some fakes hide right out in the open. When Clinton was president there was a fake antique clock right outside the Oval Office. An antiques dealer spotted it. Anyway, sometimes the fakes are deliberate forgeries that cheat the buyers out of a lot of money. Those are the ones the chief thinks Bishop—or Michael Martell can help us with."

"He's going to ask Martell for help?" I asked, surprised.

"Already did. Martell is working on one for us right

now. A Japanese Satsuma vase a dealer bought for more than two thousand dollars. Martell says it's a modern fake. Chief's bringing in the seller for questioning."

"Just like in the Antique Alley mystery books," I said.

"Pretty much," he agreed. "I just thought you'd like to know—might make you feel better about having him staying at your aunt's place, knowing that the chief trusts him."

"It's definitely good to know," I assured him. *Even if he's still a convicted killer under house arrest—with keys to my aunt's house.* "Thanks for telling me about it." I thought about it for another minute. "Can I tell Aunt Ibby?"

Pete sighed. "Between your aunt and those girlfriends of hers, I'll be surprised if they don't already know it."

"You're right. I know Martell was invited to the *Midsomer Murder* viewings. He declined the wine but accepted the invitation."

"Chief may be getting more than he bargained for," Pete said. "Between the four of them they've probably already solved the Satsuma scam."

"And moved on to the next one on the chief's list." The image of Chief Whaley trying to deal with Betsy, Louisa, Aunt Ibby, and Martell all at once made me laugh out loud. "I wish him luck."

"We'd better head for home now." Pete put our takeout wrappings into a trash barrel. "We have a busy evening ahead of us."

"Yep. We need to practice getting married."

"All we need to remember is 'I do,'" he said, pulling me close for a kiss. "And I certainly do."

"Me too." I climbed into the Jeep, waved to Pete, who watched as I backed out of the parking area. *Ever since the accident with the Corvette, I think he worries about my safety no matter how carefully I drive.*

I thought there'd be time for a quick nap before Aunt Ibby and I headed out for the rehearsal, but between phone calls to and from friends and relatives and giving a last touch-up with the iron to my dress and an extra-careful session with eye shadow and lip gloss—after all, there would be pictures—it was soon time to leave for the Old Town Hall. I said a reluctant goodbye to O'Ryan, wishing I could involve him more in the wedding festivities, but a cat can't very well be counted on to act as ring bearer, or usher as some dogs are able to do. I was sure O'Ryan *could* do those things and more if he wanted to—but with cats one can't be sure.

Mr. Pennington was well rehearsed in his role as wedding official, if a bit wordy. Pete and I practiced our "I dos" with straight faces, and walked with proper solemnity down the aisle. The outdoor food truck event met with great approval from all concerned and I could safely say the evening was a success. Pete went home with his family and I went home with mine. After all, we figured, by the next day we'd be together for the rest of our lives.

CHAPTER 28

What can I say about my wedding day that does it justice? I was about to take a lifelong vow to love, honor and cherish my dearest and closest friend and faithful lover, for richer or poorer, for better or worse, in sickness and in health, 'til death. All that, in addition to whatever embellishments Mr. Pennington might ad-lib into the ceremony. We'd chosen rings and we'd each written—and hopefully memorized—a few words to say to each other during the ring exchange.

We'd hired a limo to drive River, Wanda, Rhonda, Shannon, Marie, Aunt Ibby, and me from our individual homes to the Old Town Hall. Pete had done the same to pick up best man brother-in-law Donnie, and fellow police officer groomsmen, Jimmy Marr, Ted Costa, Paul Linsky, and Bill Andrews. Our arrivals had been timed, of course, so that Pete wouldn't see me in my wedding dress until I walked down the aisle on Aunt Ibby's arm to meet him at the altar. Our flowers and bouquets, all from Flower Fantasy—longtime advertisers on WICH-TV—had been delivered to the town hall ahead of time and were, as expected, fresh, beautiful, and perfectly arranged.

When the first strains of Mendelssohn's "Wedding March" sounded from the organ, the full realization hit me. *This is it. This is the beginning of my forever.*

Aunt Ibby and I took measured steps in time to the music as we'd rehearsed the night before. I watched Pete's face, saw his smile, and wanted to move faster toward him—but maintained the required ladylike step-pause, step-pause all the way to the altar. I handed River my bouquet. Pete and I stood side by side, facing Mr. Pennington. "Dearly beloved, we are gathered here . . ." he began in his best Shakespearian voice. He recited the well-known rites of marriage, throwing in some Thoreau— "There is no remedy for love but to love more"—some George Eliot—"What greater thing is there for two human souls, than to feel that they are joined together to strengthen each other"—even a little Elton John—"How wonderful life is when you're in the world," winding up with Robert Browning's "Grow old along with me! The best is yet to be." Everyone said afterwards that it was the best marriage ceremony they'd ever heard. Pete and I barely whispered our vows to each other as we exchanged rings—after all, these were private thoughts. They didn't need to be shouted. By the time Mr. Pennington intoned "I now pronounce that you are husband and wife," I realized that I'd been holding my breath. "You may kiss your bride," he said. Pete kissed me tenderly, lovingly, convincingly and together we turned, facing friends and family, and led our wedding party down the aisle. No measured steps then. I almost danced my way to the big open double doors.

The limos waited for us in front of the Old Town Hall. Pete's Police Athletic League peewee hockey-team kids, boys uncomfortably handsome in suits and ties—their girl goalie pretty in pink satin—stood in a row outside the doors, bubble wands ready, showering us all with rainbow-tinted millions of bubbles.

We piled into the limos for the short ride to the restaurant. There was a formal photo session on the iconic stairway in Colonial Hall, then we joined our guests for dinner and dancing. The Fabulous Fabio had outdone himself on the cake. We carefully removed the top layer of buttercream-frosted vanilla cake—to be saved and frozen for our first anniversary. The cake topper, with its bride and groom and yellow cat figures, would have a special place in our new home. We'd agreed there'd be no cake-smooshing as we fed each other the first pieces. Maybe someday we'd have a daughter who'd wear this same dress and I didn't want to risk stains. Anyway, we knew Aunt Ibby and the Angels wouldn't approve.

There were toasts and speeches and music and dancing and kissing. We found that Mr. Pennington and my aunt could do a mean macarena and that almost everyone in the room could boot-scoot with the best when it came to line dancing.

Since Pete and I weren't planning to start our honeymoon trip until the following morning, I didn't have to leave the party to change clothes. We'd arranged with Donnie to drive us to the new house at ten o'clock. The Jeep was parked out front, gassed up and ready to go and Pete's Ford was stashed in Aunt Ibby's garage. Our wedding photographer had followed us home in order to get that special shot of the bride being carried across the threshold. When Pete put me down just inside the living room I looked at the mantel clock. It was exactly 10:15. Like the clock in my vision. Same numbers. Different clock. *Still don't know what it means.*

Our bedroom had been visited somehow during the evening, and a fresh bouquet of roses and an ice bucket holding a chilled bottle of champagne greeted us there. (A plateful of butterfinger cookies revealed the identity of the "wedding fairy"—it had to be Marie.) A row of white candles—wisely left unlighted—were lined up on the edge of the tub along with a bottle of bubble bath crystals.

We sipped the champagne from monogramed flutes, nibbled on the cookies, lighted the candles, splashed in the bubbles and eventually turned out the lights on our perfect wedding day.

I woke up early. Not surprisingly, Pete was already up, dressed and making coffee. I made the bed, hung my wedding dress in the closet and tossed on a robe, following the good coffee smell and the sound of country music down to the kitchen. "Guess what?" Pete greeted me. "We have our first visitor." I glanced around. O'Ryan, seated on a Lucite chair, said "*mrrrup.*"

"Well, good morning, O'Ryan. How did you get in?" I sat beside him and ruffled his fur.

"The cat door's been installed," Pete said. "That Joanne is a whiz. When I came downstairs the cat was already curled up on a chair in the sunroom."

"I'm glad he feels at home here," I said. "I know I do."

"Me too," he said, with a kiss that lifted me out of my chair and threatened to delay the start of our trip. If we both hadn't been aware of the cat watching us so intently, it would have. We'd already packed our bags and stocked the Jeep with a few camping essentials in case we wound up someplace without a hotel; a cooler full of soft drinks, water and snacks, rain ponchos and boots, mosquito spray, flashlights, emergency flares, and plenty of sunscreen were ready if needed.

We'd already decided to go to "the place" for breakfast, avoiding unnecessary dish washing. I rinsed our champagne glasses and coffee mugs while Pete put our suitcases in the Jeep. "Ready to leave, Mrs. Mondello?" he asked.

"Ready, Mr. Mondello." My new title would take some getting used to. I looked at the new wedding ring on my left hand and at my mother's emerald ring on my right. "But let's wait for O'Ryan to leave," I suggested, "just to be sure he has that new door figured out both coming and going."

"Good thought," he said. "The old boy is going to miss you."

"I know. I'll miss him too. But we plan to do Face-Time and Skype and Facebook and all. We'll keep in touch." If Pete thought it was odd that I'd arranged to keep in touch with my cat while I was on honeymoon, he didn't say so. Within a few minutes O'Ryan considerately left via the new cat door, and with one wistful backward glance, disappeared over a neighboring fence.

And just like that, with Pete behind the wheel, we were on our way. It occurred to me that even after our several-years-long relationship, we'd never actually spent ten whole days and nights together before. I shared that thought with Pete. "We still have things to learn about one another," I said.

"I'm looking forward to it," he said. "Years and years and years of learning about each other, years of sharing everything."

"Yes," I said. "Years and years." At the same time I thought about the things we'd been hesitant to share so far. I still didn't always tell Pete about the visions. I felt sure that my scrying ability made him uncomfortable. Anyway, if I didn't understand what they meant, how could he? I remembered too, the many times he'd been unable—or unwilling—to share details about his work with me. Was it a sense of duty to his profession? Or didn't he trust me completely?

On the other hand, did *I* trust *him* completely with my strange, secret talent?

I relaxed against the smooth leather seat and smiled to myself. *Well*, I thought, *I guess we're about to find out.*

CHAPTER 29

We headed straight for Loudon, New Hampshire. It's only an hour and a half or so from Salem and we already had our tickets for grandstand seats at the New Hampshire Motor Speedway for a NASCAR cup race. The thrill of the sounds and excitement—even the smell from the engines and tires—of the race never goes away for me. This time I even remembered a couple of the drivers from my days with Johnny. Pete had moved from a casual fan of the races up to a serious one. Same thing happened to me with hockey. Go Bruins.

After the race, loading up on NASCAR souvenirs for friends and family—mostly for the nephews—and having lunch, we drove north for another hour to relive a childhood adventure we both had shared. We went to visit the beautiful bears at Clark's Trading Post in Lincoln, adding more souvenirs to the growing stash. I bought a beaded cat collar for O'Ryan. I FaceTimed Aunt Ibby so he could see it. He liked the collar. Didn't care much for the bears.

We'd decided to spend our first night somewhere in Maine, and in true road trip fashion we hadn't made any reservations or even any plan about exactly where we'd stay—just that it had to be somewhere along that "stern and rockbound coast" we'd been learning about. By the time we'd reached Portland, Pete was tired of driving—I was tired of sitting. We picked a mom-and-pop–looking motel with an ocean view and a pebbly beach within walking distance of an attractive-looking seafood restaurant. Enormous California king-sized bed—Maine lobsters—the sound of the sea nearby. What could be better?

We knew that Pirate's Island was about six miles out to sea from Boothbay Harbor, so after breakfast (waffles and sausages) we headed in that direction. I could tell from the landscape as the Jeep climbed uphill that we were close to the cliffs I'd seen in my visions. "I guess I'd better call the relatives and tell them we're in the area," I told Pete as we cruised along a typical New England Main Street. "Look at all the cute shops. Maybe there's a jewelry store here. I really should get a guard for my mother's ring. I'd hate to lose it."

"Good idea," he agreed. "Look. There's one. Joe the Jeweler. It's next door to the gas station. While you get your ring fixed I'll gas up and find out where the boat docks are and where we can leave the Jeep safely when we go to the island."

So that's what we did. A bell over the door gave a friendly *ding-a-ling* when I entered the shop. A man behind the counter looked up, one eye amazingly huge behind a bright lens attached to a glasses frame. He pushed the lens up so that it rested on his forehead. The thing was similar to the jeweler's loupe Michael Martell had shown us, but more permanent looking.

"Hello, young lady. How can I help you?"

I slid the ring from my right hand. "I need a guard for my ring." I handed it to him and he pulled the single lens into place once again and peered at the ring. "Hmmm. It's been a long time. Good to see you again, old friend," he said.

"Excuse me?" I said. "I don't believe we've met before."

Once again, he pushed the lens up onto his forehead. "Oh, no, not you, my dear. I meant this old-timer." He held the ring up. "I did the engraving on this one. *Forever.* I remember it well. Nice young couple." He squinted at me. "Come to think of it, the girl looked a lot like you."

"My mother," I managed to respond. "You remember my parents?"

"Sure do. Not every day you get to handle a piece of jewelry this old—and rare." He nodded, with an expression that reminded me of Aunt Ibby's wise-old-owl look. "I engraved it and appraised it. The young man—your father, you say? He wanted an appraisal so that he could write a check for the proper amount to the owners of the treasure. Yessir. That's what he said. 'To the owners of the treasure.'"

"What treasure?" I asked.

A shrug of bent shoulders. "Don't know. He didn't explain and I hadn't heard anything about treasure. Now I'm guessing he might have meant that place they call 'Pirate's Island' where these days they charge a pretty penny and let folks try to dig up coins and such." He attached a narrow piece of gold to my ring and handed it back to me. "Try this. See if it works for you. Come to think of it, though, I never again saw anything as pretty as this ring come off of that island. Mostly gold coins, a gold chain once. That's about it."

I slipped the ring onto my finger. "Much better. Thank you. So do you think my ring is part of some kind of pirate treasure?"

"Didn't say that. I appraised it back then for what I figured the gold and the stone was worth. Probably pretty near twice that amount now—and if anyone could prove it *was* some kind of pirate treasure—then Jenny bar the door! It's worth a lot more."

I paid the man, who said he wasn't the original Joe, but Joe Jr., thanked him again for the information and went outside to meet Pete. "Did you get it fixed?" he asked.

"Sure did, and learned some more about my parents at the same time," I reported. "Darnedest thing. The jeweler is the one who engraved *Forever* inside it."

"And he remembered them?"

"Yes. He even said I look like my mother." I felt tears welling up at the thought.

Pete wisely changed the subject. "There must be a florist here in town. When we get back from the island I'll bet we can get flowers or a wreath right here."

"Good idea," I said. "I'll call the island right now. I hope I brought that number." I reached inside my purse.

"The gas station had a brochure about Pirate's Island. The number is on it along with some history of the place." He handed me a large, colorful card. "Let's get in the Jeep. It might be better to call them when we see what the deal with the tour boats is. Maybe we can even go over there today. If not, we'll just find another motel."

I turned the card over, looking at the prices for the various types of "Pirate's Island Adventures." "Looks to me like hunting for buried treasure provides a pretty good income for Aunt Doris and Uncle Bill," I said. "I'm afraid they're planning for us to take the deluxe package. It includes an overnight stay, a home-cooked breakfast, a visit to the lighthouse, a metal detector for an hour, a shovel and treasure map and the use of a rowboat to take us to the underground cave at low tide!"

"Could be fun," he said. "If we don't like it, we don't have to stay."

"Right," I agreed. "Want me to drive?"

"Sure, if you want to. I've been hogging the wheel of your new car, haven't I?"

"*Our* new car." I climbed into the driver's seat. "Tell me the part on the card about the pirates. I read something about them in the island's TV ads and Aunt Ibby had done some research on them too. She and Dr. Martell went back and forth about the pirates who hung around in Maine. I didn't have a chance to read the whole card."

"It's a pretty good story. Don't know how much of it is true, but I'll bet it keeps a steady stream of treasure hunters showing up at the island. It starts in the early part of the eighteenth century." He faced me and smiled. "Once upon a time," he began, "long before there were any lighthouses around here, the town hired a man who lived on the island to light fires at the harbor entrance at night to help guide ships safely. So one night the fire tender on Pirate's Island—only it wasn't named that yet—saw a ship flying the Jolly Roger flag approaching. He was afraid to hide in his house, so he climbed a tree and watched what they did." Dramatic pause.

"Which was what?"

"Be patient. I'm telling this. Anyway, the ship anchored and some men got into a small boat and rowed to the island—'singing blasphemous songs and swearing horrible oaths'" Big grin. "He saw that the small boat was headed to a cave that could only be entered at low tide—which that night, it just happened to be."

"Oooh, Captain." I pretended to shiver. "You've got me hooked."

"Good one, Lee. Anyway, after a while that boat full of singing, swearing pirates swung around to the lowest end of the island and he lost sight of them until they approached the signal fire. They stood around, seeming to warm themselves. Then they approached his little house and went inside."

"Stealing and looting his meager possessions, I suppose," I suggested, turning at a sign with an arrow marked BOOTHBAY.

"That's what pirates do." Fake sigh. "That poor soul stayed in the tree until the sun came up. The pirates were long gone. He went back into his house and made an entry in his log about what he'd seen, He got into his little boat, rowed ashore and left town. Never went back to the island again."

"Aunt Ibby told me about the log. She says that my aunt Doris still has it. Are you making some of this up? He quit his fire tending job?"

"Guess so. But not before he spread the word about the pirates going into the cave. People started going out there with shovels when the tide was low enough, digging around, looking for pirate treasure. They say there's even an X carved into the rock down there. Eventually the government built the lighthouse, made some improvements in the keeper's cottage and whoever was tending the fires by then wound up owning the island with a job for life." He put the card on the dashboard. "That's the story."

"I wonder if it's true or smart advertising agency copy. Joe the Jeweler said that my father mentioned writing a check to the owners of 'the treasure' when he had the ring appraised."

Pete looked surprised. "No kidding? The jeweler thinks your ring is part of a treasure?"

"No. I'm afraid not," I said. "He says he's never seen anything that's been dug up on the island as pretty as my ring. He appraised it on the quality of the gold and the stone—but he did say that if it *was* pirate treasure it would be worth more."

"What does Martell think about it?" Pete asked. "He must have an opinion on it."

"He compared it to jewelry he'd seen at Mel Fisher's museum. He seemed open to the idea that it *could* be pirate treasure. Then he and Aunt Ibby got into a pirate name-dropping contest and I left." I pointed to a sign. "Look. Tour boats that way." I made the turn.

CHAPTER 30

We learned quickly that there would be no problem finding boat transportation to the island. There were ferryboats, lobster boats, bird-watching boats, windjammers, schooners, sloops, cabin cruisers, speedboats, kayaks, Jet Skis and more. We decided on the *Miss Judy*, a trim, 33-foot sightseeing boat, with a lobster boat hull. She carried around twenty passengers and made regular trips back and forth to Pirate's Island daily in good weather. The captain assured us that we'd probably spot seals and might even catch sight of a puffin bird or two. We made reservations for an afternoon trip, planning to stop for lunch first. We parked in the secured lot, and found a nearby park bench where I made my phone call to my newfound, island-owner relatives.

"Hello there, Maralee." William Raymond's voice was

hearty. "Been looking forward to your call. You lovebirds in Maine yet?"

"We are," I said. "We're at the Boothbay Harbor boat docks. We thought we'd take a ride over this afternoon to see you and Aunt Doris, if that's convenient for you."

"Sure is. We don't go much of anywhere. We hardly ever leave our little bit of paradise here on the island," he said. "You just come on over whenever you like. Your room will be ready whenever you are."

"Thank you. We don't want to impose, but we're anxious to meet you both. Is Aunt Doris available now? I'd love to speak to her."

"Oh, she's around here somewhere. She likes to watch the birds in the afternoon. You're right in time for puffin season, you know."

I didn't know that, but told him we'd look forward to seeing him and my aunt and the puffins later in the day, and we said goodbye.

"We're good to go?" Pete asked.

"Yep. He says our room is ready whenever we are." I was puzzled. "That surprised me. Puffin season, packed tour boats and a ton of advertising and they have a vacant room?"

"It is odd," Pete agreed. "The guesthouse doesn't look very big in the pictures. Maybe the high prices scare people away."

"Could be," I agreed. "I'll bet the gift shops have some cute puffin stuff. Let's look around and then do lunch."

Even though Pete isn't much of a gift store fan, he humored me while I bought more souvenirs. A cute, nautical-themed restaurant was nearby, service was fast and friendly and our lobster rolls were delicious. We strolled back to the boat dock where the *Miss Judy* was beginning to fill with passengers. Our reservations were for an open-ended round trip, and we found that most of our fellow passengers had signed on for the three-hour Pirate's Island tour. The *Miss Judy* would drop them off, go back to Boothbay Harbor, and return with another group three hours later and return the first group to the dock.

"I can see why Bill and Doris don't leave the island very often. There's a revolving door of guests coming and going," I said as we started to cut through the waves toward the island, where the lighthouse loomed about four miles in the distance. The captain took us for a short sightseeing ride within the harbor, commenting on the history of the area. He mentioned Black Sam Bellamy's ill-fated last trip, and the fact that legend claims some members of Bellamy's crew may have buried some pilfered treasure on Pirate's Island and—with a wink—wished the treasure hunters among his passengers good luck.

The *Miss Judy* pulled into a weathered dock, sturdy aged pilings framing a postcard view of just what an island off the coast of Maine should look like. A cute cottage was uphill from the base of an aged lighthouse. A small skiff filled with pink petunias partially blocked the doorway to a silvery-gray shingled building with a hand-lettered sign proclaiming BAIT STORE. Another was marked COFFEE SHOP. I could hardly wait to get ashore to explore the rest of the place. "Oh, Pete," I breathed. "It's perfect."

We said goodbye to the captain, promised to phone when we knew what day we'd need a ride back to the mainland, and stood aside as our fellow passengers climbed into multicolored golf carts and set out on their three-

hour adventure. I squeezed Pete's hand, glad that we'd
have more time on this magical place. "Pete, I'm glad my
parents had their last hours here."

As the golf carts clattered away, a man stepped onto
the dock. He wore khaki shorts, a white shirt, sunglasses
and one of those sunshade hats with a deep brim and a
long panel protecting the back of his neck. Even with all
the sun protection, there was no disguising the welcoming smile, the hand extended to help me up onto the dock.
Pete was close behind me.

"Uncle Bill?" I ventured, still pumping his hand. "I'm
Maralee and this is Pete."

"Welcome to Pirate's Island," he boomed. "Can't tell
you how delighted your aunt and I are to finally meet you
both. I've got a little golf cart reserved for us to take a
ride around the property. It's just over here behind the
bait store." He dropped my hand and reached for Pete's,
grasping it, firmly. "Howdy, Pete. Pleased to meet you.
Glad you're here. Come along." He picked up our two
bags.

With a quick look at one another, we followed him.
Uncle Bill took the driver's seat and Pete and I sat in the
back. The road was narrow, unpaved, a bit too bumpy for
conversation, but not actually uncomfortable. Every so
often, the golf cart would slow down while our driver-
guide-uncle pointed out something of interest. "See over
there? Wild blueberries. Doris will make you a pie while
you're here." Another stop. "We're on fairly high ground
here. Right above the low-tide cave. You know about the
pirates?" He didn't wait for an answer, but moved on.
"See over there, where all those rocks are kind of piled
up? That's a puffin roost. They like rocks. See the woman
there in the red dress?" I shaded my eyes, looked where

he pointed. "That's your Aunt Doris. Loves those birds. You'll meet her later." It didn't seem to me that we were very far away from my aunt, that we could have stopped to meet her then and there. But away we bumped. I knew that Pete was thinking the same thing. He shrugged. I did too—and we listened as my new uncle gave a short recitation on Celia Thaxter and nearby inelegantly-named Smuttynose Island—reputed to be where Blackbeard spent his honeymoon and site of the 1873 murder of two young women.

Our ride ended at the cottage. It was bigger than it had appeared at that first glance, but maintained its cozy look. "Like I told you . . ." Uncle Bill tucked our bags under his arms. "Your room is ready whenever you are. I'll put your bags inside. Doris and I live upstairs but we won't bother you. You want to freshen up, like they say? I need to get back to the tour group. Time to give out the shovels. You never know when someone might find a bit of treasure."

We followed him to our room. Rustic, beautiful, with fireplace, ocean view. "Uncle Bill, it's lovely. Thank you so much." I reached for his hand. "We can't thank you enough." He grasped my right hand with both of his. "My pleasure," he said. His expression suddenly changed. Smile disappeared. He turned my hand over, focusing on the emerald ring. "Where did you get this?" I tried to pull away, but he didn't let go. "Where did that ring come from?" he demanded.

Pete stepped between us and Uncle Bill dropped my hand. "Is something wrong?"

"No, no of course not," Bill said. "It's just I thought I'd seen that ring before. A long time ago."

"It belonged to my mother," I told him. "My aunt Ibby

has kept it in her jewelry box all these years. She gave it to me as a wedding gift."

The woman in the red dress appeared in the doorway suddenly, silently. I didn't notice her there until she spoke. "Bill? Who are these people?" She stepped into the room, moving toward me. She stopped, reached out and touched my face. "Carrie. You've come back." She pulled me into a tight embrace.

"You're confused, Doris." Bill's tone was soft. He put a hand on her shoulder. "This is Maralee. Your brother's little girl all the way from Salem. She just got married to Pete here. They're on their honeymoon and came to see us. Remember, darling?"

The woman backed away from me, putting both hands to her face. "Oh, I'm sorry. I was confused. You look so much like—somebody else I used to know."

"That's okay," I said. "You called me Carrie. She was my mother. Everyone says I look like her."

"Yes. You do. But you are Maralee and you're on your honeymoon." She smiled and made a half-turn so that she faced Pete. "And you are the husband to Maralee. Pete. Do I have that all right now?"

"Perfect," I said. Pete had slipped an arm around my waist, gently pulling me toward him, away from my aunt and uncle.

"Happy to meet you both," Pete said. "And, yes. We'd like to freshen up—maybe take a little rest. Will that be all right?"

"Absolutely." Bill's booming voice was back. "I'll show you around whenever you like. No hurry." He took his wife's hand. "Right, honey?"

"That's right," she said. "No hurry."

The two left us, closing the door behind them.

CHAPTER 31

"What do you think?" I whispered.

"What do *you* think?" he answered.

"Something seems a little off." I was pretty sure he'd found the brief encounter as strange as I had.

"I didn't like his reaction to your ring. He was actually angry," Pete said, "and his wife seems a little bit spacey, don't you think?"

"Yeah. Aunt Doris. I don't think she's drunk, though. Drugs, maybe?"

"Maybe. There's something not quite right there," he said. "I've been on enough domestic-problem calls to spot trouble."

"She looked as if she's afraid of him. He even scared me a little when he started yelling about the ring," I admitted.

"He did? Hey, we don't have to stay here. The *Miss Judy*

will be back in a couple of hours." Pete's jaw tightened. I knew he wasn't happy. "What do you say we thank them for everything, say we have places to go, people to see, and we need to be on our way."

"Then I'll be worried about Aunt Doris," I said. "What if there *is* something wrong with her? She's my daddy's sister."

"You're right. We'd better stick around for a while." We sat together on the edge of the bed. "We'll learn what we can, as fast as we can and then get the hell out of here." Cop voice. "How does that sound?"

"Can we work together on this?" I asked. "I'm not doing a field report and you're out of your jurisdiction."

"True enough. How's this? We take a walk around the island. See what the people who work here have to say about the place."

"Sure. Bill and Doris can't be running the whole show all by themselves," I said. "Let's play tourists and ask nosy questions."

"That's what we'll do." He smiled. "You call it interviewing and I call it questioning, but it's the same thing, isn't it?"

"Always has been." I returned the smile. "But up until right now we couldn't quite coordinate our talents. Want to start with the gift shop?"

"More souvenirs?"

"Strictly business," I promised. "Well, maybe a stuffed puffin toy for O'Ryan."

With that decided, we left the room. Pete pulled the door closed. "Hey, there's no lock."

"It's a guest room," I pointed out. "People don't lock guest rooms in their own houses."

"You're right. I have a suspicious nature."

"That comes with the cop business," I told him. "I have a curious nature. Comes with the TV business."

"Same thing. We have a lot in common, don't we?"

"Good thing we got married, huh?" We'd reached the little gift shop. I stopped to look into the show window. "Hey, there's O'Ryan's cat toy."

The bell over the door sounded a pleasant *ding-a-ling*. A pretty young woman with black hair and creamy café au lait complexion greeted us. "Good morning. I'm Amelia. Welcome to Pirate's Island. Please take your time and look around. I'm sure you'll find a treasure here."

"Thanks, Amelia," I said. "I saw a puffin cat toy in the window. My cat will just love it. Do you have a cat yourself?"

I saw Pete's raised eyebrow—as if to say, "What kind of question is that?"

"I used to," she answered. "But I had to give him to my mom. I live here on the island during the tourist season. We can't have pets."

"Too bad," I said. "Have you worked here long?"

"Every summer since high school." She handed the soft toy to me. It had a squeaker in it. O'Ryan would love it. "Now it helps to pay for college. I love my job."

"It seems like a very pleasant place to work—and to live. This is our first visit. Mrs. Raymond is my aunt."

"Doris? She's a sweetheart, isn't she? You'll have to meet my dad. He does the lighthouse tours. He's been with the Raymonds since he was a kid. Started summers like me, back in the seventies. Now he's here full-time. He has a little apartment downstairs in the lighthouse."

I glanced at Pete and grinned. *See what a cat question can get you? A contact who thinks my spacey aunt is a sweetheart and another who might even remember my parents.*

It was Pete's turn. Carrying the puffin toy, I browsed a jewelry display and listened. "Island life must be kind of dull for a young person like yourself." He used a nosy-tourist tone of voice. It was quite convincing, I thought. "Not much excitement out here, I guess." Sad, sorry-for-you face.

Amelia seemed anxious to dispel Pete's impression of island life. "I guess the winters can be kind of boring, but summers—oh boy! The treasure hunters keep things interesting. Sometimes there are even fistfights out here when somebody digs up some gold coins. Then the newspapers and TV stations show up. I've been interviewed plenty of times."

Not bad. The fistfights might be interesting. Pete tried again.

"Tourists, huh?" Dismissive tone for tourists in general. "But all the coworkers must get along pretty well then, don't they?"

Amelia looked from side to side and dropped her voice. "Not always. Every once in a while somebody quits or gets fired or just disappears, you know? And then, married folks don't always get along. We hear some yelling and screaming from the big house once in a while. It's normal, I guess. My folks were divorced when I was little and I'm still single, so I don't know what's normal and what's not." A shrug of slim shoulders and a pretty smile. "But I love it here and I guess my dad does too or he wouldn't have stayed so long, would he? He'll tell you. His name is Hank. Tell him I sent you."

Bingo! Disappearing people and yelling from the big house?

Pete looked my way. "It's good to be happy in your work, right, babe?"

"Right," I agreed, picked up a couple of bags of gold-foil–covered chocolate coins for the nephews, paid for them and O'Ryan's toy, thanked Amelia for her help and without further discussion Pete and I headed straight for the lighthouse.

We stepped aside as a short parade of orange golf carts trundled by, leaving the lighthouse area and heading toward the shopping complex we'd just left. A few of the passengers, people we'd met on the *Miss Judy*, waved as they passed us. "They'll load up on souvenirs and then get their metal detectors to hunt for treasure," I guessed. "It looks as if my aunt and uncle have a little gold mine of their own here."

Pete agreed. "Pretty smart operation. How long has this been going on?"

"Aunt Ibby said that the name of the place changed to Pirate's Island not long after my parents died," I recalled. "Almost thirty years." We walked up a path leading to a closed door at the base of the structure. A sign with posted hours was nearby. "Looks like the lighthouse tours are scheduled at certain times. Should we just knock on the door and ask him to show us around?"

"Sure. Why not? Being the niece of the owners ought to carry some special cred, don't you think?"

"Okay. The most he can say is no." I knocked.

A voice came from somewhere above us. "Wait a minute. I'm coming." The sound of foorsteps on metal stairs was familiar. It sounded like me running up or down the stairs between the ground floor studio at WICH-TV and the reception office. I was smiling at the thought when the man opened the door. He looked a lot like a gray-haired Tiger Woods with a neat little pencil mustache. He was not smiling. "What?"

Pete stepped forward. "Hank? Excuse us for interupting if you're busy. Amelia sent us over. I'm Pete Mondello, and this is my wife, Lee. She's Mrs. Raymond's niece."

The "Mrs. Raymond's niece" part of the introduction brought an immediate change of attitude. "Oh, wow. No kidding? Doris's niece, huh?" Hank ran a hand through thinning gray hair. "I thought you were a couple of the boat tour people. They're always coming back because they left their cell phone or their sunglasses or their hat someplace in here. Usually it's up in the light—so's I have to run all the way up the spiral staircase to the top. Come on in. No problem. You want to see the old light?"

"Thanks. We'd like to, if it's not too much trouble," I said. "Amelia says you've been working here a long time."

"Longer than most anyone else here—'cept for Mrs. Raymond. Doris. You say you're her niece?"

"Yes. My dad was her brother."

"Her brother. Wait a minute." He looked at me closely. "Kowalski. Jack Kowalski's little girl. That who you are?"

"Yes. I'm Maralee Kowalski. Lee Mondello, now," I explained. "You knew my dad?"

"Damn right. I was probably the last person he talked to before he took off in that little yellow death trap he liked to fly around in." He shook his head. "Sorry, ma'am. But how a smart cookie like Jack made such a bone-headed mistake is beyond me. I still don't belive it."

"You were there that day?" Pete asked—in cop voice. "You saw the crash?"

"Sure did. I stood on the runway. I'm the one who spun the prop for him. Got her running. Watched as he started to climb. I knew right away something was wrong. Engine sounded bad. Then she quit. They didn't have a chance." He made a zooming, downward motion with his right hand. "Down she went. Boom. Gone."

I couldn't speak. I turned toward Pete, glad of his presence as I pictured the downward-plunging *Daisy Mae*. "What did you mean by a 'boneheaded mistake'?" Pete asked. "What did he do wrong?"

"You know anything about small planes?" Hank asked.

"Not really," Pete told him. "What happened that day? In simple terms?"

"Jack Kowalski and I talked planes a lot," the man said. "I used to fly a copter when I was in the Coast Guard. After I got out, they needed somebody to tend this old light while the automated one was being installed. That's partly the reason I wound up here on the island. When the Coast Guard decommissioned this light—" he waved his hand toward the sprial staircase—"they put in the new automated light just off of the eastard end of the island. Then this one got named an historic landmark by the state, so they needed somebody to keep an eye on both of 'em. Bill Raymond hired me full-time for the tours, so I got to stay here. Sweet deal." He nodded his head. "But anyway, everybody here on the island witnessed the same thing. The plane reached an altitude of about two hundred and fifty feet before it lost power. See, there's a fuel valve handle on those planes that's *always* left *on*. When they checked the wreckage they found it was almost all the way to the *off* position. That meant that the plane operated normally for only about half a minute then—because of fuel starvation—she dropped. There was a gusty wind that day too. Jack couldn't posibly have regained control at that point, even though he tried."

"You think he tried to move that switch back to the *on* position?" Pete asked.

"I've always thought so," Hank said. "It was right there beside him on the left side of the cockpit. It wasn't all the way to the *off* position. I think he noticed the error, tried to adjust it but it was too late."

"You said it wasn't like him to make a mistake like that," I reminded him. "To move a handle that you say was *always* on to the *off* position."

"That's what I said. I said it then and I'm saying it now." Hank made a fist with his right hand and punched his left. "Not Jack. He'd never make a dumb move like that."

"The NTSA determined that it was pilot error," Pete said.

"They didn't know Jack Kowalski," Hank countered. "But there was no one else in the plane except him and Carrie. Jack in the forward pilot seat, Carrie behind him in the aft passenger seat. He took off in it. I was there on the airstrip when they left. He flew it. It was his responsibilty. What could they say except pilot error?"

"If he didn't move the fuel valve handle," I asked, "who did?"

The three of us looked at each other. For a long moment no one spoke. Pete broke the silence. "If Jack Kowalski didn't move the handle, someone else who was on the island that day must have moved it."

"Frightening thought, isn't it?" Hank said.

"But why?" I wondered aloud. "Why would anyone here want my parents dead?"

"That's just it," Hank said. "Nobody who's here now or was here back then had any reason to harm him—or Carrie."

"That we know of." Pete finished the thought.

"That we know of," Hank echoed.

CHAPTER 32

I'd nearly forgotten my original reason for coming into the lighthouse—to take the tour of the old structure. Hank, switching from his normal conversational voice to the carefully pronounced, memorized-script speech of a professional tour guide, led us up the spiral staircase, step by step, fact by lighthouse fact. From a fixed white light, fueled by ten whale-oil–filled lamps in a thirty-foot tower, he described how the lighthouse had evolved into a sturdier, taller brick structure with a flashing red light—a thousand-watt bulb that shone through glass prisms surrounded by a red shield. Unused, but still in place, it was displayed along with ten uniform kerosene lamps—white wicks neatly trimmed. "And finally," Hank sounded regretful as he pointed toward the eastern end of the island, "the keeper-tended light was replaced by the automated version that now shows a white flash every five seconds."

We stayed at the top of the lighthouse for a few minute, enjoying the view. Hank opened a narrow door, allowing us to step outside, onto a fenced platform. I smiled when I noticed an ashtray and lighter on the floor beside the door. Aunt Doris's secret was safe with me. Looking seaward, boats dotted the horizon. Looking toward land, we saw distant houses superimposed against looming cliffs. Our view of the island below was obscured by trees. I wondered if the tree the lightkeeper had climbed was still alive. Then with Hank in the lead, we retraced our steps downward as he related a few more facts, barely touching on the story we'd already heard about that first fire tender, who'd been frightened away from his job by pirates. I couldn't resist asking about it.

"What about the pirate story? Is it true that it's in an old log and that the pirates buried a chest of treasure somewhere on the island?"

"It's true. I mean, there is an old log," he said. "And every once in a while a coin or two turns up here. Personally, I think there could have been a broken chest on the bottom offshore somewhere, and occasionally the tide brings in a little something."

"Makes sense," Pete said. "But the singing, swearing, shovel-wielding pirates makes a better story."

"Exactly," Hank agreed. "Been good meeting you two. Sorry about your family, Mrs. Mondello. Damn shame. It's getting near time for the *Miss Judy* to come back and pick up the first group. You folks sticking around for a while?"

"Guess so." Pete looked at me. "Bill and Doris have invited us to stay. My wife is concerned about her aunt's health."

"Doris? She's slowed down a lot. Spends most of her

time these days bird-watching. I barely see her any more." Hank looked around and put a finger to his lips. "She used to sneak up in the tower once in a while to sneak a smoke. Bill doesn't aprove. He hardly ever comes up here anyway. Says he doesn't like heights." He opened the door to the outside. "She used to do some of the walking tours too. Even took the rowboat low-tide rides down to the cave occasionally."

"I'd like to see the cave," I said, meaning it. "I heard there's an X carved in stone down there. True?"

"True." Hank nodded. "Maybe if you asked your aunt she'd take you there."

"I think I will. It sounds like an adventure," I said.

"Maybe you'll dig up the lost pirate treasure." Pete laughed.

"The adventure will be enough, thanks. I like Hank's theory about the tide bringing in bits and pieces of lost gold and bestowing it randomly." As I spoke, it occurred to me that maybe my ring had been a lucky find—a shiny object among the rocks and sand and seaweed, spotted by my father and happily gifted to my mother—a thought I shared with Pete as soon as we'd started down the path leading away from the lighthouse.

"Makes a certain amount of sense that way," he agreed, "but if it was a random happy find, what makes good old Uncle Billy so grouchy about it? He recognized it as something he'd seen before—'a long time ago.'"

I felt an imaginary light bulb turn on over my head. "Daddy told Joe the Jeweler that he was going to write a check for the value of the ring 'to the owners of the treasure.' But he never got home to write that check. Could be that Bill is still angry because he expected to be paid for it."

"You may be right," Pete said. "Let's get a new estimate from your friendly neighborhood jeweler and pay the man. Let bygones be bygones and all that. What do you think?"

"I don't want to offend anybody by offering relatives money after all this time, but if Daddy owed a debt, it needs to be paid," I reasoned, "but it'll have to be handled carefully."

"Uncle Bill doesn't strike me as a guy who'll turn down a quick buck, if you don't mind my saying so," Pete said. "Let's just sit down and talk treasure with them. Let them know we want to do the right thing."

"We do need to talk with the two of them about several things," I said. "First on the list, though, should be figuring out whether my parents died from pilot error or not. Hank seems to think not."

"You're right. It won't be easy figuring out who was on the island that day almost thirty years ago," Pete figured. "The list of suspects may be long—and long gone. But you have the exact time and date of the accident, and the newspaper gave the names of a few witnesses. We can start there. Okay?"

"It *can* be pilot error, of course," I admitted. "Nobody is perfect. Dad could have pushed the wrong lever. I don't want to be poking around, prying into people's pasts who had nothing to do with it. But I would like to take a look at that airstrip. It showed up plainly from the drone shot. Can't be hard to find."

"Let me do that prying part," Pete said. "Prying into people's pasts is my specialty. Looks to me like the airstrip is right down the center of the top of the island up beyond those trees." He pointed. "Look! Here comes the *Miss Judy* with a new cargo of treasure hunters." We watched as the mate of the sightseeing boat tossed a line to a waiting dockhand. There was no mistaking the next voice I heard.

"Hey Moon!" Scott Palmer waved both arms in the air. "Did you guys come down to meet me?"

Pete and I waved back. Pete leaned down and whispered into my ear. "Here comes another professional prier. Let's put him to work."

"You're absolutely right." I aimed a big smile in Scott's direction. "I handed him this assignment along with that fancy camera he's got around his neck. He owes me." We waited as the passengers filed past, headed for waiting golf carts, until Scott reached us.

"Come with us," I invited. "We'll get our own golf cart." I wasn't sure where we'd get the promised conveyance, but offered it anyway. "I was surprised to see you so soon. Doan must really want this story in a hurry."

"Guess he does, and I'm glad to get the assignment." His eyes were downcast for an instant. "But nephew Howie wanted more field reporter time, so it worked out for him too."

"I can relate," I said. "Been there." It was true. My present position as program director had come about because young Howard Templeton, Buffy Doan's nephew, had wanted *my* field reporter gig. Pete had stepped aside and was talking with one of the golf cart drivers. I saw him give a thumbs-up to the driver.

"Okay. We're all set for a cart for you." Scott smiled as a bright green golf cart with a green-and-white–striped awning rolled in our direction. The driver stepped out and after a few words, Pete slid behind the controls. I sat beside Pete. Scott—camcorder in position—took the back seat.

"How'd we rate this?" I whispered.

"I dropped your name, my badge number and the fact that Scott is working on a Maine documentary for a major TV station," he said. "Uncle Bill says to take our time and turn the cart in at the garage when we're through." He looked around. "Do you know where the garage is?"

"Nope. We'll find it." I turned to face Scott. "Let's start with the airstrip. Then I'll show you some puffins. Cutest darn things you've ever seen."

"Airstrip?" He looked puzzled, but we were already on our way uphill.

CHAPTER 33

Pete found a path leading up. We followed it past another small guesthouse nestled among greenery, then upward until we came to a clearing with lots of blue sky. The grassy strip was slightly overgrown as though it hadn't been used recently—but with straight lines and white-painted rock boundaries easily visible.

Scott, plainly excited, jumped from the cart, aiming the camcorder toward the distant shoreline. "Wow! I'll bet on a real clear day you can see three states from here."

The weather report on the day my parents had flown from here had been clear. Visibility had been no problem. Gusty wind, the report had said. That shouldn't have been a problem either. *But, pilot error?* I didn't want that to be the answer. Pilot error would mean that my father had been careless. Careless of my mother's life and his own and ultimately, mine. Careless of the lives of any siblings

I might have had. All because of a simple fuel switch. If he could see three states, he could certainly have seen that the switch was in the wrong position.

"You're right," I said. "Maine and New Hampshire for sure, and maybe a tiny edge of Massachusetts. Check it out when you get up inside the top of the lighthouse. They've got a cool telescope up there."

Scott walked toward the part of the airstrip where the painted white rocks formed a border on the steepest side of the island. "Wow. Quite a drop from here." He backed away from the edge."I'll check out that lighthouse ASAP. First, I need to find out all I can about the treasure they claim people have been finding around here for years."

"No shortage of people who want to talk about that," Pete told him. "The lighthouse tour guide has some stories and so does his daughter. She works in the gift shop. We've already talked to both of them. Nice people."

"You're not doing a story on this place too, are you, Moon?" Scott pleaded. "It's not a big enough place to support two reports at the same time."

It might, if there are two different angles.

"Don't worry, Scott. I told you. The documentary is all yours," I said. "I'll be interested in whatever you find out about the island, though. After all, this was the last place my parents visited before their accident. Maybe you'll run into some people who were here on the island that day. People who saw what happened."

His expression saddened. "Sorry, Moon. I wasn't thinking. This little airstrip was where they took off from, right?"

"Yes. I guess it looks pretty much the same as it did back then."

"Okay. Now, what about those puffin birds?" He panned

the camera around. "Some of the people on the boat were all gaga about them."

"Let's go see if we can find a few. My Aunt Doris has a special spot she watches the birds from every day," I said. "I think we can find it."

"I remember," Pete said. "It's over on the ocean side. Come on." We all climbed back into the golf cart and headed down a bumpy, tree-lined road. Pete was right. We saw my aunt—wearing hot pink this time—sitting in a green wooden Adirondack chair—smoking a cigarette and tossing crumbs to the flock of brightly colored birds gathered on a nearby pile of rocks.

"Do you think it will be all right if I climb down there and talk to her for a minute? Look, there are some other people down there with cameras. Just to establish a connection for later. Maybe take her picture and a shot of the birds?"

"I think so, but Scott, see if you think she's . . . well, if she's okay. I spoke with her briefly and she seemed a little vague." I stopped, searching for the right words. "I wonder if she's medicated—or if she's just naturally a bit drifty. You know?"

"Sure, Moon. Want to wait for me up here?" He got out of the cart and started down the incline. "This won't take but a minute or so."

"We'll be right here," Pete said. "I think she's fine. Looks to me like she's just found a quiet place to sneak a cigarette."

We watched Scott picking his way carefully toward my aunt and the puffins. "He'll start by asking her about the birds," I said, "and before long she'll be telling him her life story. He's good at this."

"Does he know about the ring?"

"All I told people at the station is that the ring belonged to my mother and that she got it when she was on the trip to Maine and this island."

"That should be enough to get him started. Let's take a look around here." He pointed. "The plane must have started out at the beginning of the runway—over there." I looked toward where he pointed, picturing the small yellow plane with its cartoon girl painting and my young parents, seated single file inside the open cockpit, smiling, waving goodbye, happy to be going home.

"I wonder who was here to see them off?" I wondered aloud. "Bill and Doris must have here for sure. Hank too, of course. Maybe some of the witnesses that were quoted in the paper watched the takeoff from up here, not from down below. Maybe some of them were watching from shore. Over there." I shielded my eyes, looking across the water toward the town—toward the steep cliffs beyond.

"It was a long time ago." Pete put his arm around my shoulders. "I wouldn't expect too much, even if we can locate them."

"I know," I said. "But we have to try." We walked toward the runway's end, stopping about midway. "They probably started to lift off right about here." *I almost heard the engine, almost felt the vibration as the* Daisy Mae *became airborne.* We paced our way along the white border, back to the place where the golf cart was parked. Down below us, Scott stood beside my aunt, she looking up at him, a smile lighting her face. They'd moved closer to the rock pile. Scott aimed the camcorder toward the birds, then lowered it. He looked toward where we stood and waved. My aunt, following his lead, waved too. "It looks as if Scott has made a friend," I said, waving back.

"I'll bet he'll be able to ask her all kinds of questions that will sound totally professional, but if you or I asked the same ones we'd only sound nosy."

"We'll see. At this point, every little bit of information counts."

"Let's call Aunt Ibby and see what's going on in Salem," I said. "And we'll show her the view from up here." She picked up right away. I could tell that she was in her office. O'Ryan was there too, pushing his fuzzy face into camera view. "Hello, you two," I said. "It's a beautiful day in Maine, and we're up on top of Pirate's Island. Here's a nice view of the town from here"—I aimed the camera—"and if you look down hill a bit"—I changed direction—"there's Aunt Doris in the hot pink dress, and Scott. O'Ryan, if you look closely you can see some puffins. Aren't they pretty?" I watched their expressions— yes, O'Ryan has expressions too. Aunt Ibby smiled and O'Ryan batted a paw at the screen, maybe patting a puffin, maybe thinking of eating one. Who knows with cats?

"The island looks pretty. Have you decided to stay for a while?" my aunt wanted to know.

"We'll see how it goes. We haven't made any commitment. Aunt Ibby, Pete and I are trying to piece together that last day my parents spent here. One of their friends, another pilot, Hank, who still works here, doesn't believe the crash was caused by pilot error."

"As you know, I've found that one hard to swallow too," she said. "What's this Hank's resoning?"

I gave her a quick rundown of what Hank had told us about the operation of the J-3, especially the details about the fuel switch. "We really need some more time with Aunt Doris and Uncle Bill," I told her. "There seems to be some conflict there about my ring. They obviously both recognized it and Bill actually yelled at me. 'Where did you get this?'" I tried to mimic his angry tone.

"What does Pete think?" she asked. I handed the phone to my husband.

"Ibby? It's possible there's a bit of a domestic problem there." He used his cop voice. "I'm not sure it's confined to whatever the problem is about Lee's ring. Also, Mrs. Raymond—Doris—seems to be slightly confused. It may be from a prescibed medication of some kind, though—not unusual at her age. Generally speaking, they both look to be in good health, good spirits."

"Hmm." My aunt wore her wise-old-owl face. "Keep an eye on them. I barely know either of them—only met them a few times. I'll look up what I can find on this end. You two—and Scott—keep digging. The Angels are already on it."

The Angels? Does that mean Michael Martell may be "on it" too? So I asked her. "Is Dr. Martell still researching the age of my ring?"

Ibby answered with a smile. "Oh, yes. His historic records on lost pirate gold are far better than mine. He has acquaintances in the field, you know. He's even contacted Mel Fisher's people."

"Wonderful," I managed. "Keep us informed."

"You do the same," she said. "Wait a minute, O'Ryan is trying to get the phone away from me."

O'Ryan's pink nose looked huge as he pushed the phone across my aunt's desk toward a row of books. I recognized them as an assortment of general desktop reference books like dictionaries, thesaurus, familiar quotations, a Bible, phone books, an atlas. A yellow paw snaked out and tapped one. "What book is he trying to show us?" I asked. My aunt's hand appeared on the screen, lifting the phone so that I could read the title.

"*Field Guide to Eastern Birds*."

"Apparently he wants you to investigate birds," she said. "Seems a little off-topic, doesn't it?"

"The only birds we've been talking about are the puffins," I said, aiming the phone, zooming toward the mound of rocks where a few of the uniquely colored birds sat—almost as though they were posing for my camera— and for my cat. "This what you mean, O'Ryan?"

"*Mruup*," he said and jumped down from the desk. Cat conversation over.

CHAPTER 34

A few minutes later, Scott came bounding up the hill. "Hey, thanks, Moon! Aunt Doris is a living doll. A walking history book. And she's going to show me a three-hundred-year-old log that tells all about when the pirates landed here. Doan will flip out when he sees that footage." He put the camcorder on the seat carefully and climbed into the cart. "I suppose you guys have already seen it."

"Uh. No, not yet," I explained, trying hard not to sound miffed. "We got here on the boat just before yours."

"Oh, really?" I recognized the self-satisfied tone. "She says one of her first husband's ancestors was the first light tender out here. He kept the log."

"I read about that," Pete chimed in. "He actually saw those pirates coming ashore. Scared the poor guy so bad he rowed himself ashore and never came back."

"Yep." Scott slapped his knee. "Young Howie's going to wish he'd grabbed this one, right, Moon?"

"You bet," I said. "Lots of interest in pirates." I wondered if Scott had already been offered some fresh-baked blueberry pie too, courtesy of *my* aunt Doris.

"Mrs. Raymond is going to stay with the birds a little longer. She said to tell you she'll see you at dinner at their place. Six o'clock."

"Thanks," I said. "Will we see you there too?"

"Who, me? Of course not. I'm not family." Scott did his long look. "I think she was impressed because I arrived in the fancy golf cart. Want to give me a ride back down to the dock? I need to figure out where I'm staying tonight—on the company credit card."

We bumped our way back downhill and dropped Scott off at a small, rustic booth decorated with lobster buoys and fishnet, marked ISLAND INFORMATION CENTER. As soon as he was gone, Pete asked, "What was all that about O'Ryan and Ibby's bird book?"

"I'm still trying to figure it out," I told him.This wasn't the first time our smart cat had used a book title to tell me something—usually something important. Pete has come to accept the fact that O'Ryan isn't just any old run-of-the-mill house cat, but the fact is, my husband has no idea how extremely clever the cat actually is. I can't pretend that I even understand it myself—but I realized that since we'd taken forever vows, it was time to at least attempt to explain O'Ryan.

"I guess you know that O'Ryan has some—uh—unusual abilities." I didn't wait for an answer. "Maybe it has something to do with Ariel—her being a witch and all—I'm not sure. But I haven't always told you *everything* he does that isn't—um—normal for cats. Some of it sounds so crazy I couldn't think of a way to tell you—or even Aunt Ibby—what he can do." I moved closer to him and put my hand on his knee. "From here on—crazy or not— I'm going to tell you everything."

He covered my hand with his. "Let's start with the birds. Does O'Ryan want you to look at the puffins?"

"Something like that. I—we—have to figure it out. I showed him the rock pile where the birds roost and he let me know that's what he wants me—us—to look at."

"Mrs. Raymond and Scott were in the picture too. How do you know he didn't want you to look at one of them?"

"He would have been more specific. He could have pointed out a bottle of scotch to represent Scott, or picked up the gift card the Raymonds sent us. Nope. He means either the puffins or the rock pile is important. I'm sure."

"I'm willing to accept that," Pete said, "as hard as it is to believe. Let's see what we can find out about it. Like, how long has the rock pile been there? Three hundred years, since the pirate invasion? Or is it part of a building project here on the island? They look like natural rocks— or are they those fake ones people use in waterfall features, or the kind they have in the *Pirates of the Caribbean* ride at Walt Disney World?"

"I like the way you think," I told Pete. "Who shall we ask?

"The Raymonds, I guess. Since we're invited to dinner, it might make a good converstion topic," he suggested. "Besides, who would know better than the heir to the island and the promotor of all the Pirate's Island businesses?"

"Perfect," I said. "I think I'll give River a call and see if she has any thoughts on what's going on here." There was a time when I wouldn't have shared that with Pete, who used to humor me about my interest in River's tarot readings, while at the same time calling them River's "hocus-pocus." River's readings had been right far too often to be so easily dismissed, and Pete had—grudgingly—accepted that fact.

"You know," Pete said, "between us we might make a good investigating team. We each have degrees in criminology and if we combine my police academy fact-gathering and questioning techniques with your reporter skills, tarot readings and witch cat revelations, who knows what we can do together?"

"Don't forget my seeing things," I reminded him. "I guess I'm sort of unusual, aren't I?"

"Don't worry about it. We balance each other perfectly, don't you think so?"

"I've thought so from the beginning." I put the phone on speaker, tapped in River's number, hoping she'd be awake. She was.

"Hi, honeymooner," she said. "How's marriage so far?"

"Perfect, of course," I told her. "But we're wondering about a couple of things. Remember that five of swords that showed up in my reading? The card O'Ryan was interested in?"

"Sure," she said. "The cheater." Pete frowned, moving closer to the phone. I hadn't mentioned the sinister-sounding card to him.

"I think he may be my newfound uncle," I explained "I can't say he's cheating, exactly, but he sure is a hustler. And he's not being nice to my aunt. I'm concerned. Should I be?"

"Trust your instincts, Lee. You're good at that. And yes, that man may be the person the cards warned you about. Especially since O'Ryan tapped it."

"Speaking of O'Ryan, we FaceTimed today and he showed me a book: *Field Guide to Eastern Birds*."

"Does that mean something to you?"

"This island is famous for its puffins. You know them? There's a rock pile here where they hang out. I showed it to the cat. That was what he wanted to show me."

"Good. So you've figured that one out. Any visions?"

"There was one before we left and I may have figured that one out too. It was a gasoline pump hose on a field of daisies."

"Which means—what?" Again, Pete leaned close, listening. I hadn't told him about the vision either. *I need to get better at sharing that part of my life—even if it makes him uncomfortable.*

"The plane was named after a cartoon character— *Daisy Mae*, and the crash was due to a fuel valve being shut off." It felt good to put it into words, to share it with River and Pete.

"Is Pete there with you?" River asked. "Does he know about these things?"

"He's right here beside me," I said, "and he knows about them now."

"What do you think, Pete?" she asked. "How do these symbols add up to you?"

He paused, cop faced. "Well," he began slowly, "It

looks as though—according to one large yellow cat—we have a person who may be dishonest somehow, we have a plane with a loss of fuel, and we have a pile of rocks where birds hang out."

"All of them here, on this island, with us," I added.

"Yes," she agreed. "You have several pieces to your puzzle, and they're all close by. Remember too, Lee, that there was another card next to the five of swords."

"The high priestess," I recalled. "She was reversed." Pete looked interested, but confused.

"Hidden things," River reminded me. "Hidden things from the depth of your conciousness might appear."

"Not much help there," I said.

"On the other hand, the priestess might simply represent a selfish woman," River said. "Does that fit anywhere?"

"Not that I can think, of but I'll keep trying."

"Good. You two will figure this out. I know you will. Sending you love and golden white light."

"Thanks. Love you, River." I put the phone into my pocket and faced Pete. "So the first thing we'll ask at dinner tonight, is how long the pile of rocks has been there. You agree?"

"Absolutely," Pete said. "Seems like a good enough starting point. Then we can see where the conversation leads us."

"Hopefully it will go somewhere that makes sense. The conversational possibilites on the topic of ordinary rocks may be limited," I suggested. "The reversed high priestess as either 'hidden things' or 'selfish woman' has some appeal. I hope my aunt Doris doesn't turn out to be selfish."

"If her talk with Palmer is any example, she doesn't mind sharing information. I hope she'll be as generous with us," he said. "And if River's hocus-pocus means anything, I'm thinking 'hidden things' is a safe bet for everything on the island—including an alleged pirate treasure."

CHAPTER 35

Question: How does one dress for dinner on a private—but somewhat crowded—island when the hosts are close blood—but emotionally distant relatives? We decided on island casual—meaning jeans on the bottom and print cotton shirts on the top—Hawaiian for him, cute cats for me. Anticipating the possibility of such an invitation, we'd brought along a very nice Cabernet Sauvigon along with a sampler of Godiva chocolates to share.

So, bearing gifts, neatly dressed, and hoping Scott had been right about the six o'clock time, we knocked on the door of the upstairs section of the lighthouse keeper's cottage. Bill Raymond opened it immediately, a welcoming grin on his tanned face. My Aunt Doris stood a few steps behind him, wearing a red muumuu, a tentative smile and outstretched arms. "Welcome, kids! Come right on in," Bill ordered. "Hope you like barbecue—I'm doing the cooking tonight out on the deck."

Pete assured him that we both like barbecue, which is true, and I stepped forward to accept my aunt's lily-of-the-valley–scented hug. "I'm so glad you're here." She spoke softly. I could see a resemblance to my dad in her profile. My actual childhood memories of both parents are dim, but Aunt Ibby's many photo albums have provided me with, I beieve, accurate mental images of each of them. Aunt Doris's hair was silvery gray now and my dad's hair when he died was a rich chestnut brown. Her nose was what Aunt Ibby would classify as "patrician"—long, straight and classic, as was his. Her skin was tanned too, but remarkably unlined for her age—which I guessed to be around seventy. For a smoker who spent time in the sun, she looked darned good. I hoped it was genetic.

Bill accepted our gifts, sticking the wine bottle under one arm and depositing the candy on a nearby coffee table—which had been neatly constucted from a typical New England wooden lobster trap with a thick glass top. He threw open a set of sliding doors. "Come on out to the deck. Maybe we'll catch a pretty sunset. Doris, grab some wineglasses."

The wooden deck was long and broad, partly covered by a canvas awning, but mostly open to sky and sea view. A charcoal grill stood ready to accept thick steaks, already doused in orange-red sauce, displayed on a huge pewter platter. Foil-wrapped potatoes and ears of corn were already nestled among glowing coals. The sun was low in the west, streaking the sky above distant cliffs and mountains with pink and purple and gold. All in all, it looked as though we were about to enjoy a picture-perfect evening.

"Mind if I take a picture of us to send to Aunt Ibby?" I asked, my phone already in selfie position. "Everthing looks so pretty."

Doris deposited the wineglasses on the long picnic table, patted her hair and stood beside Bill, their arms around each other's waists, while Pete, at my side, mugged for the camera while I grinned and snapped the shutter. Doris, Pete and I took our seats at the table while Bill continued to man the grill. Pete lost no time in beginning the conversation. "Guess you've been on camera quite a lot today, Mrs. Raymond. Scott Palmer was really pleased with the footage he took of you this afternoon." He faced the couple and I knew he'd be watching Bill Raymond's reaction. Was her husband aware that Doris had given an interview to a TV station? I watched both Raymonds. The man's eyes narrowed, his face colored ever so slightly. Doris, eyes downcast, twisted the fabric of the muumuu. Neither aunt nor uncle reponded to Pete's comment.

I jumped in with a comment of my own. "I spoke with Aunt Ibby today and told her about your interest in the puffins. Amazing birds. Uncle Bill, you told us how they like to roost on rocks. Has the pile of rocks we saw today always been there? Or was it built to attract the birds?"

"Smart girl." He pulled a corkscrew from a drawer in the table and began to open the wine. "I knew how much tourists love those damned birds. Puffins poop on everything, you know. During puffin season I keep a handyman busy with a hose just cleaning up after the little devils. Anyway, a long time ago I imported a barge full of rocks from landside and piled them up good and strong and sure enough, within a year or so we had a good colony of the critters calling Pirate's Island home." He handed his wife a glass of wine. "That what the reporter was asking about, honey? The rock pile?"

"No, dear." She shook her head. "He took some pictures of the birds, but he mostly wanted to know about the pirates and the old lightkeeper who got scared and never came back and about the coins people still find on the island. I told him I'd show him the log. He was mostly interested in that."

Pete's turn. "I guess you built the rock pile for the birds after Lee's parents were here, back when the place was still Ruby Light Island, right? We met Hank down at the lighthouse and he remembers their visit very well. Said he even spun the prop on the Piper Cub when they were leaving."

"Did he?" Bill filled three more wineglasses. "Long memory, Hank. I don't remember much about that day at all. You, sweetheart?"

"No. Not really." Her eyes brightened. "Wait. I remember picking a bouquet of wildflowers for Carrie. She loved the flowers that grow wild around the island."

"That's nice," I said, completely forgetting that Pete and I were supposed to be tag-teaming helpful questions. "I like thinking that she had flowers before—you know—before the crash."

"She did, Maralee," Aunt Doris assured me. "I remember now. It was a big bouquet of them. Bluebells and black-eyed Susan and Queen Anne's lace and violets and lily of the valley and lots more. I tied them with a blue satin ribbon. I stood on tiptoe and handed them to her through the big window on the little yellow plane. I promise you, she had an armload of flowers when she went to meet the Lord."

Doris had given me a gift. The picture of my mother smiling, holding those wildflowers, would forever replace my fearful image of her terrifed face surrounded by flames.

"Thank you, Aunt Doris," I said, and immediately returned to the job Pete and I had set out for ourselves: Asking questions and getting answers. I tried again. "Who else was there, saying goodbye to my parents? I'd love to meet anybody who has memories of them they could share with me. I have so few."

"I can't think of anybody," Bill said. "Nope. It was just us, I'm sure. I don't really remember Hank being there, but if he says he was . . ." His voice trailed off. I looked at my aunt.

"Uh-uh. Can't say as I remember anybody either. Long time ago."

"I understand. Could I tag along when you show Scott the log?" I asked. She aimed a quick look in her husband's direction before she answered. He gave a nearly imperceptible nod.

"Of course you may. We don't show it around much, you know. It's pretty delicate. I've been told it belongs in a museum." She folded her arms and lifted her chin. "It's rightfully mine and I'll do as I please with it." Sly smile and a giggle. "Someday we'll build a museum to put it in, here on Pirate's Island, right, Bill?"

"Right, sweetheart," he agreed, lifting his wineglass in her direction. "Now, how do you two like your steak cooked?" I asked for rare and Pete opted for medium, as usual. "You're in for a treat after dinner too. We're having your aunt's famous blueberry pie."

The happy idea of our having that pie when Scott wasn't derailed my train of thought for a second. Pete took up the slack. "Mrs. Raymond," he said. "Hank told us that you sometimes escort visitors down to the cave where the pirates are supposed to have hidden a treasure chest. If the tide is right while Lee and I are here, do you suppose we could see that too?"

Again, my aunt darted a glance in her husband's direction. This time, he answered the question. "Not much of anything to see down there." He sounded apologetic. "Not that I'm above charging the tourists to take a look. They think it's kind of an adventure, you know? Looking for gold and at the same time knowing that the tide could come in and trap you in there?"

"Did anyone ever actually get trapped?" I asked.

He laughed. "Of course not. That would be bad publicity. Nope. It's easy enough to pick a really low tide on a calm day. I wouldn't let my wife do the tours if there was the slightest danger, now would I?"

Doris beamed. "When I was younger, I used to take the tourists down there in a rowboat. I use the Boston Whaler now. Sure. We'll check the tide table and if it's safe I'll take you down."

"What's it like in the cave?" I wanted to know. "Dark and dank and spooky?"

"Kind of," she agreed, "but we give everybody a head lantern to wear—like the miners have. Of course, we give them all shovels so they can dig around in the floor of the cave."

Bill interupted. "We *rent* them all headlamps and shovels. In a seasonal business like ours, you can't afford to give anything away. Once the cold weather sets in and the snow flies and the birds fly the coop, we pretty much close up shop until spring comes around again. Most of the tour boats stop running, so by Christmas there's no-

body around except me and the missus and old Hank—
and he keeps pretty much to himself."

"I understand," I told him. "The TV business in Salem
is seasonal too. Spring through Halloween we're jammed
full of commercials. Then it tapers off. But did anybody
ever dig up treasure in the cave?"

This time Doris interrupted. "Some really pretty gold
coins have been dug up down there, and some more have
been found in other places on the island too. Not everybody is brave enough to do the cave trip, so they like to
dig in some areas we've set up for that."

"It must be so exciting to actually find gold. I can't
even imagine it." I spoke truthfully, thinking of how excited my dad must have been if that was how my ring had
been discovered. Still, Uncle Bill had shown anger when
the subject of my ring had first come up and I had no intention of ruining the mellow mood on the keeper's cottage deck by mentioning it then. "Hank thinks there may
be a treasure chest somewhere offshore that's broken up,"
I said. "He believes a few coins wash ashore now and
then."

Bill lifted one shoulder. "He may be right. Wherever
the gold is coming from, I hope it keeps on coming.
That's what keeps us in business, right, honey?"

"Right," Doris agreed. "The gold and the pirates have
brought us good luck. Maybe someday we can pay the island back for all it's given to us."

I knew that was a perfect opening for me to bring up
the subject of my father's intention to write a check for
whatever the ring was worth, but again—thinking of
Bill's reaction earlier, I let the moment pass. So did Pete.

*Maybe we shoiuld mail them a check after we get
home.*

Pete put us back on the lightkeeper's-log train of thought "Do you have to keep the old log under special conditions? Three-hundred-year-old paper must be fragile."

"Darn right it is." Bill picked up a pair of tongs, moving the foil-wrapped vegetables onto the platter and transfering the steaks onto the grill. "We have a storage unit that keeps it at seventy degrees year-round. It has to have special humidity too."

His voice turned a little edgy. "Damned thing is more trouble than it's worth."

"I'm guessing it gets pretty chilly in the cave too." Pete switched subjects again. "What with the salt water rushing in and out of it."

"It can be cool," Doris agreed. "But I find it quite pleasant down there. I'm looking forward to showing it to you both."

"Never as pleasant as it is right here, right now," Bill interupted his wife. "Good food, fine weather, excellent company. What could be better?" He plated corn, potato and steak done rare with the dexterity of a professional chef, placing it in front of me with a florish. "Enjoy," he said, and proceeded to plate and serve three more dinners. He joined us at the table, refilled the wineglasses and nodded in his wife's direction. "Grace, darling?"

Doris promptly bowed her head, hands folded tightly on the edge of the table. "Robbie Burns okay?" she asked.

"Whatever you like is fine," Bill said, then added, "Your aunt has a vast selection of table graces to choose from." Doris closed her eyes, Pete and I bowed our heads.

"Some hae meat and canna eat, and some wad eat that want it. But we hae meat and we can eat, and sae the Lord be thankit." Doris's Scotish burr was perfect, the light-hearted delivery of the ancient blessing just right. The idea of having a selection of verses memorized delighted me and I decided on the spot that I would do the same in my own household.

"Thank you, Aunt Doris," I said, "and Bill, you're right about the weather, the food and the company. Just right." The meal was expectedly delicious, right down to the flaky, juicy, colorful blueberry pie and after-dinner coffee. We watched the sunset in companionable silence while the impersonal, automated light at the far end of the island flashed white every five seconds.

CHAPTER 36

We'd had a long and busy day and I was happy to return to our designated bedroom. Aunt Doris accompanied us partway, stopping at an enviable walk-in linen closet that smelled of sandalwood and selecting a soft, woven yellow blanket for us. "It'll turn cool tonight," she said, handing it to me.

"You'll be glad of an extra blanket. They're made in Maine. I'll bet you didn't know that Maine is famous for fine blankets." As soon as we reached the room Pete kicked off his shoes and flopped down on the big bed. "Bedtime, Mrs. Mondello?"

"Bedtime for sure, Mr. Mondello," I agreed. I put the cushy, soft blanket on the foot of the bed, undressed quickly and pulled on a white cotton nightie while Pete stripped down to boxers. "Want the window open?" he asked. "I'll bet we can hear the surf. Smell the salt air."

"By all means. Let's have the full deluxe island experience as long as we're here."

He slid the window partway up, then stood there, inhaling deeply. "Yep. It even smells healthy." He turned off the bedside lamp and joined me under the covers. "What did you think about the interaction between our host and hostess? A little tension there?"

"He's not crazy about preserving the ancestral log, doesn't mind his wife doing the cave trips, isn't fond of puffins, but spent time and money building them a roosting spot."

"For profit," he reminded me. "Everything here is for profit. They've managed to make a good income out of a pile of dirt and trees and rocks and what amounts to a handful of gold coins."

"My aunt isn't shy about reminding Bill that the old keeper's log—and the whole island, for that matter—is hers," I said.

"Maybe that's why her memory of your parents' visit all those years ago seems so much more accurate than his." Pete pulled me close. "I mean about the flowers and all."

"Yes. She seemed really sharp about most everything tonight. I wonder why she was so hazy the first time we met her," I said. "Big difference. I wonder why."

"My guess is some kind of medication," Pete said. "I've seen it before."

"I think you're right. The next question is whether or not she's self-medicating—or does she have help?"

"I guess you noticed that she looks to him before she speaks," Pete said. "Does she need his permission? Even to say a prayer?"

"I like the idea that she's learned a variety of different

blessings." I defended my aunt. "I'm thinking of doing the same thing."

"But I'm sure you don't plan on asking me if it's okay."

"You've got that right," I said. "But seriously, he speaks to her with such affection—honey and sweetheart. Is it an act? And if it is, why?"

"Maybe it's none of our business," Pete said. "After all, we're asking nosy questions because your cat is interested in a bird book. Have we asked enough?"

"You're right," I agreed. "We learned a little bit about a lot of things just by asking about a pile of rocks. But now I want to know more about the day my parents died—and why Hank says he doesn't believe it was pilot error. I still want to know who else was on the airstrip that day."

"Bill doesn't seem to remember much about it," Pete said. "Maybe when you go to see the logbook you could press your aunt a little more about what went on up there."

"I will. Listen." I cuddled closer. "I can hear the waves crashing out there—and the air smells good. But I'm cold. Let's pull that blanket up."

Nagging questions and worrisome answers pushed away, snuggling under a cozy blanket, the sound of the sea for background music—our second night together as Mr. and Mrs. was a delightful piece of the beginning to our forever.

I awoke to the sound of seagulls calling—maybe even puffins too, although I didn't yet know what puffin voices sounded like. Early-riser Pete was already awake. "Shall we head for the coffee shop and start exploring this place?" he asked. "Looks like a pretty day."

I was anxious to explore—and definitely ready for morning coffee. It didn't take us long to shower and dress in shorts, T-shirts and hiking shoes. I made our bed while Pete secured the windows. "I wonder where the climate-controlled space where they keep the log is?" I wondered. "On the island or someplace ashore?"

"Either way, you'd better take a sweater," Pete advised. "Bill said it would be cold."

"Right." I tossed a red sweater over my shoulders, looping the sleeves across my chest. "I'll call Aunt Ibby from the coffee shop and catch her up on what we've learned so far."

"Which isn't a lot," Pete said, "but O'Ryan might like to know that the rock pile was imported from landside."

"I want to tell her about the flowers Aunt Doris gave to my mother too. That was important to me."

"I could tell," Pete said. "Aunt Doris seems like a genuinely nice woman, doesn't she?"

"Definitely not the selfish woman the tarot card could mean."

Pete agreed. "I wonder if the Angels have come up with anything new," he said, "but I'm almost afraid to ask."

"And what about the new boarder? Martell? I'll bet he's chiming in too. Aunt Ibby said he knows about pirate history."

"I wonder if he knows anything about antique manuscripts?" Pete held the door of the coffee shop open for me. "Like the pirate log."

"I wouldn't be surprised." A hostess led us to a window seat overlooking the boat dock. We ordered coffee first, then pancakes. I called my aunt. She answered from her kitchen table.

"Good morning, my dears," she said. "How's island life?"

I aimed the camera toward the dock. "Every bit of this place is scenic," I said. "Every photo looks like a post-card."

"Interesting," my aunt said. "Michael has found some old postcards that show the place when it was Ruby Light Island. Got them from a fellow antiques dealer who special-izes in paper memorabilia." She held up a card. "Nothing fancy about it back then . . . See? There's the lighthouse and a small house—I guess that's the lighthouse keeper's cottage." She turned the card over. "This was about forty years ago. It couldn't have been much different when your parents went to visit up there." She put the card down and picked up another, holding it forward. "Can you see all right? This one is an aerial view. You can see the lighthouse and you can make out the airstrip at the top of the island and a small boat dock below. The place has changed a lot, hasn't it?"

"Sure has," I agreed. "And it's all happened since they were here almost thirty years ago."

"The story about the pirates and the treasure in the cave was well known back then," Pete said, "wasn't it?"

"It was," my aunt answered. "Carrie and Jack knew the story. But people had been trying for centuries to find it and never reported digging up as much as a single piece of eight. By that time it seems to be have been regarded as nothing more than local legend."

I held my right hand out and looked at the emerald ring. "And yet—here's my mother's ring."

"There's that," she said, "and Michael has discovered something else—though we don't know if it means any-thing."

"What's he found?" Pete asked. Cop voice.

"Here," she said. "I'll let him tell you about it."

He's there? The wife-killer is in my aunt's kitchen? Again?

As though she'd heard my unspoken question, she answered it. "B and B, you know, dear. Bed-and-breakfast. French toast with real maple syrup this morning." Michael Martell's face appeared on the screen.

"Hi, Ms. Barrett—I mean, Mrs. Mondello. Hi, Detective Mondello. I don't know if this is just coincidence or not."

"What have you got, Martell?" Pete asked. Serious cop voice.

"I guess I told you earlier that I'd been in touch with some friends down in the Florida Keys—coin dealers."

"About the *Atocha* treasure," Pete said. "The Mel Fisher discovery."

"That's right. Spanish gold and silver coins and jewelry," Martell said. "Some of my dealer friends have noticed more and more gold coins showing up in recent years, at auction and in dealer sales. They're being called *Atocha* coins. The dates are right, 1617 or older, but they are not Spanish. They are Peruvian. There's no doubt these are pirate treasure coins, but they may be from a New England wreck."

"Black Sam Bellamy," I said.

"Possibly," Martell said. "No proof, but I think it's worth looking into."

"I think so too," Pete said. "Thanks, Martell. Thanks, Ibby. Anything else?"

"I guess you know the Angels are interested in your island too," my aunt said. "Betsy does some modeling for a ski shop up that way and she's been asking questions of the locals."

Betsy is extremely good at asking questions—and getting answers. "What did she turn up?" I asked.

"Couple of things. A surprising number of people remember the plane crash," she said, "even though it happened so many years ago. Most remember because of the media coverage. It was big news. But she did talk to one woman who remembers actually seeing the crash from the island. She has the woman's number."

"Good job," Pete said. "We've been hoping some witnesses would turn up. Anything else?"

"Betsy said this might be more interesting than important, but she asked if the Raymonds do any skiing. The shop manager told her she'd heard that Doris and her first husband were excellent skiers, but that Doris gave it up after she married Bill. Seems he doesn't like the mountains. He's afraid of heights. Does that mean anything to you?"

"It's the second time we've heard it," I told her. "Hank mentioned it, and now Betsy. but I don't know what it has to do with anything."

"There it is, for what it's worth," my aunt said. "Louisa did a credit check. No problems. They pay their bills. I think that's all we have from this end. Want to say hi to O'Ryan?"

"Of course we do." The dear, familiar fuzzy face loomed large on the screen. "Hello, darling cat," I said. "We'll be home to see you soon."

"*Mrrup. Mrrup,*" he said and gave the screen a pink-tongued lick.

"I love you too," I told him. "We're checking on those rocks and puffin birds."

CHAPTER 37

We decided to walk off those pancake calories and chose a tree-shaded but well-trod path leading away from the boat dock. "It doesn't matter which path we follow," Pete said. "We're on an island so we can't get lost."

"I don't know." I looked around. "It's a pretty big island."

"We could get lost for a few minutes, even an hour," he said, "but it's not like we're in the Amazon jungle or even a national park. We'd still be on Pirate's Island. They'd find us."

"True." I linked my arm through his. "And I wouldn't mind getting lost with you anyway."

"For better or worse," he said, patting my hand. "Hey, maybe we'll stumble on Black Sam's treasure and be millionaires."

"For richer or poorer," I said. "However it works out."

"I wonder if we get to keep it," he said.

"Keep what?"

"Black Sam's treasure. I mean, if somebody *did* get lucky and dig up the chest, do they get to keep it? Or do they have to return it to Spain or Portugal or wherever it got swiped from in the first place?"

"Finders keepers," I said. "Why not?"

"Mel Fisher got to keep the *Atocha* treasure," he said. "Spain never put in a claim for it. And the crew that found Black Sam Bellamy's wreck of the *Whydah* put all the gold and jewels in a museum and people pay to see it. Same with some of the *Atocha* treasure."

"That seems fair," I said. "If we find it we'll make a museum and charge admission. Okay?"

"Deal. Look." He pointed ahead. "That's the back of the cottage where we slept last night."

He was right. We'd traveled in a circle. Through the trees I recognized the second-floor deck with the grill and picnic table. An outside flight of stairs led up to where my aunt and uncle were seated at the table. I began to raise my hand to wave to them, to announce our presence. Pete held my hand still and whispered, "Shhh. Wait a minute. You wouldn't want them to think we're sneaking around, spying on them." We moved a little bit closer. Close enough to hear voices but not close enough to make out words. We moved forward again, then stood still behind a clump of greenery. *We're definitely sneaking around, spying on them*.

I heard my aunt's voice—querulous, unsure. "But she's family. My brother's daughter. My next of kin. She deserves to know."

"Nonsense, darling." His voice was low, persuasive.

"Here, take your medicine. You worry too much. This will make you feel better."

"Thank you, dear," she said. "Maralee is a smart girl. She's been asking questions. Why don't I just tell her? She'll understand."

"No," he said. The edgy sound was back. "No way. This has nothing to do with her."

"I suppose you're right." Her answer was hesitant. "It's not as if she *needs* to know. It's just that Jack would have told her."

"Jack is dead and gone. He has nothing to do with this either." The smooth salesman tone was back. "The girl needs for nothing. I told you I checked on her. Plenty of money there. Jack had good insurance."

She sighed. "I'm sure he did. He loved that little girl."

"Trust me, my love. We'll do this my way. Yes?"

"Of course. Yes."

I poked Pete with my elbow, and jerked my head back toward the trail. This was wrong. I didn't want to eavesdrop—even if the topic was me. He nodded agreement, took my hand and we headed back into the covering woods. We didn't speak until we began to hear sounds from the dock—outboard motors, seagulls, somebody's radio playing rap.

I spoke first. "I feel guilty for listening to them," I said. "But what does it mean?"

"It isn't as though we set out to spy on them," he reasoned. "All we learned is that there's something your aunt wants to tell you and your uncle doesn't think you need to know."

"We learned something else too. He's feeding her some kind of medicine."

"Yeah. I caught that. It may very well be a prescription

from her doctor. Whatever they've decided not to tell you has something to do with your father." He frowned. "And your father and mother are somehow mixed up with this island and pirate treasure."

We'd reached the coffee shop and reclaimed the seats we'd vacated earlier. More coffee seemed like a logical choice at the moment. "What about the coins showing up in Key West? Coins that don't belong there. What about that?"

"I've contacted the PD down there. They were already on it," Pete said. "Whoever is selling the coins to the Florida dealers hasn't left an easy trail to follow. There's some antique jewelry showing up down there too. Same source. But none of the items are presumed stolen. Curious, but not illegal."

His answer surprised me. "Weren't you going to tell me about that? We need to work together on this."

"I know. I meant to tell you as soon as I finished that call," he said. "I'm sorry. Keeping quiet about police business is a long-standing habit."

"I know what you mean. Keeping quiet about my visions is a habit too. We'll have to do better on those things," I told him. "You're thinking my aunt and uncle have something to do with the Key West thing?"

"It's possible." Cop voice. "It's also possible that some lucky treasure hunter found the pirate stash on the island and kept quiet about it. Or maybe Hank is right and the treasure was underwater all this time and a local diver lucked out."

"You're right. Too many possibilities. I guess there's more than one answer to what Aunt Doris and Bill were talking about too. Something they aren't telling me—something that my father would have. But what?"

"Who knows? Maybe you have a secret sibling," he suggested. "Maybe your parents were government agents. Maybe it's something deeply personal and none of our business. I think we need to dig deeper, but we'd better tread lightly while we're at it."

"Agreed," I said. "What about Betsy's tip about Uncle Billy being afraid of heights. Does that mean anything to you?"

"Not yet. You?"

"I'm thinking about who was on the airstrip when the *Daisy Mae* took off. Hank seemed quite sure that Uncle Bill was there," I recalled. "Aunt Doris said Bill was there too. Remember how Scott reacted when he got too close to the edge? Seems like a place a person who was afraid of heights would avoid, doesn't it?"

"Yeah. Did I ever tell you you'd make a good cop?"

"Couple of times," I answered. "Seriously, if Uncle Bill is afraid of a ski slope, I'd think the edge of that airstrip would give him the heebie-jeebies for sure."

"It would. Let's get the phone number of that woman Betsy found who witnessed the crash from the island," he said. "Maybe she was on the airstrip. Want to call Betsy now?"

I tapped in Betsy's private number. "Hi, Betts. Aunt Ibby told me about what you learned at the ski shop. Good job. Do you have that phone number handy? The one for the woman who remembered the plane crash?"

"Sure do. She remembers meeting your parents too. Her name is Kim. Here's the number."

She read off ten digits. I repeated them, scribbled them on a paper napkin. "She met my parents? Oh Betsy, how wonderful. I can hardly wait to talk with her. Thank you."

"You're welcome, Lee. We all think this whole island

mystery of yours is facinating." There was excitement in her voice. "We're all on it. Don't you worry. Ibby, Louisa, Michael, and me—we've got it covered."

Is Michael an honorary Angel? I didn't dare to ask. Didn't want to know the answer. I thanked her again, hung up and waved the paper napkin in Pete's direction. "Her name is Kim. She knew my parents." I put the number into my phone, waited for it to ring. "Voice mail. Damn." I left my name and number and the requested brief message.

The call back came within minutes. Kim indeed had been on that island that fateful day. She'd met my parents—said they were lovely people. She'd been hiking on a ledge below the airstrip, not close enough to see the takeoff, but near enough to actually hear the engine fail, to see the yellow plane beginning the terrible descent. I thanked her for calling and wished she hadn't. I tried to shake the image of the falling plane from my mind. I was glad when Pete made a suggestion.

"Want to go back to the cottage? Pretending we weren't there earlier?" he asked.

"Certainly," I said. "Which path shall we take?"

"Maybe they all lead there. Let's take the one that goes to the front of the place so we don't look so sneaky."

That's what we did. We returned to our room, making sure we made enough noise tramping across the porch and letting the screen door slam to be noticed. That worked. It only took a few minutes for my aunt to "yoo-hoo" over the upstairs banister. "Good morning, children. Would you like to take a peek at the keeper's log this morning?"

"Sure would," I said.

"That would be great," Pete agreed. "Do we need to change clothes?"

"No," she said. "Just grab a sweater and come on up-stairs."

I already had my red sweater over my shoulders and Pete had a PAL sweatshirt handy, so within minutes we were on our way to the second story of the cottage. "Do you suppose they keep the log in the house?" I whispered.

"Nothing here surprises me." Pete tapped on the door.

Aunt Doris, resplendant in a flowing bright orange dress, greeted us with unexpected and somewhat awkward hugs. I looked over her shoulder, thinking I'd see Uncle Bill nearby. "Come in and sit down for a minute. I've invited Mr. Palmer to join us. He's very interested in our island history, you know."

He'd better be. He's here on an all-expense-paid trip. We were in an attractive beach-themed living room. "Yes." I sat in the indicated chair. "I've worked with Scott. He's quite thorough in his research."

"I could tell," she said with a self-satisfied smile. "Bill always says I'm a good judge of character."

Pete took a chair next to me. "Will Bill be joining us?"

Aunt Doris suppressed a giggle. "No. He had business ashore so he took the Whaler and left a while ago." She dropped her voice to a whisper. "I didn't take my medicine this morning. Poured it on a houseplant. Darn stuff is good for me, I know, but it makes me sleepy." Another giggle. "Anyway. I know a great deal more about the log than he does—but I don't like to hurt his feelings by showing off when he's around. The log belongs to me, you know—I mean, to my family, including you, dear

Maralee. So I decided to do this on my own." A knock on the door interupted her. "That would be Mr. Palmer," she said. She was right.

Scott, "bright-eyed and bushy-tailed" as my Aunt Ibby would say, camcorder in hand, a WICH-TV hoodie jacket over his shoulders, and an obviously brand-new white straw hat on his head, swept into the room. "Thanks so much for inviting me, Mrs. Raymond. Hi, Moon, hi, Pete. I can hardly wait to get started. Where are we going?"

"Not far." Doris crooked her finger. "Follow me."

Scott was first in line behind her. Pete and I followed. Single file, we passed through a really cute kitchen, into a large bedroom—restful in cool blues and greens. A king-sized bed with an ornate pressed-wood headboard was under a window. She paused in, I thought, somewhat dramatic fashion before a pair of mirrored sliding doors. "Here we are," she said.

Pete, Scott and I looked at one another and back and forth between us. Pete and I were silent, but Scott voiced what we were thinking. "Huh?" he said. "Huh? Where are we?"

The self-satisfied smile was back. "I had to give up my lovely walk-in closet for this." She pushed the two doors into their pockets, exposing yet another door. "But it was worth it."

The gray metal door had a keypad on one side. "It'll be cool in here. Better put on your jackets. Myself, I don't mind the cold. Follow me." Shading her right hand with her left, preventing us from watching her tap in the code numbers, she pulled the gray door open.

It was a cramped space, a small generator on one side of the area. We had a similar one in the house on Winter Street in case of power outages. A glass case was centered on top of a wooden dresser that matched the pressed-wood headboard. Doris pressed a button, lifting the top of the glass case and simultaneously casting light onto the contents. The open pages, which appeared to be about halfway through the slim book, were ragged, brown, with curled edges. The old lightkeeper had fortunately written with some sort of early pencil. Graphite survives neglect and dampness and aging better than most ink. The words on the page were distinct. We crowded close to the display. Doris pulled a pair of gloves from her pocket, slipped them on and began to turn the brittle pages, reading the words aloud as she did so.

"*I had placed three logs upon the fire when a commotion arose from below. A vessel was decernible in the light from the moon. A smaller vessel was dispatched from the larger. As it neared this island I heard loud voices shouting blasphemies and singing bawdy words. Fearing intruders, I climbed a tree, seeking shelter among the branches.*"

She read on, with dramatic expression, sharing with us the long-ago writer's chilling fear as he witnessed the maurauding band of pirates passing within feet of his hiding place, moving, climbing, back and forth between the cave in the rocks, up onto the ledge above, then warming themselves beside the leaping flames of his sentinel fire.

As she related the tale, I pictured the frightened man, huddled in the tree as he witnessed the pirates breaking into his cottage, carrying out some of his meager possesions, tossing some of them into their waiting boat, discarding others into the fire. When he'd finished his report, signed and dated it, he'd placed the log back into the ravaged cottage and—local legends reported—rowed himself ashore, never to return to the island.

No one spoke for a few moments after Doris finished reading. Scott, who'd been filming and recording the entire time, broke the silence. "That's a really good story, Ms. Raymond. Do we know what happened next? To that keeper or the one after him?"

"Not really. A substitute keeper took over until the first lighthouse was built. There is another legend—a joke really, about what happened to the original keeper. They say he put an oar over his shoulder and started walking inland. When he got to a place where people said 'What's that thing?' that's where he stayed.

"I don't believe it," Scott said, "but I like it. I'll use it for laughs. Now about the treasure, seriously. We know there've been a bunch of gold coins dug up around the island in different places. A guy I know down in the Florda Keys says the same kind of coins have been turning up down there. What's up with that?"

I couldn't help jumping into the conversation. "I heard something similar. I heard that the few coins that have been found on this island are from Peru. There are some like them turning up in Key West although the wrecks found down there are mostly from Spain." I watched my aunt's face. Her expression changed. She hurriedly replaced the glass top and closed the gray door on the air-conditioned locked space in the closet. "Okay. Everybody out. Shoo. Let's lock up before Bill gets back. I'm not supposed to show the log by myself. It's precious, you know. It should be in a museum with all the other precious things." She pulled the mirrored doors together. "The fact is, I don't know anything about the coins or where they came from or where they go. Not anything at all."

Pete and Scott exited the narrow space in a hurry. I lagged behind because of the mirrors. The flashing lights and swirling colors came first. Then the vision.

I saw a smiling Bill Raymond walking toward me, carrying something in his arms. He moved close to me and thrust the thing forward. It was a folded yellow blanket like the one on our bed.

CHAPTER 38

Pete, Scott, and Aunt Doris were already on the other side of the room when I was able to look away from the mirror—which now showed only the reflection of a confused redhead. "Ready, babe?" Pete asked with the degree of concern in his voice that told me he knew something was not quite right.

"Come along now," Aunt Doris ordered, clearly anxious to get us away from the hidden room. "Hurry, all of you. Bill will be back soon enough."

Scott was already outside of the bedroom door. "Let's go, you guys. Thanks, Mrs. Raymond. I'm gonna go find somebody with a boat to take us around to that hole in the side of the island where the pirate cave is."

Pete put his arm around my shoulders, gently propelling me toward the door. "The mirror?" he whispered.

"Yes," I answered, then echoing Scott, I thanked Aunt Doris, told her we'd see her later, and followed Scott down the stairs and outside into sunshine and salt air.

Scott, with the enthusiasm of a kid, bounded ahead of us on the path back toward the dock, the prized camcorder bouncing on his chest. "What did you see?" Pete asked, his arm still around me. "Anything bad?"

"Nothing bad. Just confusing and sort of silly, like they almost always are." I told him about seeing my uncle offering me a nice, warm yellow blanket. "Mean anything to you?"

"Nope. Sorry. But I guess it'll eventually make sense. That's what usually happens with these things, isn't it?"

"It is." I sighed. "Eventually. What did you think about Doris dumping her medicine into a flowerpot? And what was all that about Bill not wanting her to show the keeper's log?"

"Worrisome, isn't it? Tricky situation. It's one of those domestic things where something seems a little off, but it's in the 'none of our business' category. But hey, for now, let's see if Scott can hitch us a ride to the other side of the island for a look at the pirate hole-in-the-wall."

As good as his word, Scott had found a teenaged boy with a motorboat who'd give us a ride around the island for ten dollars. The boat was an open skiff with a nice fifteen-horsepower Yamaha outboard in the stern. It looked sturdy enough to hold all four of us, so we climbed aboard. "You might want to put on your sweater, lady," the kid warned. "She kicks up a little spray if I open her up." I took his advice. So did Pete. He and I sat together on the plank seat in the middle of the skiff, while Scott positioned himself in the bow, camera ready to shoot.

"The tide's not low enough to go inside the cave, you know," the boy said, raising his voice over the hum of the motor. "Not that I'd go in there anyway."

"You wouldn't? Seems like a good adventure," I said. "Why not?"

"There's a ghost of a dead pirate in there," he stated flatly. "Everybody knows that."

I hadn't heard of any ghosts on the island and I said so. "Whose ghost is it supposed to be?"

"Black Sam," he said. "He's in there guarding his treasure."

"No kidding? Who told you about it?"

"My grandpa." The boy widened his eyes in mock-fear. "He was heading out to go fishing one morning—low tide, before sunup—and he saw the cave was wide open. So he decides to cruise by and have a look, you know? He gets right close to the hole and there's the ghost, with a shovel, digging in the floor of the cave."

"A pirate?"

"Sure it was a pirate," the kid insisted. "It was Black Sam. Who else would it be? They don't allow visitors that early in the morning."

Pete and I looked at each other, trying not to smile. I wasn't about to try to talk a youngster out of such a good ghost story—especially if it came from Grandpa—and Scott was busy making notes, asking for Grandpa's phone number.

The hole in the island wall was easily visible—at least the top half of it was. Scott aimed the camcorder and Pete and I each held up our phones. I wanted to share the view from the water with Aunt Ibby and O'Ryan and I was sure Pete's nephews would get a kick out of seeing the "haunted" cave.

"Look up there." Pete pointed to the pile of rocks sheltering the puffin families. "Looks like Doris is already up there babysitting the birds. That orange dress is hard to miss."

Scott raised the camcorder. "That makes a pretty shot. See how the wind blows the dress back? Nice. I'll bet she gets her picture taken a lot."

I remembered the first time we'd seen her there on the rocks, in her hot pink dress, surrounded by people with cameras. "Every time I've seen her she's been dressed in bright colors," I said. "She must like being photographed."

"Her husband picks out her clothes. He likes her in those hot colors. She told me so," Scott said. "He told her he wanted to be sure she was safe and the bright colors would help him keep track of her."

"Seen enough?" the boy interrupted. "I gotta get back pretty soon."

"Sure. Thanks," Pete told him. "That was a good ride and I liked your ghost story too." I saw him slip an extra five-dollar tip into the boy's hand. I clicked off another shot of the island as we sped away toward the dock. Almost the entire island was on the screen. I could see the lighthouse at the east end, then the puffin roost with the growing entrance to the treasure cave below it at the island's midsection. The very top of the western end of the island almost seemed to be sheared off perfectly flat— just long enough to create a runway for a small plane.

We docked, slightly windblown and saltwater damp, all of us pleased with our impromptu tour and our photos. I particularly liked my end-to-end shot of the island. I personally deemed it almost postcard-worthy and decided I'd have a print made and framed as a souvenir of this portion of our honeymoon trip.

"It's still early," Pete said. "Next time the *Miss Judy* arrives, what do you say we hop aboard for the return trip and ask Joe the Jeweler for a current appraisal of your ring? That way, if the occasion arrises that we want to write a check for it, we'll have the numbers. Anyway, we should insure it for a fair value, don't you think so?"

"Yes," I agreed. "And while we're ashore let's find a florist and figure out what we'd like for our memorial tribute."

"None of this is easy for you, is it?" Pete said. "So many reminders of your parents—and what happened here."

"It's all what they call bittersweet," I admitted. "This island is interesting and historic and beautiful in its own way. I've enjoyed meeting my aunt and uncle, especially Aunt Doris. But at the same time, every day there's another reminder of how they died. Hank's 'Down she went. Boom. Gone' description of the *Daisy Mae*'s last minutes. It's hard to get that out of my mind—but Aunt Doris's story about my mother with her arms full of wildflowers—that's a sweet picture I'll always be able to carry."

"I'm glad some of it's good, but as far as I'm concerned the sooner we get out of here, the better. We still have a honeymoon road trip to enjoy, Mrs. Mondello." He took my hand and we headed up the path to the cottage. "Let's change to our goin'-to-town clothes and wait for the *Miss Judy.*"

We put our damp clothes on coat hangers, hung them in the shower, changed to dry jeans and shirts and returned to the dock to check the schedule of the *Miss Judy*. We had another half hour to kill. "Let's go visit Hank,"

Pete suggested. "He's someone we can talk to about ghosts in the cave and Peruvian coins in Key West and who's the best florist in town."

It semed like an excellent idea. We followed the dirt path to the eastern end of the island. Pete knocked on the lighthouse door. "I hope he won't think we're tourists who left our sunglasses in the tower," he said. The pounding of feet on spiraled metal stairs and a muffled curse told us that was just what Hank thought. When the door opened Hank's growled "What!" morphed into a cheerful "Hi guys! Glad to see you."

"You busy?" I asked. "We won't keep you long. We have some time before the *Miss Judy* docks so we thought we'd grab a little visit with you."

"*Miss Judy*?" He stood back, grinning, gesturing for us to come inside. "Going ashore? Island fever got to you already?"

"No. Not yet," Pete said, "though I can see how it could. We've got a little local business to take care of. Going to see the jeweler and look for a florist." At Hank's questioning look he explained further. "We're going to get an insurance appraisal on Lee's emerald ring and we need to find a nice wreath or plant or arrangement to put on the site where her parents died."

Hank ushered us into tiny living quarters at the base of the lighthouse. Pete and I shared a navy-canvas upholstered love seat and Hank took a matching club chair. I caught a small motion beside his chair. I gave an involuntary jump when I spotted a very small mouse. I pointed. "Mouse," I said.

Hank smiled. "That's Minnie. Sorry if she scared you." He clapped his hands and the mouse scurried behind the chair. "Bill says no dogs or cats but he didn't say I couldn't keep a pet mouse. I keep her in cheese—she loves Gouda—and she keeps me company."

"She's very cute," I said, hoping Minnie would stay behind the chair.

"Yeah. She's my mini-support animal. But about your parents—that day has been on my mind since you kids first arrived here."

"I've thought about what you said," I told him. "About how you can't belive the crash was pilot error."

"It's true, Maralee. I mean, Mrs. Mondello. Can I call you Maralee? After all, I knew your daddy."

"Of course you may, Hank," I said. "I keep seeing in my mind the picture of you all up on the airstrip. You and my mother and dad and Aunt Doris and Uncle Bill. Have you thought of anyone else who was there?"

"No. I've tried, I see the *Daisy Mae*. I'm turning the prop. Jack is in the front cockpit. Carrie's in the rear. I see Doris walking toward us with an armful of flowers."

"That's about the way I see it too," I said. "It's funny how the mind makes movies in your head." The image of Bill Raymond, his arms extended, carrying a folded yellow blanket popped into mine. I couldn't very well tell Hank, almost a complete stranger, about my vision. I could talk about a dream, though. River says the visions are almost like dreams—only I'm awake. "I had a dream about Bill Raymond walking toward *me*," I fibbed, "only he isn't carrying flowers. He's carrying a yellow blanket like the one on our bed. Silly, huh?"

Hank jumped to his feet, almost knocking his chair over. "Not silly. That was it! How could I have forgotten it? Don't you see?"

Pete and I both shook our heads. "See what?" Pete said.

"What?" I asked. "What had you forgotten?".

"It didn't seem important. I mean, the weather was cool. It made perfect sense. A nice, last-minute gesture—friend to friend." Hank remained standing, began pacing in the small area. "How could I have missed it? Damn!"

I spoke as levelly as I could, with the man practically stepping on my feet as he paced back and forth. "Hank. You missed what?"

He returned to his chair. Sat on the edge of the seat, his fists clenched, hands on his knees. "It was the last minute before they left. Bill came running up to join us. It was unusual, him being afraid of heights and all. But, like I said, it was a cool day. Carrie, being smart, had a leather jacket on, but Jack was in shirtsleeves. Carrie had the flowers in her arms already. Doris had backed away from the plane and Bill tucked that yellow blanket over the front cabin door. 'Here you go, Jack.' He was yelling, over the noise of the engine, you know? Then he backed off and stood beside Doris and we all waved goodbye."

"That was nice," I said, secretly delighted to have my vision explained so easily and logically. "Thanks for re-membering."

Hank pounded on fist on his knee. "Don't you get it?"

"I do." Pete used his cop voice. "It makes sense The blanket over the door would have covered the fuel lever."

"My father wouldn't have been able to see that it was positioned wrong," I said, "unless he moved the blanket."

"Which he must have done right away," Hank said, "but it was already too late."

I didn't like what I thought of next.

CHAPTER 39

Pete must have been on the same wavelength. "So Bill had his hand *inside* the cockpit door?"

"Where he *could have* touched the fuel lever?" I asked.

Hank's jaw was set. "Looks that way."

"Does the lever move eaily?" I wondered. "I mean, would a light tap of the hand move it?"

"No. You'd have to give it a good shove." Hank sounded positive.

I didn't like the direction this conversation was taking. I said so. "I don't like the idea that Bill—that anyone on this island—would do such a thing."

"Not saying he did, babe." Pete spoke softly. "Not saying anyone did, but it's a possibility."

"It's also possible that it was pilot error," I insisted. "That my dad actually did close the lever by mistake."

"True fact," Hank said. "But damned unlikely."

Pete leaned back in the love seat. "You don't care much for Bill." It was a statement, not a question. "Why?"

Hank looked down at the floor. "Can't really say. He's never done me wrong. Not ever. He keeps me employed at pretty good pay. He even hires Amelia every summer. Just a feeling." He looked up, eyes practically flashing. "I don't like the way he treats his missus. She deserves better."

"I know what you mean about that, Hank," I said. "Sometimes he seems . . . well, disrespectful. But why would he mess with the fuel lever? Why would he want to harm my parents? It doesn't make any sense."

"It doesn't make any sense *yet*," Pete said. "There's something we're missing. A reason for Jack and Carrie to die. We know the how and the where and the when. What we don't know is the who and the *why*."

Hank held up a finger. "Looks like we'll have to figure it out later. I hear the *Miss Judy* coming."

I didn't hear anything and said so. "All the engines around here speak to me," Hank said. "Small ones, big ones. They all have their own voices." He put his finger to his lips. "Shhh. Listen. Hear it now? She's got a little whine. Needs a tune-up."

"I hear it now," I said, after a moment. "You can tell the different boats apart?"

"Sure can. I've been here for years, listening to the boats, the island, the sea, the foghorns, the ocean." He cupped an ear with one big hand. "Hush. Here comes another one. The Whaler. Bill's on his way back. He won't tie up at this dock, though. They've got a small wharf of their own."

"That's amazing," I said. "I mean about your hearing the different engines. Let's go outside and see if you're right."

"Oh, I'm right," he said. "You going back to the cottage and talk to Bill about—you know. About what we talked about?"

I didn't want to. I looked at Pete. "No," Pete said. "We're not. Not right now, anyway. Come on, Lee. Let's grab a seat on the *Miss Judy*. Thanks, Hank. We'll be seeing you."

Hank opened the door and walked outside with us. He pointed to the dock. "See? There's the *Miss Judy* just tying up and there's a Boston Whaler just rounding the bend over there."

"That's quite a talent," I said. "Good ears."

"Yep. The hearing's still good," he said, "but apparently the memory is failing. Why didn't I remember that—about the yellow blanket?"

"It happens to all of us sometimes," Pete told him. "Don't worry about it. See you when we get back." We hurried onto the dock, standing aside while the passengers debarked, then greeted the captain and climbed aboard along with a few other people who were headed landside too.

We chose two seats in the stern, apart from the other passengers. "Do you think Hank will take your advice—and not worry about what he saw that day?" I asked Pete.

"He won't," Pete said. "And we won't either. What do you think about it? It was your dream—I mean vision—that brought it up in the first place."

I hesitated for a moment before I answered. "The reason for the vision in the mirror was meant to jog Hank's memory. Plain and simple. That's what it was for." I was sure I was right.

"Seems like a darned important detail for him to forget, doesn't it?" Pete muttered. "I wonder if anybody else on the airstrip that day remenbers it. Like Doris, or even Bill himself. And who else might have been there that day? Who else might remember?"

"What if it was Hank who moved the handle?" I said. "What if there was no yellow blanket? What if my vision gave him a handy excuse to make Bill look bad?"

"Motive?" One-word question in cop voice.

"For which one?" I asked. "Bill or Hank? Or even sweet Aunt Doris?"

"Let's start with Bill or Doris," Pete said. "If your ring is part of a treasure, then your parents knew that the pirate treasure story was true. Would the Raymonds want to keep it a secret?"

"I wouldn't think so," I reasoned. "Not being the publicity hounds that they are."

"Publicity hound that *he* is," Pete countered. "Not so much Doris. She's a secret-keeper. Look at the pains she takes to guard that old log. She wouldn't want the word to get out."

"But to kill her own brother over it? I don't think so."

"I don't really think so either," Pete said. "But, back to Hank. He knew about the fuel system on the plane. He knew exactly what would happen if it was turned off."

"What would *he* gain by their deaths?" The bridge of my nose began to ache. Even thinking about the crash could bring on tears. "I can't think of anything about it that would benefit him."

"Hmm." Pete appeard to be concentrating on the receding view of Pirate's Island. "Does he seem to be overly fond of your aunt? He's mentioned a couple of times that he doesn't like the way Bill treats her."

"I've noticed it," I admitted. "But what would that have to do with my parents?"

"Maybe if Bill got blamed for murder, Hank would think he'd have a clear field with Doris."

"Aunt Ibby would call that a far-fetched idea," I told him. "Anyway, Hank must have been married back then. His daughter Amelia isn't much younger than I am."

"You're right," he said. "It's unlikely, but I have to consider all of the possibilties. You'd be surprised by how often the least likely suspect turns out to be the guilty one."

I knew he was right. I'd seen that happen more than once myself. At the same time, I wondered if Pete remembered what Amelia had told us about her parents' marriage. "They got divorced when I was little," she'd said. Did that mean anything? I decided not to mention it.

The *Miss Judy* cut neatly through the waves. "Getting a little choppy." Pete put his arm around my shoulders. "You don't get get seasick, do you?"

I laughed. "We still have a lot to learn about each other, don't we? No. At least so far I never have. Do you?"

"Nope. Never yet. The only seafaring you and I have done together is our annual trip to Misery Island." He was right. At least once a summer we take a boat ride to Big Misery to put purple pansies on a little gray dog's grave.

"We're building some nice traditions, aren't we?" I whispered.

He squeezed my shoulder. "We have a lifetime to build lots more."

"Our forever," I said, and immediately thought of the inscription inside my mother's ring. My ring. "I wonder if Joe the Jeweler will remember anything more about whatever conversation he had with my parents."

"I was thinking the same thing," Pete said. "Let's try to jog his memory if we can."

"It worked with Hank," I said, and turned my attention to the not-too-distant shoreline.

CHAPTER 40

My first reaction when we opened the door to the Joe the Jeweler shop was disappointment. The elderly gray-haired gentleman standing behind a glass-topped counter full of fine watches wasn't Joe. "Excuse me," I said. "Is Joe around?" The man smiled. "I'm Joe. How can I help you today?"

Of course. He's Joe, Sr. Pete answered the question. "My wife and I were here a few days ago and we spoke with your son about her ring." I extended my right hand. "Joe, Jr. remembered engraving it a long time ago."

The man bobbed his head. "Yes. He told me about it. The ring belonged to your mother and Joe engraved the word *Forever* inside it. That right?"

"Yes," I said. "We'd like to ask him if he has any other memories of his conversation that day with my parents."

"One of Junior's kids has a game today, so he's not here, but maybe I can help. I was in the shop when your parents came in."

"You were here? You met them?" I was excited.

"I did, but we had a brand-new engraving machine. Junior was much better at using it than I was. He engraved the ring. I watched. And listened."

"Joe, Jr. told us that he'd appraised the ring for the value of the gold and the stone at that time."

"That's correct," Joe, Sr. said. "Its age wasn't taken into account, although because of its style, the cut of the stone, we believed it might be two to three hundred years old."

"We'd like to have a current appraisal," Pete said. "Could you do that for us?"

"Of course. I presume you still don't have any provenance of the age or origin of the piece."

I slipped the ring from my finger and handed it to him. "We don't," I said, "although we believe it may have been found on Pirate's Island."

"I've appraised a few coins folks have found or dug up out there." He picked up a jeweler's loupe like the one Michael Martell had used and held it to his eye. "Nothing like this, though."

"My father told Joe, Jr. that he wanted the appraisal so that he could send a check to the owners of the treasure. Did you hear my father say that?"

Another enthsiastic head bob. "Sure did. That's more or less what he said."

"More or less?" I asked.

"Yes, ma'am. The way I remember it was 'the owners

of *our* treasure.' I could be wrong, though. Memory is a funny thing."

"Our treasure," I repeated. "That makes a difference, doesn't it?"

"Not to me," Joe, Sr. said. "Gold is gold and emeralds are emeralds." He put the ring on a velvet pad, wrote an appraisal slip and handed it to me. "If you ever come up with some provenance of exactly where it came from, we'll appraise it differently. Meanwhile, take good care of it. It's worth quite a lot now."

. I handed the slip to Pete, who gave a low whistle. "Sure you want to wear it? Maybe it should be in a safety-deposit box at the bank."

"Beautiful things are meant to be enjoyed." I returned the ring to my finger. "I'll wear it."

"I guess we'll think twice about writing that check," Pete said. "We'll need some more answers."

We paid Joe, Sr. for the appraisal and thanked him for sharing his memory of meeting my parents. "You look like her. Your mother," he said.

"I know," I told him. "Thank you. Now, can you recommend a florist?"

He opened the cash register and withdrew a business card. "Here you go. Flower World. They're one street over. Tell 'em I sent you."

"I will," I promised.

Pete and I took our time finding Flower World, enjoying window-shopping as we passed by the colorful shops bordering the harbor. "What do you think about Joe, Sr.'s version of what your father said about writing a check for our treasure instead of *the* treasure?" Pete asked me. "It changes the meaning, doesn't it?"

"Sure does. It sounds as if my mom and dad had part-ownership of some kind of treasure, doesn't it?"

"It does," Pete agreed. "Sounds to me as though a group of people own a . . . something of value."

"So my ring is part of the something of value."

"The treasure," he said. "Might as well call it what it is. Somebody on Pirate's Island has found a treasure."

"They found it more than thirty years ago and my parents had to die because of it." I stated it as a cold fact.

"The people they were acquainted with on the island back then—the ones we know of who are still there—are Bill, Doris, and Hank," Pete said. "What if they, along with Jack and Carrie, dug up a treasure chest?"

"And what if they decided to share it equally." I hitch-hiked on Pete's idea. "And my dad wanted to give my mother a ring from the treasure, so he agreed to send back a check for its appraised value. That would be the fair way to do it."

"You make a good case for the 'our treasure' remark," Pete told me. We'd reached Flower World, so our discussion had to pause while we switched our attention from rings to roses. The young woman who waited on us came up with an excellent idea. "Why not plant a tree for them," she suggested, and we knew right away that she was right. We bought a strong young birch tree, some special fortified planting soil and promised to return for our tree the following day. It would fit into the Jeep, we'd borrow a shovel from Bill—goodness knows he had enough of them—and give my parents a proper farewell. And we'd have a tree we could visit from time to time.

Pleased with our day's achivements, even though we'd come up with more questions than answers, we went to the dock to wait for the return of the *Miss Judy*. We stood a few feet apart from the other waiting passengers, and kept our voices low.

"You still thinking about—what we talked about before?" Pete asked.

"The treasure-sharing? Yes, I sure am. Can we simply ask them about it? The most they can say is no."

"Of course, none of them have to tell us anything," Pete said. "So who do you think we should ask first?"

I didn't even have to think about it. "Doris first," I said. "Then Hank."

"What about Bill?"

"He's too intimidating for me," I admitted. "All we need is for one of them to tell us we're right. I'll bet on Hank or my aunt."

"I agree." He gave me a little fist bump. "Did I ever tell you you'd make a good cop?"

The *Miss Judy* pulled in to the dock. We joined the others waiting for transport to Pirate's Island while the mates assisted the arriving passengers, then did a quick cleanup. The captain welcomed us aboard. "You two are getting to be regular passengers. How's the vacation going?"

"Great," I said.

"Super," Pete told him.

"On the way in I saw Bill Raymond heading back to the island in that speedy little Whaler of his. You probably could have hitched a ride with him. Have you guys dug up any treasure yet?"

"Not even a nickel," Pete said. "We're starting to think maybe somebody already found it a long time ago."

He gave a short laugh. "You're not the only ones who've had that idea. Nobody ever finds much of anything except a gold coin here and there that maybe fell out of a pirate's pocket or else washed ashore from an old wreck."

"Even one of those would be fun to find." I decided to push the conversation a little further. "Have you heard anything about the coins that are turning up in Key West? We have a dealer friend who says they don't come from the Mel Fisher collection."

"Funny you should mention that," he said. "I heard a little buzz about Key West coins just this morning. Couple of fellows on the morning run out there were asking everybody on board if they'd ever seen any of the coins that were supposed to come from Pirate's Island."

"The island coins are from Peru, not Spain," Pete told him.

"Yep. That's what those guys said. They had one of them. They held it up so everybody could get a look at it. Said they paid only fifteen-hundred for it from a guy down in the Keys and that the *Atocha* gold coins were twice that much. Said they were looking to buy some more."

"Interesting," Pete said.

Interesting for sure. Does somebody think the treasure is *still* somewhere on Pirate's Island—and that some of it might be for sale? I made eye contact with Pete. He raised one eyebrow. Had we reached the point in our relationship that we could read each other's thoughts?

How wonderful!

CHAPTER 41

"All ashore that's goin' ashore," yelled one of the mates. We said goodbye to the captain, tipped the mates and promised that we'd be back for another ride the following day. We'd be armed then with a shovel for our tree-planting mission to that awful cliff site.

"Want to stop at the lighthouse? It's right here," Pete suggested as soon as we stepped away from the *Miss Judy*.

"Might as well get started," I agreed. "If Hank is home and not busy with a lighthouse tour."

"Right." Pete looked around at our fellow passengers. "That's probably exactly where some of these folks are heading."

"We can wait," I said. "I want to call Aunt Ibby and maybe the station too, and your nephews would like to hear from you, I'm sure."

"Why don't we just join that bunch and take the tour again? That way your aunt and the kids can see the light-house too?"

"Perfect." We followed the chattering group of tourists to the lighthouse where a smiling Hank greeted all of us, reserving a wink and a whispered, "Back for more?" for us. We waited in line while a departing group, one by one, said goodbye to Hank and thanked him for the tour.

I called my aunt, promising a lighthouse adventure.

"O'Ryan's here beside me, snoozing on the couch," she said. "He'll be so happy to see you and hear your voice. He misses you a lot. He's been sleeping in your old room."

"I miss that sweet boy too," I said. "Wish he was here. He'd have a whole island to explore and some cool birds to chase."

"*Mrrupp. Mrrupp.*" O'Ryan interrupted the conversa-tion, forced his fuzzy head into the picture, purring loudly.

"I miss you, boy," I told him, "and you were right about the bird book. Anything else you want to tell me about?" I heard Pete's soft snicker and looked at him. "What?" I whispered.

"You're consulting with a cat," he reminded me. "It's just . . . odd."

"Not to me," I said, a teensy bit annoyed. "Or to this particular cat." I returned my attention to the screen. "Anything else?" I asked again, watching my amazing cat carefully, as he took tiny, mincing steps across the couch, looking back over his shoulder, making sure my aunt was tracking him with the camera.

"I'm watching him," I heard her say. "I think he's heading for the kitchen." The camera bobbed along, following O'Ryan. I recognized the cat's-eye-level base-boards, the table legs, the dining room wallpaper and finally O'Ryan's special red bowl beside the refrigerator. The camera jerked upward as the cat leaped up onto the kitchen counter. He skidded to a stop beside a green plastic collander full of—blueberries.

"Blueberries?" I questioned. O'Ryan reached a yellow paw toward the collander. Tapped the edge.

Aunt Ibby answered. "My blueberry pancakes went over so well, I'm planning on blueberry muffins for tomorrow morning. My blueberry bushes are loaded with fruit."

"Same on Pirate's Island," I told her. "We had Aunt Doris's famous blueberry pie with dinner last night."

"Was it as good as mine?" My aunt's face appeared on the screen.

Oops. Tricky question. "It tasted almost the same," I said truthfully. "Maybe you both have the same recipe."

"I believe we do," she said. "I got mine from Carrie and I'll bet she got hers from Doris."

"But why is O'Ryan interested in your blueberries?"

"Don't know." She focused on the cat once again. "It might be the only thing he associates with Doris."

"I'll bet you're right. What do you think, Pete?" He'd put his phone away.

"Marie answered," he said. "She's going to round up the boys and call me back. I think we should ask him. Hey, O'Ryan. Do you want us to talk to Doris?"

The cat bobbed his head up and down vigorously, then left the table in favor of the red bowl.

"See?" I said. "You can talk to cats too. We'll see what Doris has to say about that treasure, all right?"

"All right. I wish Bill hadn't gone ahead of us in the Whaler, though. He'll be there watching her every move."

"No matter where she is."

Pete finished the thought. "He'll see her bright dress just about anywhere on the island."

"Creepy," I said.

"I'm still here," my aunt reminded me. "Are you finished talking with O'Ryan?"

"Guess he's through talking to us," I told her. "We're going to plant a tree at the cliff site tomorrow. I'll call you from there."

"A tree. That's a lovely idea. Did you want to tell me what the deal is with why O'Ryan wants you to talk with Doris?"

"Not yet," Pete said. "Hang on. We're about to climb a lighthouse."

We followed Hank up the spiral staircase while focusing our cameras downward—a dizzying experience for the photographers, but would probably be quite satisfying for the nephews and the aunt. I thought about the passing glimpse I'd had of River's late-night movie about a lighthouse and the two men struggling on the steep, curving stairs, and one being viciously smashed with a shovel. I tried to shake the bad thought away, concentrating on Hank's recitation about Pirate's Island and the evolution of the various light stations marking the entrance to the harbor—from a long-ago one-man-attended bonfire to a United States Coast Guard automated light. We reached the top and all crowded around the old lens, everyone attentive to Hank's careful description of light-tending tools of the trade over the centuries.

Hank opened the door, stepped out onto the circular

platform and invited us to join him. Pete and I moved around the glass-walled light and faced west. I looked down toward the rock pile, holding the camera out over the railing. The spot of orange was impossible to miss.

"There she is," Pete said. "I wonder if Bill can see her from wherever he is."

"Maybe he doesn't have to know where she is every minute," I said. "Only when there's some reason he *needs* to know."

"Stalking his own wife?" Pete's eyebrow went up.

"Creepy," I said.

My aunt's voice startled me. "What's creepy? Who's stalking who? What are you two up to?"

"Ooops. I forgot you were there," I admitted. "That's Aunt Doris in the orange dress over next to the pile of rocks."

"I see her. She likes those bright colors, doesn't she?" My conservatively dressed aunt who favors browns and grays and greens didn't succeed in disguising a disapproving sniff. "Not exactly age-appropriate."

"We've heard that her husband picks out her clothes." Pete leaned toward my phone, lowering his voice. "Makes it easier to see where she is on the island."

"Creepy," my aunt agreed with me. "What does he think she's doing?"

"We don't know."

"Having an affair?" The question surprised me.

"Aunt Ibby. She's older than you are."

Soft giggle. "Age has nothing to do with it, child. What do you think, Pete?"

"Can't rule anything out." Pete pulled his own phone from his pocket. "Maybe Bill just likes the way she looks in those colors. My nephews are calling. Talk to you later."

"I'll call tonight," I said. "Tell O'Ryan goodbye for me."

"I will," she said. "The Angels are coming over to-night. Talk to you then. Bye."

Does that mean Michael Martell will be there too?

We turned to follow Hank while Pete described the distant view to his nephews. "Three states," he said. I looked down once more. The white straw hat was almost as easy to spot as the orange dress. Scott Palmer stood close beside Doris. Was he bird-watching—or digging for a story? I could hardly wait to find out.

CHAPTER 42

Pete and I deliberately hung around in the base of the lighthouse, pretending to read the framed newspaper and magazine articles about the island arranged on the walls, until the last guest had left. "Either you two like my lighthouse spiel so much you wanted to hear it again, or you want to talk about something else."

"Something else," I said.

Hank opened the door to his small aprtment. "Come into my parlor."

... *said the spider to the fly.*

We followed him inside and once again sat on the love seat facing him. "Well, shoot," he said. "What's up?"

"It's about the gold coins that have been showing up down in the Florida Keys," Pete told him. "Know anything about that?"

Hank didn't reply right away. He stared silently at a

small oval window. I decided to push the envelope. "It seems as though somebody here on the island has acquired a good-sized stash of them. Maybe several somebodies—and that they're suddenly for sale." I watched his face. His expression didn't change.

"Yeah. I think you're right. What about it?"

"Somebody has dug up the treasure," Pete said.

"Looks like it. Those gold coins are coming from someplace," Hank agreed. "And they match the ones that have been showing up here for years."

I may as well come right out with it. "Did you find the treasure, Hank? Are you selling your gold?"

He made a face. "Me? Huh. I wish. I've been thinking it was you two."

"Us?" I was astonished. I could tell that Pete was too. "Us? This is the first time we've ever been here. We haven't dug up anything."

"You're Jack's kid. You're wearing that ring. Makes me think Jack and Carrie dug it up all those years ago and you're selling it off in Florida. I know you used to live down there, Mrs. Mondello, and it looks to me like you're pretty well off." He sat on the edge of the couch and looked me in the eye. "Come on. You can tell me. Did you leave some of it here? Did you come back to get it?"

I stifled an urge to laugh out loud. The closest I'd ever come to pirate gold was the gold coin necklace Johnny had bought for me in—guess where—Key West. "You couldn't possibly be more wrong," I told Hank. I looked toward Pete for backup.

"It's not us, Hank." Pete used his persuasive cop voice. "And you say it's not you. Yet, you were there when Jack Kowalski took off in that small plane with its fuel swich in the *off* position. Did you and Jack and Carrie find the treasure and leave it all here on the island except for that one ring? Did you decide you didn't want to share? Did you get rid of your partners that day?"

Hank stood up, fists clenched. "What are you, nuts? Jack was my friend. Do I look like a millionaire to you? If I had a treasure I'd be living on a yacht in the Bahamas with a supermodel, not in the cellar of a broken-down old lighthouse with a pet mouse."

I tried to hide my smile at the mention of Minnie. His denial definitely had a ring of truth about it. I looked at Pete. He hadn't even hidden his smile. He held up both hands. "Okay. Okay. It wasn't you and it wasn't us. That leaves Doris and Bill."

"Hard to believe." Hank sat down. "Jack was Doris's brother, for God's sake. They were always talking about growing up together in Salem. They were tight. Nope. No way."

"That brings us back to pilot error again," Pete pointed out. "Maybe it was. But where is the sudden rush of Peruvian gold in Florida coming from if not from here?"

Hank didn't answer. He put a finger to his lips. "Sshh. Listen. Hear that?"

Pete and I stopped talking. "Hear what?" Pete said. "I don't hear anything." I didn't hear anything either.

"The Whaler. Bill just got back and now he's leaving again. Let's see where he's heading." Hank opened the door and we followed him outside. He was right. The speedy little craft rounded the eastern edge of the island. "He's going back toward town. Must have forgotten something." He turned and led us back indoors.

"That must mean Doris is alone," I said. "That gives us a chance to talk to her without Bill answering questions for her."

"Good idea," Pete said. "Let's hurry before he comes back. See you later, Hank. We'll talk some more."

"How about I come with you? I'll put up the *No more tours for the day* sign."

Pete and I both hesitated.

"You might need me," he said. "Doris knows me. Trusts me. You two are practically strangers, blood or not."

"He's right, Pete," I said. "Hank knows everyone involved—he even knew my parents."

"Okay," Pete said. "Let's go. Can we grab one of those golf carts?" We could. With Hank at the wheel, within minutes we were bumping our way uphill toward the rock pile, hoping to catch sight of an orange dress. Would Scott's new white straw hat be there too?

Doris sat in the green Adirondack chair and her hand-to-mouth motion told us she was taking advantage of her husband's absence by enjoying a cigarette. I spotted Scott on a precarious perch close to the rock pile, a zoom lens attached to the camcorder. He'd clearly become enamored of the puffins, along with the rest of the birding world. With my mind never entirely away from my program director duties, I hoped he'd be able to put together a puffin presentation for Ranger Rob's little buckaroos to enjoy. As we drew closer to the pair, my heart pounded in anticipation of what we were about to discuss with my aunt. *Was she involved in their deaths?* I prayed not.

"Hey, Doris!" Hank brought the golf cart to an abrupt halt at the edge of the dirt road. He jumped out, waving both arms toward the two below us on the sloping island landscape. My aunt returned his greeting, stood, and walked toward us, her arms stretched wide. Scott acknowledged us with a one-handed wave over his shoulder, his attention still focused on a crack in the rocks. Was there a nest of baby puffins in there? I hoped so. The buckaroos would love it.

With Pete's steadying hand on my elbow we made our way down the sloping path. I formed questions in my mind as we drew closer. What's the polite way to ask exactly what "our treasure" meant? Had my parents and the Raymonds found Black Sam Bellamy's treasure and had they decided to share it between them? If they had, there was nothing wrong with that, was there? *Except for the fact that, as far as I knew, one gold and emerald ring was all my parents ever had to show for it.*

"What a pleasant surprise," Doris said, hurrying toward us. "I'm so happy to see you all." I stepped into her embrace, aware of the smell of tobacco, feeling a bit disloyal for harboring dark thoughts about death and deceit. "I'm happy to see you too," I mumbled, backing away so that Pete could shake her hand.

"Do you have time for a little chat?" Pete asked her. He glanced toward Scott. "Just the four of us. You, Hank, Lee, and me?"

"Of course." She scrunched up her eyes. "Is there something wrong?"

"I don't know," Pete told her. "Is there?"

Long, awkward pause. I was ready to step in and say something like, "Sorry we interupted you," or "It's nothing important." But Aunt Doris broke the silence.

"Did one of you tell Bill what we did? That I opened the closet and showed you the hiding place?" Her voice broke and she choked back a sobbing sound. "Never mind. It's too late now to do anything about it. He found out somehow and he thinks you've seen it." She covered her mouth with one hand. "He is so angry. Now it's too late. It's all gone. I'm so sorry. This isn't what Carrie and Jack wanted."

"It's gone?" Hank asked, voicing what we all were thinking. "It's gone? The treasure is gone?"

She nodded. No words, just the strangled sobs. We three, Pete and Hank and I, stood by helplessly, waiting for her to regain control. I peered past her toward the rock pile, hoping Scott hadn't witnessed the meltdown. Still facing away from us, he seemed absorbed in puffin-land. That was good. This certainly wasn't anything we'd want to see preserved on video.

Doris's breathing became even and she wiped her eyes with the backs of her hands. "I'm so sorry," she said again. "I'm sure it isn't your fault."

I thought of the bureau with the glass case behind the mirrored closet doors. She'd shown us the keeper's log, nothing more. No treasure. I spoke as softly, calmly as I could under the tense circumstances. "What did Bill *think* we'd seen?" I asked her. "He knows you've shown the log to plenty of people. It's even listed on the deluxe tour."

"Not in the closet," she said. "I've always brought the glass case downstairs before. But I figured, you being family and all, it would be all right. It's not as though I opened the safe, is it? All you saw was the precious log."

"I didn't see any safe," I said to no one in particular.

Aunt Doris answered my unspoken question. "Yes, you did. It's inside the big bureau under the glass case. It's really a safe with our old bedroom bureau built around it. Bill designed it right after Jack dug up the treasure chest."

CHAPTER 43

"**J**ack?" Hank almost shouted.

"My dad?" I said. "My dad?"

"Lee's father dug up the treasure?" That was Pete.

"Yes. It's true." Doris covered her face with her hands, muffling her voice. "After all those years, after all the people who dug in the floor of the cave, it took Jack—with his engineer's eyes and mind and slide rule—to figure out exactly where it was."

I wasn't sure I'd heard her correctly. "My father figured it out somehow? He found the treasure?"

"Jack actually dug it up?" Hank asked.

Doris dropped her hands and laughed. It was a strange, unfunny laugh. "Not exactly. Jack found it all by himself. Once he figured out where it was, we all grabbed shovels, Jack and Bill and Carrie and I. We all dug."

"Our treasure" began to make perfect sense.

"How did he find it? Where was it?" Cop interrogation voice from Pete.

"It was so simple, once he explained it to us," she said.

"Where was it?" Pete asked again.

"Up!" She laughed again. "It was up!"

Involuntarily I looked up, skyward. So did the others. Doris's laugh changed to the familiar giggle. "Not up in the sky. Up from the cave," she said. "The X carved on the wall meant that the treasure chest was buried *above* the cave, directly over the mark." She smiled the self-satisfied smile. "That's exactly where it was. It wasn't even buried very deep either."

This time I dropped my gaze to the rock pile. Scott had turned and now had his zoom lens turned toward us. "Under the rocks?" I asked.

"The rocks weren't there then, of course. Bill bought them later so no one else would get the bright idea to dig there and maybe find some trace of the chest. It was falling apart when we found it." She pointed to the rocks, surrounded by birds. "No one is allowed to disturb a puffin habitat in Maine!" Another giggle. "Not ever."

"Do you believe Bill has taken the treasure away from the island, then?" Pete stayed on topic as usual.

"I'm sure he couldn't have taken the chest," she said. "But I'll bet he took whaever was left of the treasure."

"What do you mean—'whatever was left of the treasure?'" Hank insisted. "Did somebody else keep some of it?" He shot an accusing glance my way. "Did Jack and Carrie get more than that emerald ring?"

She frowned. "Oh Hank, what an idea. Of course they didn't. Carrie fell in love with the ring and Jack wanted to give it to her. He planned to have it appraised so he could send us a check for the value. That was going to be the seed money for the museum." A long sigh. "That never happened."

Three voices in unison asked the obvious question. "The museum?"

"Yes. Oh, dear. Bill is right. I do talk too much—especially when I don't take my medicine. I need to sit down." She turned away from us and walked toward the green chair—and Scott's camera. We followed, like an obedient row of puffin chicks. We stood in a half circle around her. Scott joined us.

"What's going on?" he wanted to know. "You okay, Doris?"

"I'm fine, Scotty," she said. "Just needed to sit for a minute. I didn't take my medicine."

Scotty? Really?

"Should somebody run up to the house and get it for you?" he said, concerned.

"Nope. I don't need it, but thank you."

"Okay, then. I'm on my way to get a boat ride to the cave. The tide's almost dead low. I want to get a shot of the X on the wall down there. Anybody want to come with me?"

We all declined.

"I thought for sure you'd want to see it, Moon," he said. "What happened to your sense of adventure?" Disappointment must have shown on my face. I really *did* want to see the X, but I wasn't about to walk away from Doris's tale of missing pirate treasure.

"Have it your way, Moon," Scott said. "Bill's taking me out in the Whaler. Hundred bucks a head, but Doan's paying, so who cares?" He scrambled up the incline. "See you all later."

Doris's face had gone pale. "He's back? Bill is on the

island? I need to get home right away. He told me not to leave. I should be on the porch where he can see me." She stood, chasing after Scott. "Can you give me a ride in your golf cart, Scotty?"

Scott extended a hand and politely helped her into the front seat. Our next decision didn't require conversation. While Doris climbed into Scott's cart, Hank, Pete, and I walked quickly back to ours, then proceeded to follow them at a discreet distance.

"If Bill's as angry as she seems to think he is, we'd better stick around to be sure Doris is all right." Hank sounded worried. Almost frightened. I was afraid for my aunt too. I wanted to tell her that we had her back—that we weren't about to leave her alone with Bill until we had a full understanding of what was going on between them. I didn't have a chance to speak to her. As our golf cart came to a stop, Doris had already left Scott's cart and dashed up the outside stairway to her deck.

"There's no way of knowing if the Whaler is at the dock for Scott's cave tour yet or if Bill knows that Doris isn't where she's supposed to be," Pete said. "Let's go up there and sit with her."

"You two, go ahead," Hank said. "I'm going to beat it back to the lighthouse. I don't want Bill to see the *No more tours for the day* sign on the door. He likes me to be where I belong too and he's still my boss."

"Got it," Pete said. "We'll check back with you later." We got out of the cart and approached the staircase. Doris's orange dress was already out of our sight. I could visualize her sitting at the table up there, trying to look as though she'd been there all day instead of watching the birds, sneaking a smoke and getting acquainted with a straw-hatted photographer.

I didn't want to startle her by appearing on the deck all of a sudden, so I called her name. "Aunt Doris, yoo-hoo! We're coming up." She didn't reply. Pete stepped ahead of me on the stairs, with a one-handed motion for me to stay behind him. Without question, I did. Had she gone inside the house? Was she okay?

Close to the top of the stairs I peeked around Pete and breathed a relieved sigh. Aunt Doris was seated at the table just as I'd pictured her, the sweet-smiling image of the innocent, obedient stay-at-home wife.

It made me furious.

What had Bill Raymond done to intimidate the woman? I could hardly believe she was my smart, strong, take-charge father's sister. My blood. My closest relative besides Aunt Ibby.

I couldn't help myself. I spoke out—too loudly. "What do you think you're doing?"

Her expression changed immediately. Eyes widened. Lips trembling. "Oh, it's you. I heard footsteps. I thought— I was afraid it was Bill—come home early. If I wasn't here, he wouldn't like it."

Pete put a restraining hand on my shoulder but I couldn't stop. "So what if he didn't like it? This is *your* house just as much as it is his. Why do you think you need permission to come or go as you please?"

"You don't understand."

"You bet I don't," I told her. "What's going on here? You told us that you and my parents had found some kind of pirate treasure—and now you think Bill has taken it somewhere? Has stolen it?"

Pete's voice in my ear was steady, calm, reassuring. Professional cop voice. "Let's all try to make some sense of this," he said. "Doris, Lee and I are concerned about you—and Bill too. We're here to help. To listen. Let's sit down, shall we? Doris, if you can, tell us what's wrong."

Pete and I sat side by side, facing her. With her elbows on the table, her hands folded beneath her chin, she began. "What's wrong? I'm not sure. It all seemed so right. We decided on a path to take and as far as I'm concerned, we took it."

There was a pause. Doris looked away from us. Neither of us interrupted. We waited for her to continue. "We all agreed—it was the right thing to do. The Pirate's Island Museum. It would make us famous—we'd all profit from it and the treasure could be seen by everyone." She smiled a sad little smile. "Your parents were all for it, Maralee. Carrie even made some little pencil sketches of different ways we could display the jewelry. I saved them. It was going to be so beautiful. Now, it's ruined. Maybe it's my fault. I don't know."

"Where did the coins come from?" Pete asked, his voice gentle. "The ones people dug up sometimes."

"Salting," she said.

"What?" I asked.

"That's what Bill calls it. He'd take a few coins from the chest once in a while and put them where people could find them. It's called salting. It keeps the hunt going. Everybody gets more interested when they think they might be the next one to find gold."

"Yes. I can see how that would work," Pete said.

"Is that okay?" I asked. "I mean, is it legal?"

"I don't see why not," he said. "The coins and the island belong to Bill and Doris. They can do whatever they want to with them."

"I thought all of the treasure should be preserved for the museum," Doris said. "I wasn't crazy about the salting thing, but I agreed to it. But lately, when he thought I was asleep, I'd hear the doors sliding open and I knew he was getting something from the chest. It happened too often for him to be taking just a coin or two." She shrugged. "So one day when he wasn't home I opened it myself. Almost all of the gold coins were gone."

"Did you tell him what you'd found?"

"I didn't have to. He came home early. Caught me looking at the treasure chest—the half-empty treasure chest." She looked down at the table. "He said he was moving it to a safety-deposit box onshore. It would be safer there."

Pete looked puzzled. "Did you believe him?"

"I wanted to. I tried to. I told him I believed him—but he knew I was lying. Last night I heard the doors slide open again. He didn't even try to be quiet. *Clink clink.* I heard the jewelry going into his big canvas bag. He left before breakfast. He was carrying the bag. It looked heavy." She turned away from us, looking out over the water. "He took away all of our dreams for the museum—the dream I shared with your parents, Maralee. I'm surprised that he's come back."

"Are you sure he's taken it all? Have you looked in the safe yourself?"

"He's changed the combination. I can't open it."

"Can he do that, Pete? Can he take all the valuables and just leave?" I demanded. "That's not fair."

"I don't know," he said. "Perhaps what he told Doris about the treasure being safer in the bank is true."

"Or maybe he's selling it to somebody in Key West," I said. "What about that?"

"Also a possibility." Reasonable cop voice engaged. "I'm not an expert on marital law in Maine, but it's likely that the treasure belongs to both of them equally. If he's left half of it here he may be able to do that. Let's give opening the safe another try, Doris."

With another wistful glance toward the ocean, Doris stood and led us into the house. We followed her to the bedroom. I tried to avoid looking at the mirrored doors. It didn't work. By the time she'd pushed them halfway open, the blinking lights and swirling colors had appeared. Just before the last edge of mirror slid behind the wall I caught a glimpse of something I'd seen before: the clock on the wall of my old kitchen. It still said quarter past ten.

Doris poked nervous fingers at the keypad with no result. "Slow down," Pete advised. "Concentrate on the combination. Take your time."

Aunt Doris closed her eyes. Took a couple of deep breaths. Stood silently for a moment, then slowly, deliberately, hit one numeral at a time.

Nothing happened.

"Looks as though he did change the combination after all." Pete sounded disappointed.

"Ten-fifteen," I said. "Ten-fifteen."

"What did you say, babe?" Pete asked.

"The combination," I said. "It's ten-fifteen or maybe one, zero, one, five. Anyway, it's those numbers in some sequence or other. Try it," I insisted.

Doris's look was one of disbelief, but Pete knew I'd just looked at a mirror and did as I asked. He called out the numbers as he tapped them into the pad. "One, zero, one, five."

The door slid open silently, the glass case lighted, the air grew cold.

CHAPTER 44

Doris picked up the case with its precious contents, carried it carefully and placed it gently.onto the bed. "The top of the bureau lifts off, Pete. The treasure chest is right underneath it." She stood beside the bed, unmoving, watching.

All of my field reporter insticts kicked in. I moved close to Pete, wishing for better light—wishing for Marty with her big camera—wishing for the true money shot—a treasure chest brimming with gold and jewels.

The chest itself looked just about as I'd envisioned it. It was not very large. The top was rounded, encrusted with barnacles. I even thought I caught a whiff of what could have been seaweed or kelp but maybe I imagined that.

"Want to give me a hand lifting the cover?" Pete asked. "It looks pretty rickety."

I wedged myself in beside the bureau and put both hands on one curved end of the chest, where rusted metal bands and bolts looked loose and unsubstantial.

"One, two, three, lift!" Pete called.

We lifted the rounded cover of the empty chest.

Neither of us spoke, just quietly, carefully lowered the lid back into place.

"I was right, wasn't I?" Doris broke the silence. "He took it all away."

"It looks that way," Pete said. "We'll need to talk to Bill as soon as he comes back from the boat tour. Hopefully, he'll have some good reason for this." He replaced the bureau top.

I hoped so too. "Want to put the log back in the safe, Aunt Doris?" I asked.

"Yes. At least he didn't take that away from me." She lifted the case once again and almost reverently centered it on the bureau and closed the gray door. "What was that combination again, Maralee, in case I ever need it?"

"One-zero, one-five," I told her, hoping she wouldn't question me further about it.

"Lucky guess," she said. "Some people just seem to have a gift that way. Your mother could do tricks like that sometimes too."

My mother? It had never, ever occured to me that such a so-called *gift* might run in families. I'd certianly ask Aunt Ibby about it at the first opportunity. Maybe, at some future, less stressful time, I'd ask Aunt Doris for more details. Maybe. "Do you want to go back out onto the deck?" I asked, "in case Uncle Bill is looking for you?"

"We'll be right here with you," Pete reassured her.

"Chances are there's a good explanation for what's go-ing on."

I sure hope so. So far, nothing about this made much sense.

Aunt Doris faced us. "If he's taking the cave tour he'll be able to see this place from the Whaler. I'd better be out there when he looks this way." She led us from the bed-room back to the doors opening to the deck. "He uses binoculars to spy on me, you know."

Creepy.

Once again we sat at the table. "Look there." Doris pointed. "There's the Whaler. He's on his way back."

I looked where she pointed. I didn't see a white straw hat. "Do you have binoculars here, Aunt Doris?" I asked.

"Sure. They're hanging on a strap right behind the door there."

I found them, held them up to my eyes, twisted the center knob and adjusted the focus. I was right. There was no white straw hat. Bill Raymond was alone in the Boston Whaler.

"Where's Scott?" I was alarmed. Pulling the phone from my pocket, I hit Scott's number. The unavailable message played. I tried again. "He's not answering."

"If he's in the cave his phone won't work," Doris said. "I know. I've tried it."

"In the cave? Alone? How can that be?"

"Calm down," Pete said. "It can't be. Maybe they didn't do the tour for some reason. Lee, take the cart and run down to the dock and see what's going on with Scott. I'll stay here with Doris. Bill will probably pull in to the pri-vate dock. I don't want to leave her alone."

"Good idea," I said, handing him the binoculars. "I'll be right back." I hurried down the outside staircase and started the cart. The only time I'd driven one before was on the golf course. This terrain was bumpier, but still fun. I saw the green golf cart Scott had been driving as soon as I reached dockside. I parked and scanned the area, looking for the telltale white hat.

Maybe he's in the coffee shop, I told myself. I checked my watch. "It's almost dinnertime. The sun will be setting pretty soon."

No luck in the coffee shop. A waitress told me Scott had been there for lunch. "He was excited about going to see the treasure cave," she said. "I told him not to expect much. I've done the tour. It's no big deal. Just a hole in the side of the island with an X up high on the wall."

Did Scott ever get on the Whaler for the tour? Maybe he went on another boat. Maybe he found a cheaper ride. I quick-walked to the dockmaster's office. "My friend was going on a treasure cave tour," I blurted. "I saw the boat he was supposed to be on coming in. He wasn't on it. He's not answering his phone." I could hear hysteria creeping into my voice, and tried to slow down. "Where's the tide?"

I'm from Salem. I live and work close to the ocean. Tides vary. Some are orderly. They march into the shoreline on time, then turn themselves around and leave the same way. But sometimes they roar ashore and carve out great hunks of sand and rock.

"Tide's coming in," he said. "What tour boat was your friend on?"

"Not a regular tour boat," I told him. "It was Bill Raymond's Boston Whaler."

"Bill takes private parties," he said. "Check with him or Doris."

"He's on his way in right now," I yelled. "I saw him. My friend isn't on that boat."

"He probably took one of the other boats, then. Ain't nobody gonna leave a passenger in the cave, lady. Calm down." He gave me a pitying look. "Nothing to worry about. Sit down. I'll call the other captains and figure out who took him. Name?"

"Scott Palmer," I told him. "He's a reporter." I didn't sit down.

"Oh, yeah. Seen him around. Nice camera." He took a phone from his uniform pocket and put in a number. Slowly.

"How many tour boats are there?"

"Six or seven," he said.

"I'm going over to the lighthouse and check with Hank," I told him. "He knows Scott. He might have seen who he went with. I'll be right back."

"Good idea, lady," he said. "You do that. I'll keep checking from here. You find him, you call me, okay? You got my number?" He rattled it off and I put it into my phone.

"Thanks," I said, turning and heading for the lighthouse. It was well past five o'clock, so I knew the lighthouse tours were over for the day. Just beyond the lighthouse the automated light flashed bright every five seconds. I hoped Hank would be at home. I knocked, knowing that he'd probably expect a sunglasses- or hatlosing tourist on his steps. Maybe he'd pretend he wasn't there. I couldn't blame him for that. "It's me, Lee Mondello," I called. "Please open the door, Hank."

He answered almost immediately. "What's going on, Lee? Something wrong?" A frown creased his forehead, eyebrows gray against dark skin. He looked behind me. "Where's Pete?"

"He's up at the cottage with Doris," I said. "He didn't want to leave her alone. Something's going on with Bill. Looks like he's grabbed the treasure and stashed it someplace. But I'm worried about Scott. Bill was going to take him to see the cave. The Whaler is back but Scott isn't in it. Pete thought you might know where he is. Do you?" I pleaded. "Do you know if Scott was in the Whaler or not?"

Hank pulled the door shut. "He sure was. I looked outside when I heard that engine start up. It's got a whine. Scott and Bill were alone in the Whaler. No other passengers. I thought that was strange. Bill gets a hundred bucks a head for that trip and I know he left at least five or six willing customers at the dock. That's not like old Bill at all."

"What should we do? Is it possible he could have left Scott in the cave? My God, Hank. The tide is coming in."

"Call Pete, Lee," he ordered. "Tell him I'm going to grab a boat and get around to the cave. It's only about half-tide right now. We have time. You stay right here. I'll call the Coast Guard. Do you know where Bill's at now?"

"No. Pete thought he was heading for the private dock."

"Okay. Go up to the light. There's a good telescope up there. You'll recognize the Whaler if you see it, right?"

"Sure. But it's getting dark."

"Call Pete," he said, and closed the door, leaving me all alone and scared to death. I pulled out my phone and began to climb the spiral staircase, thinking about River's late-night movie of the same name and how poor, mute

Dorothy McGuire had been attacked on the stairs. *I'm not mute*, I thought with satisfaction. *I can scream my head off.*

Go ahead and scream your head off. There's no one here to hear you except a mouse.

I was relieved to hear Pete's voice. "Hello, babe. What did Hank say?"

I related as quickly, and as clearly as I could, what Hank had told me. "He's gone to the cave," I said, "and he's calling the Coast Guard. I'm on my way up to the light to see if I can spot Bill and the Whaler. Is Aunt Doris all right?"

"Yes. But the Whaler is tied up at the dock and Bill is nowhere to be seen. I've called the sheriff and he's sending a cop over to stay with Doris while a couple of deputies and I search for her husband. Any news about Scott yet?"

"No. The tide's coming in. I'm worried."

"If Hank's gone to the cave and he's got the Coast Guard on it, Scott will be all right. You'll see."

He didn't sound convinced.

CHAPTER 45

The telescope Hank had mentioned was a stationary one attached to the railing around the light. Its sweep covered the eastern tip of the island including the automated light, and the inner and outer harbor from a lighted marker buoy to the north and part of the shoreline to the south. Fortunately, that included a close-up view of the Raymonds' cottage. Even in the dimming daylight I could see activity there. Aunt Doris's orange dress stood out among the several uniformed men congregated on the deck.

I lowered the viewer to ground level. More men. I saw Pete among them. This was more than the "cop and a couple of deputies" that were supposed to safeguard Doris. This was a manhunt. They were looking for Bill Raymond. Once again I raised the telescope, swiveled it and focused on the rock pile. I knew that the cave entrance was directly below it. My engineer father had figured that out. Where was the tide? Would Hank get there in time? Where was the Coast Guard?

The last question was answered when a speeding motorboat with the familiar orange and white stripes of the USCG, lights flashing, sirens screaming, sped into view, then disappeared behind the island's edge. I realized I'd been holding my breath. It felt like the point in a movie when the cavalry arrives to save the hero. Scott was going to be all right. Probably wet and angry, but he'd be alive. Hank should be back any minute and I'd learn all the details—like why would anyone leave another person alone in a below–sea level cave with an oncoming tide?

Once again I focused on the cottage where I could no longer see anyone on the deck. Lights were on inside the house and there were moving lights among the trees and bushes surrounding the place. There was a serious search going on over there. I wished I could call Pete, to find out what was happening. Naturally that was impossible under the circumstances, but maybe the dockmaster would know something.

I secured the telescope and stepped back inside the light tower. In the fading daylight and the intermittent flashes from the automated light, I found the dockmaster's number. I was about to hit *send* when I heard the entrance door far below open. Hank must be back. Relieved, I went to the head of the spiral staircase. I leaned over the iron railing, about to call his name.

Somebody beat me to it.

"Hank! Where the hell are you?"

It was a man's voice. It was Uncle Bill—and he was angry.

"Hank!" The shout echoed, reverberated throughout the rounded building. I felt the phone slip from my hand—heard it hit the metal treads of the staircase below me. It bounced. *Clink. Clink. Clink*—from step to step. It stopped. Silence. I held my breath again.

"Hank? You up there, you worthless SOB?"

Silently, I peered over the edge. There was a light down there, its moving glow casting giant shadows on the white walls of the tower. Bill Raymond had turned on the bulb in the miner's hat strapped to his head—the kind he rented to cave explorers. I wondered if Scott had one. I hoped so. Bill's shadow looked huge and there was no mistaking the shape of the thing in his hand. He was carrying a shovel.

"Hank!" he shouted again. I backed away from the edge. What if Bill looked up and discovered it was me—alone at the top of the light? Desperate, I looked around. I could go outside and scream—but I knew the wind would carry the sound of my thin voice away. I had no phone now to call for help and I was sure my call to the dockmaster hadn't gone through. I stood very still and listened to the sounds coming from below.

Bill had begun to climb the stairs. "What's the matter with you, Hank?" he shouted. "You finally told Doris about me moving the lever on Jack's plane, didn't you, you ungrateful bum. After all I've done for you. All these years I was sure you saw me do it. It was so easy—my hand under the blanket—it only took a second. I figured all I had to do was give you a job and place to live and you'd keep it to yourself. Hell, I even hired your kid every summer. What made you rat me out after all this time? Did that cop worm it out of you?"

Poor, innocent Hank had no idea that you'd done it until I saw the blanket in the mirror.

Another step on the stairs. The light moved closer. I backed away as far as I could get from the railing.

He's afraid of heights. Maybe he won't come all the way up.

Hank had told Doris about what he remembered from that day. Why would he do that? Did he simply want her to know how dangerous her husband really was?

"You're about to have a bad accident, Hank. A terrible fall from—how tall is this thing—fifty feet?" No longer yelling, his voice was even more chilling. "Nobody's going to be worried about you. I left the TV guy in the cave and called the Coast Guard to go get him." Bill's laugh was chilling, terrible. "Look over that way. You'll see all the lights and hear all the boats and bells and whistles. Nobody's worried about you. They all want to be heroes—saving the guy who'll have it all on camera, ready for the eleven o'clock news. Nobody's going to worry about me either—until they figure out that all the gold is gone. All the jewelry too. I've even got a helicopter all loaded up and waiting."

Clink. Clunk. Another step—and the shovel bumping along at his side. "Nobody cares what Doris says about me. Everybody thinks she's half nuts, anyway. I'll be long gone out of the country. Rich as Croesus!" Again, the awful laugh.

Another sound from below. The door opened again. *Someone is here. I'm going to be all right.* I peeked over the edge of the railing once more. It was a man. Not Pete. The miner's lamp picked him out. "Hank!" Bill screamed the name, then swung around, looking upward. "Then who—?" The light stung my eyes. He'd seen me. I watched, horrified, frozen as he began to climb the spiraling stairs.

Hank followed, succeeding in grabbing one of Bill's legs. The shovel caught his arm, then crashed on his shoulder. Bill climbed higher but Hank didn't give up. In the dim light, the two men scuffled. I had no weapon. If Bill succeeded in reaching the light, I had no chance of defeating him.

My foot hit something. The ashtray. Doris's secret ashtray and lighter were at my feet, and a dozen oil lamps were right in front of me. I moved quickly, the sounds of struggle getting louder—closer.

I lighted the wicks, one at a time, watched as each one caught the flame, each one burning brightly. Hands shaking, I pulled the magnifying red shield into place.

For the first time in over thirty years, the Ruby Light illuminated the harbor, the island, the mainland. I dared to look below again. Bill Raymond held the shovel over his head and brought it down hard on Hank. I heard and saw Hank's body tumbling down the stairs. The scene was an eerie duplicate of River's late-night screening of *The Lighthouse*, the movie Aunt Ibby had said was too scary to watch.

In real life, it's even worse.

I knew that I was the only person standing in Bill's way—the only obstacle in his path to wealth and freedom. He began to climb the stairs again, faster than before. He'd dropped the shovel and used both hands to steady himself on the upward-spiraling stairs.

He paused, about halfway up. Had his fear of heights kicked in? I hoped so. I couldn't move. Couldn't speak.

"Well, little Maralee," he said. "I guess Hank told you I killed your parents too, didn't he?" He didn't wait for an answer. I didn't have one.

"I didn't want to do that," he said. "There was just no other way. I hope you understand. They were going to insist that we put all our beautiful gold and fabulous jewels into a museum. It was three against one. I had to narrow the odds." He began to climb again. "You and your cop husband showing up here put a little crimp in my plans. You're Jack's kid. That means you and the cop get a vote. It'll be three to one again for the museum." He sounded closer. "I don't want any damned museum, with cash coming in in dribs and drabs. I want all of it and I want it now. I've got it sold. I just have to deliver it. You're not going to stop me."

Pete, where the hell are you? Don't let this be the end of our forever!

I didn't have a chance to find out what Bill planned to do about me. It didn't take very long for the brightly gleaming Ruby Light to signal to thousands of people—on land, sea and air—that something was very wrong in the Pirate's Island lighhouse.

My cavalry arrived—in the form of my husband, a dozen deputy sheriffs, the dockmaster, the captain of the *Miss Judy*, a wet but still working Scott Palmer, our bruised and bloody friend Hank, along with a significant representation from the United States Coast Guard.

Bill was taken into custody. Hank was taken to the hospital. Pete and I were politely escorted to the dockmaster's office, where a sheriff took our statements, after first assuring us that Doris was safe at home with a policewoman companion.

Pete and I tried as well as we could to put into words all we'd learned and experienced since we'd arrived at the island such a short time ago. A court stenographer took our statements while Scott, with our permission, filmed the entire procedure.

We knew it was going to take a while to sort it all out—to accept that my parents' deaths had not been caused by pilot error, but by terrible design—to do what we could to help the aunt I'd so recently met to adjust to some hard facts no wife should ever have to deal with—and to figure out what to do about the possibility that I was now an heir to whatever remained of Black Sam Bellamy's treasure.

Good thing we have our forever.

EPILOGUE

We were able to keep our appointment at Flower World. We carried our memorial birch tree to the edge of that tall cliff and together we dug in the dark, loamy soil and buried the root ball. We prayed together there while birds sang and squirrels frolicked and wildflowers bloomed. It wasn't such a terrifying place after all and I felt quite strongly what might have been that elusive thing they call "closure."

Aunt Doris accepted Aunt Ibby's invitation to "come down to Salem for a while until this unpleasantness gets straightened out." She left all of the island businesses in Hank's care. I turned to Aunt Ibby's financial advisors to unravel the complicated chain of custody of the gold coins and assorted jewels—some of which apparently belong to me—so we get a vote on what to do with it all. Pete and I vote solidly with Aunt Doris. It appears that enough of the treasure will remain unencumbered by any of Bill Raymond's "business deals" to establish a small but beautiful treasure museum on the island. My mother's sketches have been turned over to the architects for incorporation into the design, and Pete and I have donated the appraised value of my ring to get the project underway.

Bill Raymond faces assorted charges—including grand theft, assault, kidnapping, false imprisonment, and more. He has admitted to tampering with the fuel lever on the *Daisy Mae* and it will be up to the courts to determine his punishment. The NTSB has removed *pilot error* from their report.

Pete and I continued our honeymoon just about as we had planned. Bar Harbor, Kennebunkport, Ogunquit, Old Orchard Beach. We made it all the way up to Mount Desert for the earliest sunrise in the country. Pete said if I wanted to we could drive straight through down to Key West to catch it where it sets last. I voted that we do that another day. I was anxious to get back to Salem and move into our new home.

I called the station a couple of times, mostly curious about what was happening with Wanda. Rhonda reported that our weather girl/meteorologist switches her costumes randomly. No one ever knows whether they'll see cute-shorts-and-crop-top Wanda or sophisticated pin-striped three-piece-suit Wanda. Scott beat us home and texted me that people are actually placing bets at lottery locations before each weather forcast.

Aunt Ibby called to let us know that Michael Martell will be moving out of his apartment sooner than he'd anticipated. Seems that our real estate agent Joanne has found him the perfect home.

He'll be moving in to the other side of our house.

RECIPES

Aunt Ibby's Pistachio Nut Cake

Ingredients:
1 package yellow cake mix
1 package Jell-O pistachio instant pudding
4 eggs
1 cup water
½ cup cooking oil
½ teaspoon almond extract
½ cup sugar
1 teaspoon cinnamon
½ cup finely chopped nuts

Put cake mix, instant pudding, eggs, water, oil and almond extract into a large mixer bowl; blend. Beat at medium speed of electric mixer for 2 minutes. Combine sugar, cinnamon and nuts. Pour half of the batter into a greased and floured 10-inch tube pan; sprinkle with half of the sugar mixture. Repeat layers and top with remaining batter. Bake at 350 for 50 minutes or until center springs back when lightly touched. Cool fifteen minutes before removing from pan.

(Aunt Ibby likes to top her Pistachio Nut Cake with a dusting of sifted powdered sugar.)

Marie's Butterfinger Cookies

Ingredients:
1¾ cups all-purpose flour
¾ teaspoons baking soda
¼ teaspoon salt
¼ cup sugar
½ cup butter, softened
1 large egg
36 pieces of bite-sized Nestlé Butterfinger candy,
    coarsely chopped

Combine flour, baking soda and salt in small bowl. Beat sugar and softened butter in large bowl until creamy. Beat in egg, gradually beat in flour mixture and stir in the Butterfinger pieces. Drop by slightly rounded tablespoons onto ungreased baking sheets. Bake for 10 to 12 minutes at 375 or until lightly browned. Cool on baking sheets for 2 minutes. Remove to wire racks to cool completely.

(Marie says she makes these after Halloween by snitching the bite-sized Butterfingers from the kids' bags.)

Aunt Doris's Blueberry Pie

Ingredients:
1 recipe of your favorite plain two-crust pastry
1 quart fresh blueberries
1 cup sugar
1 tablespoon flour
$\frac{1}{8}$ teaspoon nutmeg
2 tablespoons butter

Wash blueberries and drain well. Roll out half of the pastry and line 9- or 10-inch pie plate, trimming pastry so that about half an inch hangs over the edge. Mix 1 tablespoon of the sugar with flour and sprinkle on the bottom crust. Fill crust with blueberries and sprinkle with nutmeg. Cover with remaining sugar and dot with butter. Roll out the crust to cover top and also overlap edge by about half an inch. Tuck top crust under overlapping bottom crust and seal by crimping crusts firmly together. Prick the top of the pie to let the steam escape.

Place pie in bottom of hot oven (450 degrees) for ten minuites. Move to middle shelf and reduce heat to 350 degrees. Continue baking for about 30 minutes, or until crust is golden and blueberries smell amazing.

Love the Witch City mysteries?
Make sure you read them all!
And don't miss the first book in a new series from
Carol J. Perry
The Haunted Haven Mysteries
BE MY GHOST is available now
Wherever books are sold